I0639666

"Through the eyes of church mice, observations are made. Using their voices, author Sandra Voelker has told in diary form delightful and divine stories about life in a church, in a parsonage, and life as a pastor, the pastor's wife, and their children. The reader meets a variety of personalities (aka church members) and becomes involved in both church and town incidents, problems, and occasions. Open the pages now and enjoy a journey that is perceptive, evokes compassion, causes smiles and laughter, reveals wisdom, and touches the soul. In other words, enjoy a bit of real 'heaven on earth.'"

—Rev. Dr. David H. Ritt
President and Bishop Emeritus
English District, Lutheran Church – Missouri Synod

"Under the observant eye of Finley Newcastle (aka F.N.), the church mouse living at Historic St. Pete's Church, the comments and activities of Pastor Osterhagen, his wife Aia, their family and congregation are carefully recorded. Thank you, F.N. You put a smile on a reader's face as you record life in the parsonage and bring to mind the ups and downs, trials and triumphs of the church as a family of families… warts and blemishes, sweetness and grace. I love it!"

—Rev. Steve Wagner
Associate Pastor, Concordia Lutheran Church, San Antonio, Texas
Past Director, *Pastoral Leadership Institute*

"A charming 'tail' revealing a church's congregational life through the sharp eyes of its own church mice. A delightful read!"

—Mount Olive Lutheran Church's Monday Night Book Group
Rochester, Minnesota

Heaven on Earth

Church Mouse
Musings at
Historic St. Peter's

Sandra Voelker

HEAVEN ON EARTH
FINLEY'S TALE - BOOK II
Copyright © 2019 by Sandra Voelker

Print ISBN: 978-1-4866-1666-4

Word Alive Press
119 De Baets Street, Winnipeg, MB R2J 3R9
www.wordalivepress.ca

Cataloguing in Publication may be obtained through Library and Archives Canada

This book is dedicated to my Robert, my husband, my love.
I treasure the way you are, especially that you give and receive God's grace, through Christ
our Lord, cheerfully, thankfully, and persistently. You give me strength to do the same.

"I would be happy just to hold the hands I love."
—Gordon Lightfoot

GREETINGS!

Welcome back to those of you who have read *Finley's Tale — Book I: In the Beginning*. I have profoundly missed you! Thank you for devoting your time to reading the first part of my journal, as minutes and hours are precious and best not treated carelessly. Now that the second part of my trilogy is in your hands, let's get going and dive into more happenings at Historic St. Peter's!

PLEASE NOTE: To those who have not read *In the Beginning*, kindly let me enlighten you with some brief information. First of all, my name is Finley Newcastle. I am honoured to be a church mouse at Historic St. Peter's in Oswald County. Currently I am in the process of writing a journal recording one liturgical church year at St. Peter's. The entries into my journal come from various happenings around the church, writing down only those of paramount noteworthiness.

My gem of a wife, Ruby, and I reside in a perfect location, right next door to the Pastor's home that is called a parsonage. There is a very small opening in their dining room wall, behind the hutch, where we are able to peek into the parsonage to observe all that is going on, as well as hearing conversations. The clergy residence is attached to the church proper by a long-windowed breezeway which allows us to observe everything that goes on at church, too. The mice village that dwells at Historic St. Peter's is a tight-knit community. Of crucial priority is our safety, as we do not want to be discovered. Frequently the mice living here gather together for a village meeting, where we open and close our meetings with the singing of our theme song, "Safety First." This is our home and we want to remain here, in God's house.

I encourage you to band together with me on this journey where you will need no luggage. There is no need to fret about being behind, or that you might have to pass an examination, or that you will be bombarded and buried in details. Fiddlesticks on all of that! Please begin by taking my straightforward advice to simply read what is in front of you. After only a few pages you will adore Pastor Clement and Aia (pronounced I-ya) Osterhagen and their darling daughter Gretchen. Not long from now twins will arrive at the Osterhagen home, as Aia's due date is in late June. You will also become familiar with many delightful parishioners that belong to Historic St. Peter's, and, just as importantly, the re-markable mouse village that resides here.

Now, once again, before any more time is frittered away, let's get going! I have a tale to tell, and you may follow my tale.

Your old friend or your newest friend (chose which one is applicable),

Finley Newcastle
(F.N. for short)

On Saturday, May 9, the last entry was recorded in *Finley's Tale – Book I: In the Beginning* (I used a blank journal with J.S. Bach on the cover). Entries briefly came to a halt because every single sheet was brimming full of handwriting. Thankfully, I enlisted help from St. Pete's mice village and immediately the team of Ellsworth and Zeb stumbled upon a spiral notebook located on the bottom shelf in the Sunday School craft supply room. The cover was completely ripped off, but that is of no mind, the blank pages are what I need to continue my writing.

Recognizing that today is Mother's Day, Pastor Osterhagen and Chairperson Bill Tiederman stationed themselves at the front door of St. Peter's, ready to honour all mothers. By offering them a warm greeting and smile, along with a carnation, most of the women were delighted. A couple of village mice observed the delight on Pleasant Lerwick's face when she attended Historic St. Peter's for the very first time today and received a carnation. However, several times this was an uncomfortable task for Bill Tiederman. Sometimes he could not distinguish whether or not a woman is a mother by simply glancing at her.

As I was tucked away behind the large faux ficus tree located near the church entryway, I observed Bill making several missteps today. However, a colossal error occurred when he wished the elderly spinster, Lillian Thompson, "Happy Mother's Day!" After hearing those cheerful words, Lillian instantly burst into tears. It was a blessing that her Irish linen handkerchief (adorned with multi-coloured tatting) was tucked into her blouse sleeve, as it made her fully prepared to mop up her cascade of tears. Being of delicate countenance, Lillian has not keep it to herself that she has yet to find her true love and get married. But, she has several times revealed to others that it is far too late in life for her to have a baby, a dream of hers that was shattered decades ago. After seeing Lillian's reaction, Pastor's facial expressions showed his misgivings about whether or not this Mother's Day tradition of doling out flowers is far from being a grand idea. I heard him quietly mention his thoughts to Bill Tiederman, after which Bill's head shook up and down in agreement with Pastor's remarks. At this evening's village gathering, the mice community concurred with their thoughts on this delicate issue, too. We predict the carnation give-away has just died, at best, or at least taken a year off.

One benefit of this will be that the flower fund line in St. Peter's annual budget will be dropped significantly.

Yesterday Clement and Gretchen shopped for a Mother's Day gift for Aia. On their way home, they drove past Aia as she was carrying a cookie sheet and heading to her friend Annette's home. After Clement and Gretchen returned home, they began to wrap gifts, remarking to each other that the parsonage was filled with the delicious aroma of a sweet pastry. It was not until later that we heard Aia tell Gretchen that the cookie sheet she dropped off at Annette's home contained freshly baked baklava. Gretchen was disappointed that her mama gave all of the baklava to Annette, but Aia told her she only gave half of it away, reassuring her that there is plenty for the three of them to enjoy.

During yesterday's shopping spree, Gretchen spotted a slippery blue and purple floral nightgown that she said was really, really, big and wide enough for her mommy's tummy, so Clement purchased it. After that they drove to Victor's Greenhouse where Gretchen selected a large purple gloxinia plant that she thought was the prettiest flower she had ever seen. Gretchen suggested that they prepare spaghetti, garlic toast, olives, and chocolate cake for their Mother's Day supper. Clement agreed. After that they drove to Grocer Dan's and purchased groceries to prepare the feast. Ruby mentioned to me that Aia really enjoyed tonight's supper, her gifts, but especially the thought put into the special day. Aia thanked Clement for encouraging Gretchen to plan everything. Aia mentioned that next Mother's Day she will be the mother of three children.

Something happened at St. Peter's this morning that I am thoroughly ashamed to reveal. But, remembering that it is my duty to make reports in my journal, I plow forward. Copper, one member of our village, overheard one of the young adult parishioners, Jodie Bernard, whisper to her friend, Abbey Whitelaw, news that she was going to ask Pastor Osterhagen for a $20 donation to her basketball league for their upcoming trip to Niagara Falls. Jodie let Abbey in on the scoop when she said, "Asking for donations is a super easy way to increase our family income." She also declared that she has successfully done this with others. Today she will try her trick out on Pastor Osterhagen and use the donation to treat her mother and herself to dinner at Sarah's Farmhouse, the newest restaurant in town. Because Aia overheard snippets of Jodie's master plan, she speed walked over to Clement to warn him not to give any money to Jodie Bernard, adding that later on she will explain her reasoning. Copper pointed out to us that Aia must be the best pastor's wife in all of Oswald County, as she is Pastor's biggest supporter. Plus, he added that Aia is thrifty and careful with their money, just as she was today. Copper noticed that when it comes to money, Aia is brimming full of common sense, and when it comes to spotting monkeyshines, she is chock-full of perceptiveness.

At 11:30 p.m. Ruby and I travelled to the parsonage upset that Jodie Bernard is raising money for herself, not charity. We don't think anyone should support Jodie's fundraisers. Besides that, Ruby has been in a funk today because it is Mother's Day. A deep sense of sadness comes over her that she hasn't had even one baby, while so many in our village have one after the next. We talked about her crushed feelings as we snacked on a piece of Italian angel hair pasta found under the dining room table. I noticed that as Ruby was chewing she seemed consoled and her tears stopped.

– F.N.

THE HANDBELL GLOVES REAPPEARED TONIGHT, JUST AS SUDDENLY AS THEY WENT missing last December. The mice in our village wondered why the church gremlin, Griffin, couldn't have been kind enough to return them prior to Easter Sunday. Cadence Davis, the director, was so agitated that she unloaded her complaints to Pastor Osterhagen shortly before the 7 p.m. worship service celebrating "The Ascension of Our Lord." All of the complaining before church tonight must have affected Pastor's thoughts because he looked like he had something weighing heavily on his shoulders. He also made small flubs and said "um" several times during his announcements. Cadence was visibly upset and sour at the handbell rehearsal held after worship tonight. A majority of the mice in the village have their minds made up that Griffin has a wicked stripe inside of him, one that is just plain evil.

Having placed an order at Christian's Church Goods for a dozen pairs of handbell gloves, the bell ringers had been able to wear white gloves during their anthem on Easter Sunday. Now that Griffin has returned the gloves he captured in December, there is an abundance of them. Cadence is appalled by this and fears that the church treasurer will blame her for this extra expense. Although she does dedicate a lot of time carefully selecting quality music, she also prudently watches over the expenses of music and supplies. Each piece of music costs a couple of dollars. This unnecessary expense for gloves is what has her frazzled.

At the village meeting tonight some of the mice reported that Cadence took the handbell gloves home with her when she left the church. It is evident that she does not trust leaving them in the building any longer. The mice think Cadence's next step will be to haul the four big heavy grey bell cases home with her after every rehearsal. She'll most likely take the entire library of bell music with her, as well. She has become a safety first gal.

The mice ended the village meeting tonight with the singing of "Safety First," which led to a discussion about giving Cadence Davis a copy of the mice theme song. Because she is so interested in the safety of the gloves, the sheet music, and the bells, the mice envision that safety is definitely one of her priorities. The mice also discussed the enjoyment the bell ringers might find in playing our theme song. As the discussion was unfolding, some of the mice got goose bumps imagining our song being played by a handbell choir, especially under Cadence's direction that includes a good amount of gusto and flair. Cadence might appreciate receiving a free song, as it would be of no expense to the church. We all agreed to help Cadence in that small way. Immediately a committee was formed to orchestrate a way to deliver a copy of the music to Cadence. This would be a gift, not adding a penny to her concern about being over the budget.

At 11:30 p.m. Ruby and I travelled to the parsonage and found a potato lump that dropped on the floor from a Southern fried chicken dinner with gravy and lumpy (on purpose) mashed potatoes. We commented that we had no idea potato lumps tasted that savoury.

– F.N.

THE FIRST THING THAT AIA DID TODAY WAS TO STRIP THE SHEETS FROM THEIR BED AND put them in the washing machine. Prior to the Osterhagen's morning coffee, the colourful sheets were already blowing in the wind, suspended from the old-time clothes line. The mice have noticed that Aia generally prefers to hang bed sheets outside whenever possible to pick up the natural fresh scent from the air. Also, it cuts down on utilities. According to Clement and Aia, the fresh air fragrance is so heavenly that it is indescribable. The only time that the outdoor drying method is disrupted is when Gaynor Babineaux starts up his manure spreader sending a load of aroma not just throughout Oswald County but far into infinity.

While she was outside, Aia noticed that someone had entered their backyard before they woke up this morning and helped themselves to the first pickings of the healthy rhubarb plants that are located in one corner. The established rhubarb plants in their backyard are from an inherited rhubarb bed given to the previous pastor and his wife by some former members of St. Pete's, the Fletchers. Both Mr. & Mrs. Fletcher are gone now, but their daughter, Constance, who is in her mid-sixties, lives in the house located on the heritage farm. She lives up to the meaning of her name, "firm of purpose." Both Clement and Aia tried to figure out who the thief might be, but they keep coming back to Constance Fletcher as the main suspect. Both have a hunch she will return a few more times to glean more of their rhubarb before the end of the season because she just can't see that rhubarb go unharvested.

Constance, "The Rude Rhubarb Thief," as Aia refers to her, got the very first of the rhubarb when its taste was at its peak. She took only the pinky red rhubarb stalks, dropping the leaves on the ground for the Osterhagens to dispose of. It is a stroke of luck that Aia discovered the rhubarb leaf mess the first thing this morning while Gretchen was still asleep. Gretchen could have gone outside to play in the backyard and seen the leaves and would not have known that the leaves are poisonous. If she was inquisitive about them, she might have taken a little bite and consumed the lethal chemical oxalic acid.

Aia had planned to cut rhubarb today to cook a simple rhubarb sauce for their Syttende Mai May 17 Norwegian Constitution Day Celebration. She aimed to do the exact same thing last year for their dinner, but they suspect it was Constance who snatched the rhubarb at that time also. Now the Osterhagens are completely without rhubarb. Even though rhubarb is a perennial, Aia said that she will have to be extra quick acting when it grows back so that they can enjoy rhubarb sauce at least one time this season.

Aia went on and on complaining to Clement that Constance is constantly picking the springtime rhubarb, suggesting that she must suffer from constipation. Aia told Clement that rhubarb contains laxative properties which are extremely useful for relief of constipation. She mentioned that the Chinese have known this healthy benefit of eating rhubarb for thousands of years.

Aia also hinted that perhaps Constance is entering a rhubarb festival, as one person alone could never consume that much rhubarb, but they both ruled out that suggestion, as rhubarb easily freezes. Constance could use frozen rhubarb when she bakes any old time of the year.

The third and final part of Aia's Trinitarian (due to being a graduate of Trinity College) speech was to bring forth the idea that Constance might be using the sweet, crisp, and tart goodness of the rhubarb to make something far better than rhubarb crumble, that being home-brewed rhubarb wine. Constance just looks like her moonshine of choice might be rhubarb wine.

Clement advised Aia to keep quiet about this when she is around Constance or she will end up getting herself into a fuss over such a trivial matter. Aia nodded her head in agreement, calmed down, and thanked him. Since Aia had grumbled far too much about the loss of "their" rhubarb, Clement drove down to Grocer Dan's and purchased a big bunch so Aia could make her sauce. After that, Aia was so pleased with her rhubarb supply that Ruby and I noticed she never mentioned Constance again.

At 11:30 p.m. Ruby and I travelled to the parsonage where we came across several little mustard seeds on the kitchen floor. Aia must have whisked up her favourite mustard seed vinaigrette today, accidentally spilling a few seeds on the floor. We wondered if we would now possess the faith and strength to move mountains like we heard about in a Bible reading from Luke 17. We probably could move mountains, but decided against it as Maryland's Sugarloaf Mountain, Arizona's Mount Bigelow, and Colorado's Cathedral Peak are too distant and far-flung from us. Ruby and I prefer to stay put. This is our preferred stomping ground.

– F.N.

THE PARSONAGE DOORBELL RANG EARLY THIS MORNING. CLEMENT OPENED THE FRONT door and found Constance Fletcher standing on the bottom step, greeting him with her hands full, wearing a friendly, warm smile. Also warm was what she handed him, a homemade rhubarb pie. Pastor was delighted to receive the pie and gratefully thanked her. Constance couldn't stay and talk because she had two more pies to deliver to two of the members of St. Pete's that are homebound.

After Clement closed the front door, he brought the pie into the kitchen, got out a knife, the pie server, three little plates and forks, and cut three pieces of rhubarb pie. This morning's breakfast of rhubarb pie was unusual for the Osterhagens as they usually make pancakes on Saturday mornings. Today's breakfast was an exception to that pattern because the pie was warm and smelled sensational, so they decided to eat some of it right away. Before taking a bite of the rhubarb pie, Aia's attitude about Constance sounded accusatory, centering on three things: first, how flabbergasted she was that Constance had the audacity to steal their rhubarb; secondly, how Constance had the gall to bake a pie from their rhubarb; and, thirdly, how Constance had the pluck to present them a pie made from "their" rhubarb. After Aia tasted her first bite of the pie, she no longer had critical words to say about Constance, adding that from now on Constance was welcome to pick their rhubarb as much as she desires, hoping that she will bake them a rhubarb pie every once in a while. Noting that her baking ability was magnificent, Aia remarked that it doesn't take very many ingredients to make a rhubarb pie. One only needs sugar, butter, rhubarb, and a pie crust, but Constance has the supreme ability to take those few ingredients and magically create an utterly perfect sweet and sour creation tenderly wrapped in the flakiest, best quality homemade double crust. From now on, the "The Rude Rhubarb Thief" nickname was buried and became vastly transformed to "Constance Fletcher, The Best Rhubarb Pie Baker in the Entire World."

In mid-May of each year, several church ladies groups throughout Oswald County have been gathering together for a workshop that is referred to as "A Spring Social for Christian Gals." It is a time to listen, learn, laugh, pray, and sing. But, basically, it is a big get-to-see-and-know-each-other event that, of course, has a Christian theme. The churches involved in it are in a rotation to host the annual event.

This year it was Historic St. Peter's turn to be the super-friendly, welcoming, hospitable, and entertaining church. The mice village voted unanimously that we needed to assign one or two from our village to be on duty for this event. Cécile-Claudette volunteered her services lickety-split, followed by Hadden promising to partner with her. Hadden's enthusiasm mostly stems from being wildly infatuated with Cécile-Claudette. Thankfully, their volunteerism completely eliminated the need for the village to appoint two mice to oversee the event.

HSP's Ladies' Guild put effort into searching for the perfect speaker for this gathering and they were confident that they found one. Dr. Ellen Kam is a university professor of psychology who also is a Christian with a colossal funny side. Her topic, "A Humorous Look at the Human Mind," delighted her audience today, bringing in lots of laughter while reminding them that the mind is a spectacular blessing from God. Dr. Kam's presentation engaged the audience in an amusing way by describing how men's and women's brains are wired differently. She brought along with her two visual aids. They were large drawings mounted on plywood, one of a man's head, the other of a woman's head. The back of the plywood had been drilled with dozens of holes with red and green Christmas lights poking through them, which Dr. Kam was able to control with a switch. The lights would go off and on during her presentation when different topics were mentioned. The lights between the two brains were extremely varied, showing that what bothers or delights the female brain is often far different than what has an effect on the male brain. The laughter from the audience was enormous during some of the red/green light show. She told everyone that the human brain has so much depth and complexity, it is anything but simple. Dr. Kam received a standing ovation from the gals.

After that, Aia was called forward to lead the group in prayer. Ruby had heard that she was delighted to be chosen to do this by the Ladies' Guild but was also shocked that they selected her. Usually the closing prayer at the "Spring Social for Christian Gals" is done by someone who is an extrovert and enjoys listening to the sound of their own voice in the microphone. The entire church knows that Aia is not like that.

Aia prayed: "Dear Heavenly Father, we give you thanks and praise for all of the women who have come to Historic St. Peter's today to open their minds to learn something new, while being filled with the joys of laughter. We know that each of us is precious in Your sight because You have given us the gift of life, making us each unique. Help us to keep our minds and hearts on Christ our Saviour. Hold us in Your hands and help us to live our lives day to day for Jesus

Christ. When the time comes that You gather us in your arms and take us to our home that You have prepared for us in heaven, we will then be able to listen to the angels sing their songs of glory and praise. In Your holy name we pray and give you thanks. Amen."

In Woolcox Hall, the women of St. Peter's Ladies' Guild had prepared a reception charmingly decorated with a spring theme. Each member baked a Poke Cake at home and brought it to the church. We found out that Poke Cake is a plain white cake that, after cooling, has had holes poked into the top of it with a fork at half-inch intervals. In those holes gelatin is poured, followed by placing the cake in the refrigerator to set the gelatin. Before serving, the cakes are frosted generously with whipped cream. When the cake is cut into serving pieces, there are ribbons of colour up and down the sides of the cake. All members of the Ladies' Guild used the same recipe for Poke Cake, but each used a different flavour of gelatin, resulting in a rainbow of beautiful cakes.

The tables were set for eight and were covered in cheery yellow plastic tablecloths with fresh tulips and pussy willows forming the centerpieces. Earlier today, Judith Haugen, President of St. Peter's Ladies' Guild, profusely thanked the ladies for their efforts to create the spring table settings in a kaleidoscope of colours. After that, she reminded the women that they will be carrying trays consisting of eight slices of Poke Cake, one of each colour, to distribute at each table which will complete the artistic colour show.

One guest meekly raised her hand and signaled for a St. Pete's Ladies' Guild member to come over to her, getting close enough so she could whisper something in her ear. Because of what was told to her, she straight away spread the news to another member of the Ladies' Guild. News mushroomed quickly within the group, and soon the guild members moved throughout Woolcox Hall like a herd of galloping antelopes scooping up every plate of green-coloured Poke Cake. In the church kitchen, Cécile-Claudette and Hadden peeked out and saw the ladies inspecting the empty glass cake pan that contained green Poke Cake crumbs, and, sure enough, there was a thin layer of green dish soap stuck to the bottom of the pan. It must not have gotten rinsed thoroughly the last time it was washed.

The ladies whose green Poke Cake was whisked away were quickly given an applesauce muffin because no more Poke Cake was left. The muffins were intended for the coffee hour the next day, but the ladies decided that some people will just have to make a sacrifice and be muffin-less. After all, no one should presume that they can have a muffin every single time they attend the coffee hour. The ladies were very thankful they had muffins for backup.

The intense embarrassment about presenting a soapy dessert at an event made Claudia Cooke, the soapy cake baker, so ashamed that she told everyone she will not volunteer to bake anything for church ever again, as that was the last straw. Claudia is the same woman that brings homemade cookies to Vacation Bible School in corrugated cat food cartons. The box is probably clean enough, but just the thought of it once being in a cat food factory is not very appealing to the human appetite. The mice think that there is probably more to the story of Claudia and her disastrous cooking, but we don't know anything more about it. We did hear that the ladies seemed relieved when they found out that Claudia will not be bringing food to St. Peter's from now on. To the mice it seemed sad, but we heard that the ladies appeared as though they were trying to restrain themselves from rejoicing.

At 9:30 p.m. Ruby and I travelled to Woolcox Hall and snacked on crumbs of applesauce muffins that had fallen to the floor. I reminded Ruby to stay away from any crumbles of green Poke Cake as we need to put safety first, emphasizing that we are not about to eat anything that is flavoured with dish soap. We do not want to come down with something.

    – F.N.

As Aia and Gretchen strolled down the breezeway this fine Sunday morning, they stopped to admire the beauty of the spring flowers that were blooming brightly in the courtyard. Three members of our mice village, Apple Blossom, Fleur, and Amaryllis, prefer to reside in the courtyard throughout the spring and summer months as a way to recover from the depressingly long winter. Now they feel uplifted and refreshed by spending time outdoors. The church courtyard was radiant today with blooming tulips, daffodils, crocuses, and a few hyacinths, a real collage of colours. Just looking at them gave a person a twinge of La Primavera Festivity of Zest and Jubilation (a more accurate way of saying spring fever). Gretchen asked her mother if they could enter the courtyard to see and smell the flowers up close. Aia told Gretchen that she had a fine idea, but they couldn't stay very long, as they didn't want to be late for church. Aia unlocked the door to the courtyard and together they walked through it, admiring the purple, orange, pink, red, and yellow colours of the flowers, plus the sharp, distinct, appealing aroma of the hyacinths. Apple Blossom told us that Aia complimented Gretchen by telling her that it was a really good idea that they got this chance to see the flowers the first thing today. She assured Gretchen that other flowers will bloom in the summer that will be just as beautiful as the spring flowers.

They stayed a little bit longer in the courtyard than they should have, so they speed walked to arrive at their pew in time for worship. Fawne, the mouse in our village that has the most ravishing eyes, watched them hurry into the sanctuary, sitting next to Mrs. Whyte. Gretchen said, "Good morning, Mrs. Whyte." She remembers her name easily because everything about Mrs. Whyte is, well, white. Fawne told our village that Mrs. Whyte has snow white hair, wears a white blouse, a white sweater, an off-white pearl necklace with matching earrings, a white skirt and shoes, and carries a big white handbag. HSP's Mrs. Whyte is not to be confused with the American actress Betty White, or the brand of cornbread, muffin, and pizza crust mixes, or Mrs. Blanche White, a suspect in the Clue board game, or Vanna White, the famous Wheel of Fortune hostess. St. Peter's Mrs. Whyte has a first name, but no one seems to know what it is, not even Pastor Osterhagen. Because she is only known as Mrs. Whyte, some people and mice might assume that she doesn't care for her first name and wants it kept unknown.

During the opening hymn, Gretchen noticed that Mrs. Whyte had a little slip of white hair out of place on her forehead, so she reached over with her fingers to fix it. When that didn't work, Gretchen reached for her church activity bag and found one of her hair bows, one that was multi-coloured. Gretchen gently moved forward to be near Mrs. Whyte and gently clipped a hair bow into place, which kept that strand of hair off of Mrs. Whyte's forehead. Mrs. Whyte beamed at Gretchen and glanced over at Aia, smiling at her, too. Mrs. Whyte continued to wear Gretchen's hair bow the remainder of the morning and seemed proud of it, almost as though she had been crowned with the title of H.M. (Her Majesty) of Historic St. Peter's. Gretchen whispered to Mrs. Whyte how pretty she was in the colourful bow, instead of being dressed in just plain white. Mrs. Whyte squeezed Gretchen and then Gretchen sat back down on the pew, returned to her activity bag and busied herself with several of the items.

At the coffee hour following worship, Gretchen told her mother that she would be right back. Speed walking down the breezeway, Gretchen soon entered the church courtyard, witnessed by Apple Blossom, Fleur, and Amaryllis. Unfortunately, before worship, Aia had been in such a hurry that she had neglected to lock the door. The mice were fully aware that Gretchen was about to do something that might result in trouble. Gretchen hurried to hand pick many tulips, but only the cup part, not the stem, and one by one placed them in her activity bag. Quickly Gretchen returned to the coffee hour in Woolcox Hall and found her friend Mrs. Whyte. She sat down next to her and told her that she wanted to give her flowers. Gretchen opened her activity bag and placed all of the tulip cups on the table, telling her that they were especially picked for her. Mrs. Whyte was thrilled to receive them, but expressed bewilderment as to how to arrange them once she got them home. Gretchen told her that they are floating flowers that should be placed in a big fancy glass bowl with some water, just like her mother does using the crystal that they were given a long time ago as a wedding gift.

Chadwick, one of our village mice, was hiding behind the choir risers that are temporarily being stored in Woolcox Hall, when Lorinda Hastings hastily came over to Gretchen and in a not so nice, almost blistering voice, asked her where she got those tulips. Gretchen told her that she had just picked them from the courtyard to give to her friend Mrs. Whyte because she needs more colour in her life. Lorinda became even more noticeably irritated and annoyed at Gretchen, speaking to her in a razor-sharp way when she said, "You shouldn't pick the church's tulips!" This seemed to stun and bewilder Gretchen. Aia saw what was happening and straight away came to Gretchen's rescue by holding and pressing her hand with the Trinitarian squeeze, most likely a nonverbal way of communication invented by Aia. It consists of three gentle hand squeezes: I (squeeze) love (squeeze) you (squeeze). Gretchen looked up at her mama and clearly felt supported and loved by her, so she reciprocated her love back by giving her mother the Trinitarian squeeze.

Chadwick reported to us that Mrs. Whyte stood up and soberly advised Lorinda to pipe down and zip it, adding that a lot can be gained by learning from the generosity of Gretchen's young heart. Mrs. Whyte told Gretchen that because they are true friends she can now call her Auntie Crimson. Everyone within earshot clearly heard Mrs. Whyte publicly announce that her first name is Crimson. She revealed that she has changed inside because of Gretchen's kindness. Admitting that she no longer needs to be known as Mrs. Whyte, she is determined to fully embrace the beauty of her first name. She also added that from now on she is going to wear colourful clothing. Her plan is to head to one of the thrift stores first thing tomorrow morning to begin searching for a new wardrobe, hopefully finding a bright red sweater. After everyone heard Crimson's announcement, they clapped for her and also for Gretchen, all while Chadwick delighted in noticing that everyone in the room was smiling, with the exception of Lorinda. One of the kind ladies at the coffee hour approached Lorinda and softly spoke to her, perhaps to help her anger melt away, and it must have worked! Within a few minutes, Lorinda asked to sit down next to Gretchen and Auntie Crimson. She sincerely apologized, admitting that she easily gets agitated which results in her becoming ill-mannered. Gretchen immediately forgave her for her sharp words and jumped up from her chair to give Lorinda a hug. Chadwick said that he noticed tears coming down Lorinda's face during that embrace.

After that, Gretchen sat at the table and polished off a donut hole and so did both Auntie Crimson and Lorinda.

At 11 p.m. Ruby and I travelled to the parsonage and snacked on tidbits from the Osterhagen's Syttende Mai celebration. We found a tiny cubed potato that was dropped from their Lapskaus Stew and also a bit of buttered Hardanger lefse under Gretchen's spot at the dining room table. It tasted incredible! Ruby and I concluded that we favour the taste of Hardanger lefse twice as much as the regular lefse that Aia made last December.

While we ate, we quietly talked about the subject of yelling, the pros and cons of that behaviour. We decided that it is damaging to people because it harms feelings and makes people afraid and worried instead of feeling loved, secure, and safe. We thought that children especially shouldn't be yelled at because they need opportunities to try new things and to explore, just like what Gretchen did today when she went to the courtyard and picked tulip cups. We finished talking about the subject, but Ruby had one final word on the matter. She is certain that today was the first time that Gretchen has ever been scolded, adding that she hopes it will never happen again.

    – F.N.

YESTERDAY STELLA ANTONELLI WAS TAKEN BY AMBULANCE TO OUR LADY OF LOURDES Hospital in critical condition. Pastor Osterhagen was immediately notified to come and be with her as she was all alone. Her son, Marcus, had not arrived yet, but was on his way. Clement told Aia that he got there within a few minutes and was able to hold Stella's hand and pray with her. After Confession and Absolution he gave her Holy Communion. When Marcus and his wife, Gail, arrived, Pastor met them, visited with them, and prayed with them. They waited to see if Stella would pull out of it and turn the corner for the better. Pastor's words of comfort helped not only Stella rest in peace, but also helped Marcus and Gail let go of his mother. A short while later Stella died.

Marcus explained to Pastor that he had visited with his mother on the telephone and she sounded weak, telling him that she felt certain she was dying. After Marcus hung up the phone, he called for an ambulance and told them about the condition of his mother, giving them her home address. Immediately the two of them jumped into their car and headed to the hospital. Marcus told Pastor that he was so thankful that he was already there with his mum before their arrival. When Marcus and Gail saw her, she was hooked up to machines but already looked like she was dead. Marcus and Gail listened to the doctor's words in the hallway and heard him say that nothing more could be done for her and that it is now her time to die. Pastor's words of comfort helped Marcus and Gail as they went through the shock of his mother dying. They were already walking on the path of grief. Stella believed that because Jesus died on the cross for her sins God would carry her to heaven, knowing that she would again see those whom she loved, especially her husband, Sebastiano, who went before her and promised that he will wait for her there, saving her a place.

Losing his mother happened in an instant for Marcus. He cried while Gail asked Pastor if he could come over to the house the next morning to talk things over, as Marcus would perhaps be in better shape.

At 11:30 p.m. Ruby and I travelled to the parsonage to find a snack on the kitchen or dining room floor. We came up empty handed. Aia was spring cleaning the house all day today, that's why.

– F.N.

WHEN PASTOR ARRIVED AT THE ANTONELLI RESIDENCE TO CALL ON MARCUS AND GAIL this morning, he was absolutely unaware that one expeditious village mouse, Presto, had hurry-scurried into his vehicle. When he got out of the van, he turned to reach into the back seat for his home communion kit and noticed that the Antonelli's garage door was open. While he turned, Presto scooted from the van and hid in the garage in a spot where he could stay and listen to all upcoming conversations in the house and the garage. Pastor later told Aia that, as he walked into the garage, he noticed to his left several metal garage shelving units bolted to the wall. To his astonishment, the shelves contained hymnals, dozens and dozens of them. Presto saw him pull one off of the shelf to examine it and spotted "Historic St. Peter's" embossed on the cover in golden letters. Pastor put the hymnal back and, as he stood there in awe, proceeded to count just how many hymnals were in Stella's garage, coming up with a total of eighty-three. Presto told us that Pastor looked puzzled, so we think he suspected that Stella Antonelli might have had an impulse control disorder.

Ruby and I recalled that six months ago the church council was neck deep in the dilemma of there not being a sufficient number of hymnals in the sanctuary. There was such a shortage that everyone had to share hymnals, which is not an easy thing to do if your eyesight is weak, or worse, you are sharing a hymnal with a "hymnal hog." You know the kind, someone who selfishly monopolizes the hymnal, making it impossible for the other person to see, let alone to sing along with the hymns and the liturgy. The council did discuss whether or not to purchase more hymnals, but decided against it after Pastor told them that the Synod's Commission on Hymnody had recently published a hymnal, the newest one in twenty-eight years. Pastor suggested to the council that the church purchase enough of the new hymnals and to abandon the idea of replacing the old ones. Everyone voted unanimously for that plan. Within five weeks the new hymnals arrived and found a home in the hymn racks. But, the most welcoming place the hymnals found was in the hearts, hands, and minds of the worshippers. The mice have observed that everyone seems to be pleased with the new hymnal. The first hymn sung was #592, "All Are Welcome Here." Some of us sang along in our quiet singing voices until a few of us began feeling emotional. The mice at our village are deeply moved when this welcoming hymn is sung in worship. It has the power to make us feel as though we deeply belong here, in this place, right now.

We heard Clement mention to Aia that Stella Antonelli attended church alone every Sunday because her deceased husband, Sebastiano, faithfully attended Holy Angels Catholic Parish. Being one of the rare parishioners who sat in a different pew each week, Clement recalled seeing Stella's sizable beige handbag that she toted with her each Sunday. He also remarked to Aia that he thinks the mystery of the disappearing hymnals has now been solved, as he is certain that Stella cleverly, without being detected, stowed away one of them in her spacious handbag each time she attended worship. This accounts for the eighty-three missing hymnals that are parked in the Antonelli garage.

Aia suggested that if Stella was a shoplifter or a kleptomaniac, she must have deposited many other things in her big beige handbag in addition to St. Pete's hymnals. Aia asked Clement to recall what it looked like inside Stella's house, quizzing him if he caught sight of anything outlandish or that appeared out of the ordinary. He talked mostly about several collections of items that seemed to be everywhere that were stacked on tables, chairs, windowsills, kitchen counters, even piled on the floor, with most flat surfaces overflowing with odds and ends. Ruby and I heard Aia probe him further, asking if he remembered what any of the stacks were made up of. Clement told her about a pile of index cards that looked like it belonged to an old Dewey Decimal System from a Carnegie Library, a large antique glass peanut jar filled with paper matchbooks, a cardboard box that held dozens and dozens of toothbrushes, about fifty miniature booze bottles lined up on one kitchen counter, a basket containing boxes and boxes of paperclips, and a shoe box filled with nothing but pink artificial sweetener packets. He knew there were more bits and bobs, but that's all he could recollect on the spur of the moment.

After Marcus invited Pastor Osterhagen into his parents' home, Marcus revealed a lot about his mother. He did not recall that they ever had anyone over to the house, no company of any sort. He admitted that she had a mental health issue and that he feared she might someday get arrested due to some of her actions, especially stealing. But, somehow she escaped the law. He knew that she was secretly ashamed of her problem. Marcus wanted assurance and a promise from Pastor Osterhagen that none of what he told him would be mentioned at her funeral. He said he loved his mother and he didn't want her reputation to be spoiled. Remembering that his mother would occasionally steal things when they went shopping, he told Pastor that it did benefit their family by saving on expenditures. Stella stole the perfect shoes for him, school supplies, and clothing, anything that would fit in one of her trademark jumbo-sized handbags. More importantly for his mum, however, stealing gave her a personal rush that ignited something inside of her, making her feel vital, alive and happy. At some point, she became addicted to that rush. His mother spent years stashing things away in their house, which didn't bother his dad, Sebastiano, one bit. He seemed proud of her and the loot she gathered.

Presto told us that Marcus proceeded to tell Pastor a bit about his Dad's past. When he was in his mid-twenties he settled permanently in the United States, having left Parma, Italy, after which he daily missed the charm of his rustic, down-to-earth hometown. Shortly after immigrating, he met and married Stella, beginning young married life with very little money, barely enough to make a go of it. Because his grandparents were poor when they were growing up, his mum worked fervently to go beyond living in that type of poverty. They went from being have-nots to people of prosperity, thanks to her expertise in breaking the Seventh Commandment. Marcus divulged to Pastor that the most common item stolen by his mother was parmesan cheese from the dairy case at the grocery store. She certainly saved their family thousands of dollars over the years, as parmesan cheese daily held a place of honour on their supper table. His dad so appreciated the cheese imported from his hometown, referring to it as not your "average" parmesan, but the highly recognized and praised Parmigiano-Reggiano.

After returning home, Clement told Aia that he has no idea how or where to hide the eighty-three hymnals that Marcus will be returning to St. Peter's once he discovers the church's name emblazoned on the covers. It is an awkward subject now that the new hymnals have been purchased. Clement told Aia he will hide them under their bed. Tomorrow he will contact organizations to help him discretely find a new home for the hymnals.

At 8:30 p.m. Ruby and I travelled to the church kitchen and snacked on Macaroon cookie crumbs on the floor. There was a Ladies' Guild meeting this afternoon and, thankfully, there was a quantity of spillage.

– F.N.

BEFORE LUNCH TODAY CLEMENT SET OUT TO REFILL THE SUPPLIES IN HIS TRAVELLING communion kit. Taking a shortcut to the sacristy where the communion supplies are kept, he entered the sanctuary and discovered two three-foot tall green plants that were not there yesterday. They had been positioned in the chancel, one on each side of the altar, placed on attractive maple plant stands. Somehow they arrived on the premises without his knowledge and had been positioned in a very prominent place. Returning to the parsonage after refilling the wine and the wafers in his communion kit, he sat down with Aia and talked over this unusual addition to the formal, well-appointed sanctuary. He voiced to Aia that Historic St. Peter's is considered to be the most aesthetically attractive and historical church in all of Oswald County. Clement seemed troubled that these plants somehow look odd, out of place, a strange match for the formal sanctuary.

Aia asked Clement to watch the children for a few minutes while she speed walked to the sanctuary to see what he was talking about. Upon returning home, she told Clement that they are called "Money Tree" plants and are meant to bring good luck, fortune, wealth, and prosperity. Aia reminded Clement that Money Tree plants are often part of the decorum in Chinese restaurants, adding that she agrees with him that they look completely out of place at St. Pete's. On the bright side, she added that they are a hearty plant that doesn't need much light.

Ruby and I heard the thoughts Clement was focusing on, not just on who donated the plants, but his concern that there might be a hidden message, a behind-the-scenes agenda to this. Clement mentioned that perhaps the person who donated them assumes that the church needs much more money, is greedy for money, or that the pastor unfortunately thinks that money just grows on trees, especially when it comes to purchasing new hymnals.

For now, Aia suggested patience be applied to this situation because sooner or later it will come out who donated the plants. She told him that perhaps they could become portable plants, often leaving the sanctuary to be placed in Woolcox Hall, the Fireside Room, the entryway, one in each washroom, or various other places. She also told him to forget about it and be thankful for them. Her words to Clement concluded by telling him that they were having egg rolls and chicken fried rice for supper tonight and that she would like to borrow the Money

Tree plants to add ambiance to the parsonage at suppertime. They can pretend that they are in a Chinese restaurant. Clement thought that would be a good idea, so he offered to bring the plants home later this afternoon, cautioning that they will need to be returned to the sanctuary after supper.

At 11:30 p.m. Ruby and I entered the parsonage with hopes of finding a piece of fried rice that we could split. Thankfully, we found two kernels of rice along with one diagonally cut slice of celery. They were so tasty that we once again commented on Aia's exquisite culinary skills, especially when it comes to stir-fry cuisine, which is a once-a-week mainstay at the Osterhagen's supper table. We are fully aware that the Osterhagen's are not financially well off, but Ruby and I thought that if Aia borrows the Money Tree plants frequently, perhaps fortune will find its way into their lives and ease up the tension and anxiety of making it until payday each month. If good fortune happens, perhaps they could even go out to a Chinese restaurant on payday with their new wealth. Ruby and I are thankful that two Money Tree plants have arrived at HSP and are certain that the Osterhagen's will be blessed in many ways by them.

– F.N.

TONIGHT AIA AND GRETCHEN ATTENDED A "FRESH FRAGRANCE EVENT" THAT WAS assembled in St. Peter's Woolcox Hall. Most of the ladies purchased several fragrances that were available in cranberry, citrus, vanilla, cinnamon, apple, lavender, and rose. Gretchen enjoyed progressing from one fragrance to the next by smell-testing them, giving her opinion of which aromas were worth whiffing. The scents seemed to have no appeal to Aia, probably because her sense of smell is askew during this pregnancy. She did like the electric simmer pots, so she purchased a moss green and brown pottery pot for their home. She told Clement that she will create her own fragrances for now, aromas that appeal to her pregnancy cravings, like roasted garlic, fresh oregano, blackened chicken, and licorice. She said that she and Gretchen will go to Green's Natural Food Market tomorrow and pick up some unusual scented oils to create unique fragrances that are not available at Grocer Dan's. Aia said that she is looking forward to creating high quality concoctions and Gretchen (aided by her discerning nose) will be second-in-command.

At 11:30 p.m. Ruby and I travelled to the parsonage and snacked on one whole chocolate chip. We discussed what an advantage there is in having a crack in the wall in the Osterhagen's dining room. When Aia whips up simmering pot scents, the aroma will drift through the crack, thereby freshening up our dwelling, too.

– F.N.

Saturday, May 23

THIS MORNING RUBY AND I AWOKE TO THE APPETIZING AROMA OF BACON FRYING AT THE parsonage. We tumbled out of bed and rested near the crack in the dining room wall eavesdropping on the Osterhagens' breakfast conversation. Each one talked about their personal plans for the day, relating tidbits of news, almost like an old-time radio program. We were not precisely aware of what they ate for breakfast, except that it included hickory-smoked bacon.

Aia shared with Clement and Gretchen her thoughts and plans regarding the large woodland garden area at St. Pete's that is located on one side of the church, the shady side. Mentioning that it is now a glorious carpet filled with dainty, sweetly-scented lily-of-the-valley, in both the white and pink bell-shaped varieties, she said that she had an idea. She wanted to cut enough of them to fashion three floral arrangements; one as a centrepiece for their dining room table, one to place on the antique mahogany Victorian side table that is located in the narthex, and one to place on top of the sanctuary piano. Gretchen added that her plans for the day were all about helping her mama with the flowers. Clement finished the conversation by announcing that his day was so full that he hopes he has time to stop and smell the roses and the lily-of-the-valley.

After Ruby overheard the Osterhagen's breakfast conversation, she unveiled her plans for the remainder of the day. The first item on her agenda was to search for Willow, the current president of the Garden Girls Club, which consists of six bachelorette mice that are now of prime marrying age, each with the same thing on her mind. Willow was advised by Ruby that this is perfect lily-of-the-valley season as the garden patch is in its efflorescent prime. Willow spread that news to Cherry Blossom, and then it catapulted. Cherry Blossom spread it to Linden, Linden to Skye, Skye to Brooke, and finally, Brooke to Lark, thereby notifying all six female members of the Garden Girls Club to journey to the lily-of-the-valley flower patch.

The Garden Girls primary mission and vision is to spend time in the church flower beds in order to pick up the evocative scents of the blooming flowers on their fur coats, which makes them smell appealing to the mice bachelors. The bachelor mice do almost the same thing, but they prefer to spend their time in the bachelor button garden to acquire that fragrance, a more masculine aroma.

Having had no idea exactly what time Aia and Gretchen would be cutting some of the lily-of-the-valley, the Garden Girls Club decided to postpone their journey from 10 a.m. to 4 p.m. The new time of 4 p.m. turned out to be unfortunate after all, as they incorrectly assumed that Clement, Aia, and Gretchen would be inside at that time for tea or coffee. However, that was precisely when Aia, equipped with garden shears, and Gretchen, provided with children's scissors, appeared at the garden, ready to give the lily-of-the-valley a trim, which was more like a substantial haircut.

After Aia and Gretchen arrived, the Garden Girls Club scampered into hiding, moving so fast that Brooke lost her breath and Skye was so shook up that she started crying. To calm them down, Willow suggested that they gather in a circle and hold paws, huddling together to sing "Safety First" by mouthing the words instead of making a peep of noise.

It wasn't long before Gretchen came over holding her child-friendly scissors. Before she could take her first snippet of lily-of-the-valley, she spotted the mice. With a quick reaction all six mice synchronously placed their index fingers to their lips. Gretchen saw their reaction but didn't make a sound. Everyone in the club expected her to scream, but she was hushed and calm and simply moved to another area. After obtaining enough lily-of-the-valley, Gretchen found them once again, gave them a big smile, and waved goodbye. The last they saw Gretchen and Aia, Gretchen was carrying a wicker basket filled with lily-of-the-valley and heading to the back door of the parsonage with her mother.

The Garden Girls Club spent a good hour in the flower patch soaking up the aroma of the lily-of-the-valley. During that time, Cedric, one of the bachelor mice in our village, paid a visit to the Garden Girls Club. Willow told Ruby that Cedric appears to be infatuated with Lark. Cedric is a kind and loving mouse. Lark seems to be very receptive to Cedric. They might make a Mr. & Mrs. Match.

Willow told Ruby that prior to the Garden Girls Club afternoon spent in the lily-of-the-valley patch, she went to see Dr. Theodore Simonsen, the mouse village head librarian, but she couldn't meet with him because he had a toothache. So, she met with the assistant librarian, Dr. Christoff Kikkunen. Asking him for information about lily-of-the-valley, he was happy to research and inform her that he shares interest in that flower also, which made Willow wonder if he was possibly single and unattached. Shortly after her request, Dr. Kikkunen told her that the only church information that he was able to find referred to the flower also being named "Mary's Tears." That information stems from a legend that when Christ our Saviour was crucified, tears sprang forth from Mary's eyes and landed gently on the ground resulting in lily-of-the-valley flowers springing forth and blooming where each tear had dropped. Dr. Kikkunen also said that he found a hymn in an old Salvation Army hymnal where the text of the refrain goes like this: "He's the Lily-of-the-Valley, the bright and Morning Star. He's the fairest of ten thousand to my soul." Another bit of knowledge that Dr. Kikkunen added was that lily-of-the-valley is the national flower of Finland, but he only knows that information because he happens to be of Finnish descent and it is common knowledge in his family. After that, Dr. Kikkunen asked Willow if she would ever like to spend an afternoon with him. Willow told Ruby that she was favourable to that, so Dr. Kikkunen said he would contact her in a few days to make the arrangements. Willow was already hearing wedding bells and proclaiming that soon she hopes to be Mrs. Willow Kikkunen. Ruby did her best to discourage this type of talk, as she is concerned that Willow's hopes will be shattered if Dr. Kikkunen does not find Willow to be the one with whom he wants to tie the wedding knot.

At 11:30 p.m. Ruby and I travelled to the parsonage and snacked on a morsel of a cheese puff. While we ate, I asked Ruby if she would have enjoyed spending some time today in the lily-of-the-valley garden, even though she is a married mouse and no longer a spinster. She quickly replied by saying, "Ixnay." I asked her to explain herself further. She revealed that "Ixnay" is Pig Latin for "nix" which evidently must mean "not." I shook my head in agreement, even though I have never heard of Pig Latin before. Remembering that Ruby is allergic to many aromas, I figured out the reason why she couldn't go with the others. At first I thought she might be uncomfortable trying to click with the clique of spinsters, but realized the real reason is because of her hypersensitivity to scents. I am fine with the fact that she didn't pick up the lily-of-the-valley scent, since my Ruby's natural scent is sweet enough for me and brings about a lot of pleasures.

I must remember to pay a visit to Dr. Theodore Simonsen or Dr. Christoff Kikkunen tomorrow in order to find out exactly what this Pig Latin is. I don't have the first idea what it is, but I certainly did not want to admit that to my Ruby. Until I know more about it, I'll assume that pigs must be highly intelligent if they have the ability to speak Latin.

– F.N.

It was expected that today's attendance at St. Pete's would be below par. Being that this is Memorial weekend, many parishioners left town after work on Friday to travel north to open up their lake cottages while others headed off to their preferred campground where the adventure begins by setting up a tent. This is time to gather around the first campfire of the season where everyone can try out their outdoor cooking skills on hot dogs, hamburgers, brats, s'mores, and any other food that can be prepared over an open flame. Scary stories are spun around that fire while hands are lifted up to point out the Milky Way. Memories of embracing the great outdoors on this time-honoured weekend seem to travel home with everyone along with a trunk load of dirty laundry. Today the Osterhagens, just like the parishioners, were in the spirit of getting going on the summer season.

Ruby and I have remarked to each other that during this last trimester of Aia's pregnancy, she is not quite like herself. She has gone soft when it comes to practicality and frugality. Perhaps the twins are already a blessing to her in that she does not get as bent out of shape emotionally, even though she says she is out of shape physically.

Diana's Dairy Delight, located in the neighbouring small town of Roselle, opened up for the season this weekend. During this morning's breakfast the Osterhagens made a plan to drive out to Diana's this afternoon to treat themselves to soft serve ice cream cones with chocolate sprinkles. I informed Samson (one exceptionally strong and long-haired mouse in our village) about this adventure, so he seized the opportunity to quickly scoot into Gretchen's activity bag during worship this morning, knowing that each time Gretchen travels in their van she is equipped with her activity bag. Joining in on this outing made Samson privy to all that took place at Diana's.

After arriving at the "Triple D," the carhop approached their van and the Osterhagens were greeted by none other than Gretchen's babysitter, Christine. Happy to see each other, Gretchen asked permission to get out of the van so that she could hug Christine. Hoping to fetch good tips this summer, Christine mentioned that she is saving up for college expenses. Christine visited primarily with Gretchen, telling her there is newly-installed wallpaper printed with colourful ice creams cones in the washroom. After hearing that, Gretchen instantaneously needed to use the washroom, and so did Aia. Samson revealed to us that Gretchen asked to use the washroom three times during their short stay at Diana's. When it came time to order, Aia requested a banana split plus a family-sized order of onion rings. Ruby mentioned to me that Clement must be wondering what else his wife will crave before this pregnancy is completed.

Earlier in the day Aia was clearly upset. When she was approached after worship about preparing homemade potato salad for the annual church picnic by a representative of the church council, Henry Wallace, she tried to be civil when he asked her if she would prepare two hundred servings for the picnic on Sunday, June 1. She looked at him in absolute shock. She calmed down by remembering that Henry is a bachelor who has no clue what it is like to be pregnant, especially with twins, and to peel that many potatoes. She told him, "No, I can't do that, but I'd be happy to supply all of the ketchup for the picnic." Thoroughly irked, Aia complained to Clement that a pastor's wife is supposed to have the word "yes" tattooed on her forehead, along with a constant smiling happy face, and right now she is incapable of doing that. She did her best to give Henry an answer but is afraid, due to reading his facial expression, that he felt offended. Henry looked like he had just had an unpleasant visit with a real ice queen. Aia admitted to Clement that she can occasionally be an ice queen. Clement agreed with her.

Aia put Gretchen to bed tonight by reading stories together and praying, "Now I lay me down to sleep." After that, Aia changed into her extra-wide Mother's Day nightgown. Telling Clement how overheated and clammy she was, she headed outside to cool off and to view the moonlight. As soon as Aia walked outside, Ruby and I headed toward Woolcox Hall so we could keep an eye on her through the big windows. We watched her for fifteen minutes and then watched Clement go outside to find her, carrying along with him the baby monitor just in case Gretchen woke up. He found Aia at the church playground equipment swinging back and forth on one of the swings, her nightgown blowing in the evening breeze. We feared, for a moment, that she'd get sick or fall off of the swing, but realized that she was doing just fine. The look on Clement's face seemed to say that he was thinking he may never again see his girl-like, very pregnant, unusual, beautiful, and complicated wife acting like this. In most ways we have noticed that Aia does not resemble other women that Clement has known. Her moods are sometimes in the medium category, but most often they are either fire or ice. She is like a burner on a kitchen stove where the medium setting is shot, probably due to overuse.

After Aia returned from swinging, she told Clement that she was ravenous for some state fair food, especially the deep-fried creations. Clement heard so much about her food craving that he ended up driving down to the gas station, returning home shortly with three corn dogs, one for himself and two for Aia, which made her doubly giddy. After enjoying their treat, we heard her ask Clement if he would return to the gas station to pick up a couple more corn dogs. He gently refused her request by telling her that if she ate another corn dog she would need antacids before she would be able to fall asleep. After hearing that, Aia held Clement's hand and guided him to the refrigerator where there was a plate of chocolate walnut fudge that she and Gretchen had whipped up this afternoon. The homemade fudge turned out to be irresistibly tempting to Clement. Ruby and I were taken aback when we heard both of them forgetting their usual good manners as they smacked their lips, licked their fingers, and talked with their mouths full while carrying on and on about the delectableness of the fudge. As they ate, they became very chatty, probably due to the sugary content in the sweetened condensed milk and chocolate chips that were included in Aia's recipe.

At 11:30 p.m. Ruby and I travelled to the parsonage and munched on a tiny morsel of home-made fudge. As we ate, I became very talkative and told Ruby a bit more about my mum, something I have never told her before. What I had to say is important to me because not one day goes by without something happening that brings forth a memory of her. Just this morning I happened to glance at a picture postcard in the Sunday School craft supply room. It was a photograph of an old-time blue speckled enamel colander that was loaded full of freshly picked and washed strawberries. Suddenly, from the back of my mind, I remembered my mum singing a little song to me about a patch of wild strawberries that she found in a wooded area that grew alongside a stream. To this day I am still puzzled as to why my mum's tuneful little folk song focused solely on the distinctive fragrance of wild strawberries and did not even mention the mouth-watering tang of the berries. Their flavour is so delightful that one's taste buds simply explode during the first bite. It's as though the palate has been in hibernation all winter and suddenly awakens anew with the first bite of a wild strawberry. Mum might have been on to something though, considering that consumers now purchase many products that have a strawberry scent. There are a wide variety of bright strawberry pink candles, soaps, air fresheners, lip glosses, and body washes that smell identical to strawberries, the sought-after fruity feminine smell. That memory really perked up my day and after I told Ruby about it, it brightened up her evening. Ruby doesn't know the wild strawberry song, but after we crawled in bed she hummed me to sleep with the restful tune of "All Through the Night."

– F.N.

Friday, May 29

THE DOVER FAMILY, ALOYSIUS "TIP" DOVER, EILEEN DOVER, AND THEIR SEVEN-YEAR-old son, Ben Dover, kindly volunteered to plant all of the annual flowers at the church this spring. They filled two big planters, four window boxes, and planted annuals around the lighted church sign located in the front of the church. They have a personal connection with one of the greenhouses in the area, which cut them a great deal on the price. The Dovers are also owners of a big red pickup truck that came in handy to haul the flowers to church. It was crystal clear that they were like children with a new toy eager to oversee the planting project, to-day's efforts resulting in a stunningly beautiful display of flowers at St. Pete's.

The Dover's were given the go ahead to select flowers and plant them any way they thought would look the most attractive. It was special to see them arrive with so many flowers, ready to spend the morning dressing up the church prop-erty. Some of the mice decided to entertain themselves by resting on an inside basement window ledge to occasionally peek out to watch the Dover Family at work. The Dovers also brought along their two little dogs, Roll Dover and Rover Dover. As they were working, we thought that Rover Dover might have gotten a glimpse of us, but most likely he did not. We lay down flat on the window ledge for awhile, completely out of sight, as we needed to calm down our nerves. After a while we softly sang our theme song, "Safety First," reminding us to be extra careful, which made us all feel better. We all like living here and don't want to upset the flower cart. When the coast was clear, we went back to entertaining our-selves by taking a gander at the Dover Family planting flowers. We realized that this family must be meant to do what they are doing as they all have names that perfectly fit the job, even the two little dog names are a match. The Dover Family spent the entire day being tipped-over, leaned-over, bent-over, rolled-over, and rovered-over until all the flower planting was over.

At 11:30 p.m. Ruby and I travelled to the parsonage and snacked on a tiny morsel of a chicken enchilada. While we munched, I asked Ruby which one of flowers planted today by the Dover Family was her favourite. She could not an-swer the question because the Dover Family did not plant her most adored and wished-for flower, the *Leucojum aestivum*, the only flower that she is not allergic to. I asked her if that flower goes by any other name and Ruby told me that it is sometimes called the St. Agnes' Flower or the Summer Snowflake. Mentioning that it is a tiny and dainty white flower with a delicate perfume, she told me that the one time she sat under some *Leucojum aestivum* she became enamoured by their fragrance, so much so, that the aromatic bouquet has never left her memory. To this day, if she closes her eyes, she can still smell them no matter where she is. At that point, Ruby closed her eyes, breathed deeply, and told me that she could still smell their aroma even though she is completely surrounded by whiffs of enchiladas. After Ruby said all of those words, I asked her again to tell me her favourite flower that the Dover Family planted today. She looked up from her enchilada and replied, the *Tagetes*, but before I could ask her if the *Tagetes* go by any other name, she replied at the speed of light, "The Marigolds."

– F.N.

For several days, Laurel-Leigh and Luna-Leigh, twin sisters from our mice village, have been anticipating today's annual church picnic. They told me that their favourite part about the picnic is to observe the elderly members sitting outside in God's creation enjoying picnic foods. They think it must be something most of them look forward to, as it is the one and only picnic of the year. The elderly members with their canes, walkers, and wheelchairs know that life itself is often not a picnic. But today there was a real church picnic at Historic St. Peter's.

Most people mentioned how perfect the weather was for the event. When the weather happens to be ideal the day of the picnic, someone always concludes that God wants the tradition to continue. Whereas, if it rains on the day scheduled for the picnic, maybe God doesn't want St. Peter's to hold the picnic every single year. The few times it has rained they seem to have forgotten.

It was up to the church council to host the picnic this year. Because there are several of them, everything went very smoothly. The only hitch was due to the council members being absent from the worship service as they were outside grilling, jabbering, and having fun wearing shorts and sandals today, instead of being dressed in their regular church clothing. Several members of the congregation questioned whether "quality" members belong to St. Peter's Church Council, pointing out that they must not have their priorities straight. It was obvious that they found it of greater importance to prepare the details of the picnic than to be in the sanctuary worshipping with everyone else. The sanctuary windows were open wide this morning letting in the aroma of grilled hamburgers and hot dogs. Most worshippers admitted that it smelled so exceptionally good that it was almost too much to handle while the worship service was in progress.

Chairs from Woolcox Hall had been set up all over the church property and the food, beverages, and desserts were on long tables set up end to end. Aia and Gretchen went outside to the picnic area and waited in line, hoping that Clement would soon join them. He apparently was tied up, so they went ahead and got their lunch. While glancing at the food on the table, Aia noticed that the four bottles of ketchup that she donated were alongside the mustard. Laurel-Leigh and Luna-Leigh told us that the ketchup and mustard were not what Aia appeared to be focusing on. Instead, it was the potato salad. There were three institutional-sized pails of potato salad (store bought, not homemade) sitting in a big bucket of ice. It was evidently purchased from the deli at Grocer Dan's. Perhaps they were donated, as owner Dan Berry is a member of Historic St. Pete's. When Aia saw that extra-large quantity of potato salad, which must be two hundred servings, she was stunned, as she had been asked to prepare the potato salad for this event. She told Clement later on that she couldn't even imagine peeling and cooking that many potatoes. Still, there needed to be a tallying up of the money that they would have spent to purchase the mayonnaise and other ingredients, let alone counting up the hours spent chopping and crying over so many onions, plus how many eggs that needed to be hard cooked and peeled for the recipe. Aia appeared to be so thankful that she said no to Henry's request, because if she had attempted to prepare that quantity of potato salad at home, she surely might have gone into early labour and held Henry Wallace responsible.

Entertainment for the children was provided by the youth group. Available were face painting and the traditional children's picnic game, the gunny sack race. Both those things got very little attention as they paled in comparison to the new game, the rental dunk tank. The lineup to try the dunk tank was continual. This was an idea of the new youth group leader, Grey Neilson. Grey was having more fun than anyone else, taking more than his share of turns sitting on the stool and getting dropped in the tank when the ball hit the bulls-eye. Laurel-Leigh mentioned to us that it looked like he wanted to be a youth again, even though he's hitting forty, nearly bald, and doesn't look especially handsome all wet.

There was also entertainment for the grownups. A local chain saw artist was asked to use his skills to carve out a cross from a very large Cedar tree stump. The grownups were entertained watching him do his work, but after a while they disliked that the chain saw was so loud it interrupted their ability to visit with each other. The finished work is just beautiful and will hold a place of honour in the church garden.

After the picnic Aia and Gretchen went home. Much later Clement showed up, disturbed that he had missed the church picnic altogether. He explained that one of the members wanted to talk to him for a minute, but it ended up taking two hours. He told Aia he's going to watch out for the phrase, "I just need a couple minutes of your time," because it doesn't ever seem to turn out that way. Aia told him about the three large institutional containers of potato salad from the deli at Grocer Dan's. Because Grocer Dan's deli potato salad was served at the picnic, they both wondered why Dan wasn't asked in the first place to supply the potato salad.

When teenager Summer Harris noticed the abundance of beautiful flowers that the Dover Family had planted on the church property yesterday, she spoke with Pastor Osterhagen and asked him if she could volunteer to water the flowers. She explained that she would come over three times a week during June, July, and August to make certain all the flowers got a good drink. Pastor thought that was a great idea. She thanked him and told him that she would begin tomorrow.

At 7:30 p.m. Ruby and I travelled to the yard at the church and snacked on morsels of picnic droppings. No one saw us. We returned home for the night with full tummies and thankful hearts.

– F.N.

Monday, June 1

Carrying a full picnic basket, the Osterhagens took off today on what they call an "adventure." Ruby and I do not know what they did or where they went, but we did hear details about their return trip as Clement and Aia sat in the living room trying to unwind from what had just happened. As they were driving on the highway coming back into town, Clement slowed down to observe the lower speed limit. As soon as he did that, they were followed by a police cruiser. There were no twirling lights to motion for them to pull over. Instead, the officer followed them all the way to the parsonage. Clement and Aia assumed that he must have had a lead foot, which would result in a speeding ticket. All the way back home they were daunted and unnerved as to why the police officer was right on their tail. Driving into their driveway, they remained frozen in their seats, wondering if the officer had been notified by someone that their home had been busted into, or if their speedometer was defective, or some other tragedy had taken place. The police officer approached their car as Clement rolled down his window. At that point, Gretchen got all excited as she personally knew the policeman, Officer King. Gretchen said that he is her friend Maribel's dad.

Both Maribel and Gretchen happen to have the exact same pair of running shoes, which they removed, along with their socks, before playing a game at Maribel's birthday party last weekend. All of the birthday guests sat on the floor attempting to pass an empty sucker stick from neighbour to neighbour by using their toes. When Gretchen was picked up from the birthday party, she accidently grabbed two left shoes, leaving Maribel behind with two rights. It turned out that the Osterhagens nervous and frightful trip home had nothing to do with breaking the speed limit or being victims of a crime, but was about straightening out a shoe predicament. Aia said that it was very kind of Officer King to solve this problem, but would have preferred him to do this when he was off duty. It would have been far less harrowing if he would have been dressed in regular clothes and driving his family van instead of doing this errand in such an official way.

At 6:45 p.m. Ruby and I travelled to the Youth Room where we found a few mini-chocolate chips and teeny-tiny multi-coloured sprinkles that had dropped on the floor during a Build-Your- Own-Sundae-Sunday party that the youth enjoyed yesterday. The youth at St. Pete's are both ingenious and practical in that we read the letters BYOB on the poster, which means bring your own bowl (and spoon, of course.)

— F.N.

RUBY AND I WOKE UP FAR TOO EARLY THIS MORNING BECAUSE AIA WAS MAKING A racket of noise in the kitchen. She must have had an abundance of energy, as we saw her beginning a home improvement project, probably hoping that it will be accomplished before the twins are born. We guessed that Clement did not hear her slip out of bed. We peeked through the hole in the wall and saw Aia stripping off ugly kitchen wallpaper, using hot wet rags to make its removal easier. Under the wallpaper were walls painted flame red, probably influenced by decorating fads in the 1960s. Even though she seemed pleased at her accomplishment so far, it is evident to us that Aia is in a big mess that is much more sizable than she ever expected a re-wallpapering project might become.

When Clement woke up, he walked into the kitchen, saw the disorder, and told Aia that he couldn't believe that she was attempting a jumbo project like this right before the babies are due. We heard Clement softly say to himself that he wants his old Aia back, the pre-pregnant Aia, one who is sensible, practical, and thrifty, the Aia that thinks over things logically before proceeding. She excitedly told him about the new kitchen wallpaper that she has stored in the twins' bedroom that she special ordered from Trina at Steensen's Paint & Wallpaper. Together they walked into the twins' bedroom and she showed Clement the wallpaper with great delight. Clement really liked it, but he mentioned that this particular wallpaper needs to have a neutral wall colour underneath it or the red paint on the walls will show through. After hearing that, Aia's mood became downcast, for this project has become too mountainous for her to achieve before the twins arrive. She cried and asked Clement for help. He held her and reassured her that they will work it out, somehow, but that it most likely will not get done before the twins are born.

When Ruby heard Clement's kind words for Aia, she started to cry just like Aia. It was then that Ruby told me that she wants one of the walls in our dwelling wallpapered but she has been too timid to bring the subject up. I asked her if she already has some wallpaper. She told me that she found a greeting card on the floor in Woolcox Hall one day following a birthday party. The decorative card has a painted lighthouse, a sailboat, and an array of seashells. Printed on the top of the card are the words, "A Seaside Day." I told Ruby that we will work together to hang the wallpaper, but that it most likely will not get done before the twins are born.

At 11:30 p.m. Ruby and I travelled to the parsonage kitchen and accidently snacked on morsels of old wallpaper and wallpaper glue. We felt lighthearted, woozy, and were having dizzy spells so we immediately returned home, thankful that we made it home safely to sleep in our own bed. We were so confused, we almost lost our way. From now on we'll be more careful about what we eat. We decided that the wallpaper glue, even though it was tasty, is too overwhelming for our systems.

  – F.N.

Friday, June 5

Before bed tonight, Clement walked down the breezeway in his pajamas and bathrobe. His purpose was to place some important papers on his office desk that were essential for a meeting scheduled for early tomorrow morning. While walking past the choir room, Clement detected a beam of light shining underneath the door. Since the choir finished rehearsing at the end of May, he must have been perplexed as to why the choir room lights were shining brightly on a Friday night in June. Opening the door to turn the lights off, he encountered something that future pastors never learn a thing about during four years of seminary.

The mysterious person who vandalized the choir room had deliberately emptied the fifty-two-inch-tall filing cabinet of its contents, an extensive quantity of choral music octavos, along with choir book collections. These scores are loved by the choir members and by those who listen to them sing, as they contain sacred texts and scriptures. The role of the choir is to be a mouthpiece in presenting God's Word to worshippers each time an anthem is sung in church. The music was anything but treasured tonight as it was plunked in a big pile in the centre of the room. On the bottom of this paper heap were several of the red choir robes. It was as though the perpetrator of this crime was preparing the octavos and choir books for a book burning, but thankfully, did not light a match. A pointed message was written on the chalkboard which read, "Who do you think you are – The Mormon Tabernacle Choir?" It was difficult for Clement to speculate whether this crime was motivated by a practical joke, or if whoever did this fully intends to shut down St. Peter's adult music program by deliberately making a shamble of the choir room. The mice village has a hunch that the damage was most likely done by Griffin the Gremlin, but is open to considering other suspects.

Harmony, Spinet, and Celesta are three mice from our village that form the outstanding a cappella vocal trio, "The Sing-it-Thrice-Mice." The trio recently took up residence in the far corner of the choir robe closet. They were at home during the vandalism but remained out of harm's way by hiding silently. Not one of them dared to peek out to see who it was that sabotaged the choir room. They were far too terror-stricken to take even an itty-bitty peek at who was ruining with this havoc their most favourite room at St. Peter's.

Clement turned off the lights, shut the door, and went home and dialed 911, after which he spilled out everything he had seen to Aia. The responders arrived immediately, scanned the room and locked the door. They said that a crew would be back in the morning to take fingerprints and look for evidence as to who did this crime. Clement went to bed but couldn't sleep, so he got up and called the choir director, Stacey McKinney, even though it was 10:30 p.m. He apologized for phoning her so late, but he needed to tell her about the vandalism, also asking her if she knew of anyone that is upset at the choir or at her. She explained to him that the adult choir sings challenging music and that there was one person, Sheldon Cunningham, she had to take aside and ask him to step down from the choir because he lacked the ability to learn and perform the music. Because of this musical weakness on his part, he was throwing other choir members off. To make it worse, she had several complaints from the altos who sit in front of Sheldon about his bad breath. They didn't want his halitosis whirling and wafting, floating and gliding right on top of their hairdos. Pastor told Stacey that he has not seen Sheldon for a few weeks. Stacey added that he has not been back to choir since she talked to him. Pastor thanked her, hung up, and told Aia that he doesn't think this vandalism is the work of Griffin, but maybe of Sheldon Cunningham. In talking about it, they realized that Griffin always steals something and returns it later. No, this couldn't be the work of Griffin. Thank goodness that whoever made this mess was not cruel enough to take a match to it.

At 11:30 p.m. Ruby and I travelled to the parsonage and snacked on a small morsel that dropped from a Rueben sandwich. Especially divine was the uttermost important ingredient included in the sandwich, the Swiss cheese. It was fit for royalty.

– F.N.

Saturday, June 6

AIA AWAKENED THIS MORNING WITH A PREPOSTEROUS IDEA THAT WE HEARD HER SHARE with Clement. Her objective was to carry out a plan whereby the twins would be born on Canadian soil, thereby entitling them to dual citizenship instantly, with absolutely no effort on their part. She told Clement that all he had to do was to cross the Canadian border while her labour is underway. As Aia spoke, she described that the advantage of that scenario would provide the twins with the privilege to live and work in either country. Aia admitted to Clement that she is a bundle of nerves when she thinks about their future, not knowing what shape the world will be in by the time they are grown up. Convinced of her idea, we heard Aia say that doors would open up for them in the future. Aia relayed to Clement that the twins might one day aspire to be chefs in Quebec, pursue ballet training in Toronto, or perhaps become professional Lacrosse players in Calgary, a trinity of examples.

Clement listened to Aia's proposal, but told her that he will not drive all the way to Canada with her bellowing in agony. He spoke clearly by saying that it would be too demanding of a situation for him to handle. He reached out and held Aia, calmed her down, told her that she had a very clever and pioneering idea, but that the babies will have to be born right here in the United States at Our Lady of Lourdes Hospital, just a few blocks down the street from the parsonage. She agreed that it was a nonsensical, cockeyed idea. Blaming everything on her constantly changing emotions, she told Clement that she feels a little lopsided and cannot wait for the babies to be born so that she will feel like herself once again.

At 11:30 p.m. Ruby and I travelled to the parsonage and snacked on morsels of banana chips, potato chips, tortilla chips, shoestring potato chips, and corn chips that we found on a dreadfully untidy kitchen floor. Aia was not careful when she ripped open the chip bags, plus, she might not have had the energy to sweep up the spillage. We surmised that Aia didn't feel like cooking or cleaning today, let alone watching her calorie or salt consumption. Ruby and I were delighted to enjoy the melange of chips, but stopped short as we were worried about our blood pressure soaring through the roof.

– F.N.

THIS DAY BEGAN EARLY IN THE WEE HOURS OF THE NIGHT. CLEMENT AND AIA WERE awakened by telephone calls, four in all, until they finally left their telephone receiver off of the cradle. The first telephone call rang at 12:30 a.m. and the last call was at 2:45 a.m. Aia was wide awake during that time because she was puzzled as to why their telephone was ringing at inappropriate hours. This hasn't ever happened before, so it seemed baffling to her.

Aia answered all four of the telephone calls. Ruby and I assumed that Aia wanted Clement to rest so that he would be at his best for leading Sunday morning worship in just a few hours. As Aia later recounted to Clement, all four of the callers were men. These men each asked about our "services," to which Aia told them the service time is 10 o'clock on Sunday mornings. When they heard that, they hung up. Aia said that they all sounded like New Yorkers, mentioning that the fourth caller sounded like a really sweet guy. During the third telephone call Aia invited the caller to attend the service at 10 o'clock on Sunday morning. Aia said that he seemed especially confused by her answer, plus her invitation. He told her that it was very peculiar that their service is provided on Sunday mornings, asking if she was talking about a church service. Aia told him that he was correct. She also asked him if he needed directions to Historic St. Peter's. After he heard that, he apologized for calling and hung up. Aia mentioned to Clement that no one ever calls a parsonage in the untimely hours of a Sunday morning inquiring about the worship service, so these calls must be a big blooper, suspecting that these men were not interested in church services at all, but about another type of service.

When the fourth call rang, we heard Aia ask the man how he obtained their telephone number. He told her that he had gotten it from a magazine display ad. As she later talked it over with Clement, we heard her say that it dawned on her that their number must have mistakenly been printed in some advertisement selling "adult" conversations. A typo, as small as a misprint of just one number, could have resulted in telephone calls to their home telephone. Aia told Clement that on Monday morning she will call the telephone company and talk to them about it. She said that she has to get this straightened out, as this cannot be happening after the twins are born or she will never get any sleep.

Aia later talked to Clement about the third caller and told him that she noticed he was somewhat unlike the other three callers as he was kind, polite, and had a pleasant speaking voice. He differed from the others because when she told him the worship service was at 10 o'clock every Sunday morning, he seemed confused, but mostly humiliated and embarrassed, like he felt guilty about something and needed forgiveness. She told Clement that this man was in a conundrum about what he was doing. Aia hoped that her words inviting him to attend church at Historic St. Peter's might have helped turn him in another direction, a direction towards faith, forgiveness, understanding, and love, all through Christ our Saviour.

Ruby and I skipped snacking tonight and went to bed early, sleeping until the parsonage telephone rang at 12:30 a.m. We were awake the rest of the night because of the telephone calls at the Osterhagens. Even though we were too tired to go to church this morning, we went anyway because we didn't want to miss out on seeing whether or not the third caller came to church after Aia so kindly invited him. We would most likely recognize him because he would be a stranger.

– F.N.

JAYNE BROWNTON, THE WIFE OF HSP's JANITOR, CHUCK, ARRIVED AT PASTOR Osterhagen's office right on time today for her 9 o'clock appointment. She needed to speak with Pastor privately about something that is causing her ongoing agitation. Before she opened up about her predicament, Jayne reminded Pastor that for many years she has voluntarily assisted Chuck with his janitorial duties by cleaning out the debris from the sanctuary hymnal racks, which contain far more items than hymnals and Bibles. Jayne revealed to Pastor that the hymn racks often become a yucky garbage slot. Over the years she has found such items as chewed gum, partially-eaten sticky suckers and sucker sticks, pencils, lozenge and gum wrappers, cookie crumbs, old bulletins and inserts, pens, pieces of dry breakfast cereal, contaminated facial tissues, broken crayons, fragments of crushed crackers, and, occasionally, a forgotten baby bottle with milk or formula that has turned totally rancid. Mentioning that such a disgustingly filthy job requires industrial strength disposable gloves, she informed him that she always donates an extra-large box to St. Pete's. Explaining further how much work it is to clean the hymn racks, she remarked that it would be better for St. Pete's to have a dozen or so wastebaskets positioned on the sanctuary floor in the dead centre of every pew in order to collect the various rubbish that accumulates during each worship service.

Prior to the private consultation happening in Pastor's office, Winky, a dapper, winsome, and outgoing male mouse in our village, happened to be putting his feet up and resting behind the large oak cabinet located in Pastor's office. This cabinet houses the treasured glockenspiel unit that was donated many years ago by one of St. Pete's older members, Ziggy Zirkelbach. Ziggy contributed the glockenspiel in loving memory of his parents, Hans and Lisbeth Zirkelbach. St. Peter's glockenspiel happens to be the latest carillon system that electronically rings church bells playing familiar hymns that are programmed into the system. These hymns are heard throughout the neighbourhood twice daily, precisely at noon and at four o'clock. When Pastor and Jayne arrived this morning, Winky dropped out of his comfort zone, became noiseless, uncomfortable, and sat up straight and attentive, at first for personal safety reasons, but later on out of curiosity regarding what the two of them were discussing so seriously.

Winky told me that he grasped tightly onto the words he heard of the conversation between Pastor and Jayne. He said that he did this for my sake, as he was certain their dialogue was of prime importance and needed to be shared with me, an insightful contribution to the recording of *Finley's Tale*. I thought that was very judicious of him, and thoughtful, too, to give me some scoop to include in the telling of my tale.

Ruby and I feel heartbroken for Winky, as he must be totally exasperated. Word has spread throughout our village that each one of our available female mice has been daydreaming that one day he might choose her to become his wife. Normally this would be stupendous for an attractively available bachelor, but not in this case. Winky's misfortune stems from bearing a rare medical eye condition that he has had since birth. He told Ruby and me that this condition causes his right eye to uncontrollably open and close speedily to an excessive degree, resembling the flirting type of winking technique that shines as brightly as Oswald County's snowplows projecting their blindingly blue flashing lights. Even though he cannot help it, Winky's winking condition conveys to the female mice that he has an irresistible attraction, appeal, and warm affection for them, even though he barely even glances their way.

Jayne told Pastor that this appointment was because she was having a difficult situation with one of the members, Ted Williamson. She described Ted as a bachelor in his mid-seventies who dresses in one of his three bowling shirts on Sundays, an odd form of church clothing, but somewhat dressy and far better than a sweatshirt or a T-shirt. Jayne mentioned that prior to Ted's retirement he was a member of just one bowling league, but now that he has more time, he belongs to three. The three individual team bowling shirts have really ballooned up his wardrobe choices. So at every worship service Ted sits in his preferred spot wearing one of them. Jayne explained that Ted's bowling shirts are beside the point. The real problem is toothpicks.

Five years ago Jayne nicknamed Ted, "Toothpick Ted," but has kept her mouth quiet and never revealed that to anyone. The nick came about because Ted incessantly has a toothpick in his mouth every time he attends church. Jayne pointed out to Pastor Osterhagen that even when the most recent church photo directly was produced, Ted had his photograph taken wearing a bowling shirt while sporting a toothpick in his mouth. Jayne went on to elaborate about Ted's toothpick life.

Jayne began by saying that toothpicks must be one of the oldest instruments for removing fragments and debris from teeth, probably even used by Adam and

Eve when they needed to remove hundreds of tiny raspberry or strawberry seeds stuck between their teeth. After that she got to the real point. Jayne said that every single Sunday morning, Toothpick Ted continues to be a long time faithful breakfast customer at Art's Truck Stop on Highway 19, being certain to pick up a free toothpick or two after feasting on a homestyle breakfast. Jayne mentioned that Art's Truck Stop has a reputation throughout Oswald County for their big and affordable trucker breakfasts served on Sundays, plated with bacon, sausage, and ham. She added that she understood just why a person might require a toothpick after chewing that overgenerous amount of meat. Along with the friendly service at Art's are fresh farm eggs, crispy home fries, and California sourdough toast. The "Trucker Special" lacks all silly garnishes like a sprig of parsley or a paper thin slice of cantaloupe. The servers at Art's have a stellar reputation for keeping mugs topped up with freshly brewed coffee which they pour out along with a pleasant smile.

Toothpick Ted told Jayne one Sunday morning that he occasionally sets up a flavouring station on his dining room table to hand dip toothpicks into a variety of flavouring oils. Telling Jayne that he prefers cinnamon, clove, or peppermint oil, he added that his favourite preference are toothpicks dipped in cinnamon oil because they produce a sweet and pungent flavour. Jayne told Pastor that she doesn't want to, or ever will want to, know that much information about toothpicks.

Jayne disclosed to Pastor that she supposed Toothpick Ted might be keen on a toothpick hobby. He could handcraft objects using ordinary toothpicks and glue, a better and safer use of toothpicks. She thought he could begin toothpick art by making a simple windmill, ship, or even a replica of the Eiffel Tower. If he got really advanced, he could try to creatively craft the Tower Bridge in London. After thinking about it thoroughly, she said that she decided not to share her idea with him. Jayne added that there is also a safety issue involved, as she has seen Ted throwing his flashy inferno-red bowling ball (which he has named Fire Storm) at Crosley's Lane & Lounge with a toothpick in his mouth, risking swallowing it or getting it stuck in his throat. (Off of the subject, Jayne took a couple of minutes to inform Pastor that the Coney Island hot dogs served at Crosley's are nothing but first-rate. They are topped with drizzled mustard and a generous amount of diced onions. Plus, if you want to make it fancy, shredded cheese can be added for an additional charge of only twenty-five cents.)

Jayne brought to light another concern. Toothpick Ted completely confiscates the job of the Sunday morning acolyte by lighting the altar candles himself before the acolyte arrives. This does not give anyone else a chance to be an acolyte, even though the confirmation students have voluntarily signed up on the schedule posted in the narthex. Winky added that the boys and girls arrive at church, immediately put on a white robe, but quickly become crestfallen after they see that the altar candles are already burning brightly. Nevertheless, Jayne said the acolyte situation was really beside the point of this meeting, which was to tackle the vicious ongoing toothpick dilemma.

Toothpick Ted has been depositing his castoff toothpicks in the hymnal racks his entire adult life, according to Jayne. She divulged to Pastor that for the last five years she has gathered up Ted's toothpick each week and added it to her ongoing collection that she keeps in a plastic sandwich baggie. Without counting them, Jayne estimated that she has amassed approximately two hundred and sixty or so discarded toothpicks in the baggie. She has become so annoyed with Ted and his toothpicks that she took action. Attaching a plain white address label to the toothpick bag, she printed the words, "Contains Deadwood, Return to Litterbug," followed by placing the bag in Ted's church mailbox. Last Sunday Toothpick Ted emptied out the contents of his pigeonhole located in the narthex and discovered the Deadwood bag. He assumed that Jayne had done it. Approaching her before the worship service, he asked her to kindly step outside. Jayne said that he was clearly hurt and told her that because of this he will find another church to attend where toothpicks are permitted. He distinctly told Jayne that she is a toothpick herself because she is sharply picking on him. Jayne said that this confrontation has bothered her very much, even disturbing her sleep.

Pastor Osterhagen wisely suggested Matthew 7:5 to help them both with their sore feelings. The verse touches on putting a stop to making judgements of others. Jayne cannot sleep at night because of the hurricane she caused and Ted now wants to flee from St. Pete's to a toothpick-friendly church. Pastor offered that he would telephone Ted and make arrangements for both of them to come into his office to work this out. The purpose of the meeting would be to forgive one another. Jayne liked that advice. Winky peeked out from behind the glockenspiel cabinet and saw the heavy burden absolutely fall off of Jayne's shoulders. Jayne thanked Pastor for helping and also inquired as to what was in Matthew 7:5. He told her that it was about first taking the plank out of your own eye so it will be easier to help remove a speck from the other person's eye. Jayne looked at Pastor Osterhagen and said that she was sorry that she hurt Ted's feelings and she wants to apologize to him. After all, a toothpick is only a speck of wood and that even after collecting two-hundred and sixty of them, they didn't amount to much. Lastly she added that she will be able to sleep tonight, adding that she'll be back on Friday to clean out the pews, which is really a cinch, one that she shouldn't complain about.

Before Jayne left, she turned around and told Pastor that many years ago she and Ted were engaged, but she broke off their engagement because every time they were about to kiss he had to remove a toothpick from his mouth. It doesn't seem like much of a reason now, but when she was twenty-three years old she was persnickety and Ted's overabundant toothpick usage seemed like too much to overlook. On her way out her last words to Pastor were to tell him that she guessed that toothpicks were the reason that she ended up marrying Chuck. She said that Chuck never uses toothpicks and that all of the toothpicks in their home are used only to check to see if the cupcakes are done or for making a relish tray using midget sweet pickles, pickled garlic cloves, green olives, and pickled pearl onions, one of each ingredient threaded onto a toothpick. Jayne said that there is a Spanish name for them but she can never remember it, so she just calls them "Spanish Bliss."

At 11:30 p.m. Ruby and I travelled to the parsonage and snacked on a small piece of a dropped deep fried cheese curd. Ruby told me how thankful she is that toothpicks were invented, as they make the best knitting needles for her projects.

– F.N.

Friday, June 12

SUMMER HARRIS, A LOCAL HIGH SCHOOL STUDENT, HAS BEEN STOPPING BY ST. PETER'S several times a week to water the outdoor summer flowers. In order for her to develop her suntan, she arrives at HSP wearing a skimpy bikini top with short shorts. It did not take very long for two elderly men to figure out her watering schedule. The two arrive ahead of Summer and post themselves in Woolcox Hall so they can observe the watering show that she puts on. She is a lovely girl with the appearance of a pretty blond movie star from the 1960s.

Hiram Holmes and Carlton Ferguson are acting just like a couple of lonely old men as they sit in Woolcox Hall three times a week with a cup of coffee waiting for Summer to arrive. Watching Summer appears to be the pinnacle of their week. From the windows in Woolcox Hall, they have a perfect view of her. Clement doesn't know if he should approach Summer and suggest that she wear a cover-up, or to not say anything. Aia advised him to just let it go, reminding him that summer only lasts three months and then the flowers won't need any more watering. She informed Clement that just as soon as Hiram's and Carlton's wives find out about their summertime entertainment watching Summer, their viewing time will expire.

At 9:30 p.m. Ruby and I travelled to the church kitchen. We were disappointed that we didn't find a bite to eat. We are aware that the church janitor and his wife put extra effort into cleaning the kitchen today. Delivered to St. Peter's kitchen last week was an extra-large refrigerator with glass doors. Due to the interior illumination from the refrigerator, we could see that the kitchen glistened and was squeaky clean. Ruby and I made a clear-cut decision that we will travel here more often to consume sweets, as there is generally a plethora of inviting cookie crumbs to be found on the kitchen floor. Sadly, that was not so today.

– F.N.

THE FIRST CULTURAL SURPRISE THAT THE OSTERHAGENS HAPPENED UPON AS NEWCOMERS to Historic St. Peter's was possibly the worship behaviour on Sunday mornings. Clement and Aia's conversation centered on what seems to be a lack of common sense, respect, and decency during the worship services, which lead to behaviours that they would like to see disappear. Socializing during the worship service, whispering, and slurping of both hot and cold beverages are just a few behaviours. They even wonder if parishioners are really wearing their Sunday best attire. Ruby and I listened in at the Osterhagens' conversation after church today as we were curious to hear them discuss the topic of church etiquette.

Aia let Clement know that she has an idea that might help raise the bar on church etiquette during the worship services. She will compose a list that can be printed in the weekly bulletin confronting this touchy subject. Clement encouraged her with a thankful go ahead and said that he's looking forward to seeing what she comes up with. After all, he mentioned that Gretchen has better manners while attending church than most any of the adult members. Clement noted that Gretchen readily stands up and sits down at all the right times, opens a hymnal and sings along, even though she cannot read, does not know the words to the hymn, or how to find the correct page number in the hymnal. She makes certain that she goes to the washroom prior to entering the sanctuary so she never has to get out of the pew for that reason. She has already memorized much of the liturgy and loudly sings or softly hums her favourite church song that is called the "Kyrie." We often hear Gretchen sing, "Lord, have mercy; Christ, have mercy; Lord, have mercy," at home, especially when she is holding and rocking Grace, her baby doll, or changing Grace's diaper.

The primary reason that Clement and Aia are askew about church etiquette today is due to Charmaine Reyes, nicknamed by Aia, "The Coupon Queen." Charmaine must be addicted to coupon collecting, delighting in the friendship pleasures it brings her. Every Sunday she comes equipped with a small satchel full of clipped coupons. As soon as Clement begins his sermon, she nudges the person nearest her and whispers to them, "Help yourself to whatever coupons you want and when you are finished, please pass the bag around the room." She has made many friends this way by saving the members cash on common items. On the outside of her leopard printed satchel she has taped the words, "Please help yourself and return to Charmaine Reyes when finished." The people in the pews watch for her satchel to come their way and quickly take turns sorting through the coupons to see if there are any they can use. There are coupons for shampoo, bug bite ointment, easy squeeze cheese, cereal, oil changes, potpies, frozen lemonade, bar soap, prune juice, hairspray, margarine, laundry detergent, etc.

Another topic is Fritz Schmidt and his flip flops, or, shall we say, lack of flip flops. As it is now warmer weather, it seems to be fashionable at HSP to wear plastic flip flops to church. Fritz shows up every Sunday from June through August in his printed Hawaiian palm tree shirt, khaki shorts, and bright green flip flops. That's not so bad, but when he gets settled in his pew, he removes his flip flops and rubs his feet on the cool wooden floor underneath the pews. All Aia and Clement can think about is that the floor in that area is thoroughly saturated with Fritz's toe jam, which he deposits every Sunday morning during the hot summer months. *"Uff da," "Fy da," "Ish da," "Uff da fy da,"* and *"Ish da fy da"* are five exclamations that Clement, Aia, and Gretchen apply to this particular behaviour. These Norwegian derivative expressions perfectly describe what no other words in the English language can begin to convey. No other head-scratching words of puzzlement, confusion, and bafflement are able to give a better description of Fritz's behaviour than these words of Norwegian origin.

Aia urged Clement to mellow out as she will help him by writing down a general church decorum guide. She also told him that right now she was too tired to move around a lot, but that won't stop her in the next few days from sitting down to compose this list. She emphasized that this subject is vitally important to the life and health of Historic St. Peter's.

Aia prepared a special supper tonight, starting by setting up a card table in the living room. We have heard her lovingly call rainy days, "In-Clement Weather." Even though it was a wet spring day today, it did not interfere with the Osterhagens' lighthearted fun. Their meal included crab cakes, tartar and cocktail sauce, lemons, green grapes, potato chips and dip, and French bread. To match the food with the seaside theme, Aia set each place setting with a paper napkin that depicted a sailboat. "My Heart Will Always Be in Carolina" was played several times from their tape deck. All together, the meal looked and sounded similar to the ambiance that just might be found at a place somewhere on the East Coast that is called "Jack's Crab Shack."

At 11:30 p.m. Ruby and I travelled to the parsonage kitchen and happened upon a crab cake crumb that must have dropped to the floor when Aia lifted them from the frying pan to the platter. It was so delicious that we hope Aia will make them again soon. When we peeked out of the slit in dining room wall, we could see some of the living room. We noticed that Gretchen did not eat her crab cake right away, but used her knife to carefully spread tartar sauce on all areas of her crab cake. We did not know what she was doing, until we heard her say that she was "icing" her cake before eating it. Ruby and I discussed how happy the Osterhagens were tonight, as they were anything but crotchety, miserable, or cross, unlike the name of the cakes that they ate for supper. It was beyond us to figure out why their patties were called crab cakes. I guess we will never know. Anyway, the best thing for us to do is to remain sweet-natured, just like the Osterhagens.

   – F.N.

AIA HAS COMPLETED HER "CHURCH DECORUM GUIDE." WE HEARD HER EXPLAIN TO Clement that she has written the etiquette list in a fashion somewhat similar to the Ten Commandments and their meanings. After she handed the guide to Clement, he sat down at the dining room table where Gretchen was colouring in her favourite colouring book. He began reading Aia's composition out loud. After he began, Gretchen put down her crayons and listened attentively to his every word.

Church Etiquette Behavioral Guidelines

Rule #1: Use the washroom before the worship service begins. *(Explanation: If a child can hold it, so can adults.)*

Rule #2: Arrive on time for the worship service. Don't walk in late during the first hymn, the reading of the lessons, the choir anthem, the sermon, the prayers, or during Holy Communion. If need be, set your alarm to wake up earlier on Sunday mornings, making it a priority not to be late for church. *(Explanation: You wouldn't dream of being late for work or school. Why are you consistently fifteen or twenty minutes late for church? Does your alarm clock work every day of the week except for Sunday? If you are spending your time making waffles, pancakes, or a farmer's breakfast on Sunday morning before church, why not eat those foods instead for lunch when you arrive home after church!)*

Rule #3: Adults, please do not whisper during church. *(Explanation: When you are whispering in front of other people, it is noticed. Others feel excluded from your conversation and wonder if you are saying something nasty about someone else or them!)*

Rule #4: Wear your Sunday best to church and look in a full length mirror at both your front and backside before leaving home. Consider how you and your outfit look to others. *(Explanation: A tank top paired with happy face printed pajama bottoms and slippers do not even fit under the widely used phrase, "Come as you are," originally used to promote church attendance. Leave your favourite leather jacket with the words emblazoned on the back at home and save it for another occasion. Ladies, your low-in-the-front tops* really aren't appropriate church attire. When you wear low cut attire to church, it's only natural for the men to be distracted. Please attempt to change your dressing habits to a conservative Sunday best. Another excellent reason to check your appearance in the mirror before leaving home every single day, not just on Sunday mornings, concerns TP. There have been actual occurrences where people have had from four to twenty sheets of toilet paper sticking out of their waistbands or stuck on the bottoms of their shoes. It is not only uncomfortable and embarrassing for those caught in this situation, but it is completely awkward for anyone to point out what they see. Recently one woman in Oswald County walked the length of main street with her tail of TP blowing freely in the wind from her backside. She went into the bank and stood at the teller window to do her business, all the while being completely unaware about the dragging TP. News of this unfortunate incident travelled all over Oswald County. Please note to check your physical appearance, both front and back, before leaving your house each day.)

Rule #5: If it is so important to socialize at church, do that before you walk into the sanctuary or after the worship service is over. Don't visit while you are in the sanctuary. *(Explanation: Hold your thoughts and jibber-jabber inside yourself until the worship service is over. If you have trouble remembering what you were going to say, take out a small piece of paper, like a sticky note, or your bulletin, and jot down your thoughts. Hold whatever it is inside, be quiet and attentive, and save the socializing for after church. For your information, your bulletin and the monthly newsletter are meant to be read before worship begins, or after worship is over. When it's time for the sermon, listen and pay attention, and don't spend that time reading the latest church news. Keep in mind that your church has hired the best possible organist that they can afford, and you are supposed to quietly listen to the prelude and not drown out the music by big whoops of laughter and loud talking. The choir also has worked hard to prepare a special anthem to match the theme of the day, so use your two ears, close your one mouth and listen to the praises they are singing to God our Father!)*

Rule #6: Don't walk in and out of the sanctuary once the worship service is underway. Once you have chosen your pew, stay put. *(Explanation: This repetitive coming and going in and out is disruptive to everyone but you. Remind yourself that you are not at a sporting event, a buffet restaurant, or a lively concert. This in-and-out behaviour applies especially to church ushers who look at their watches, jump up from their pew and walk to the narthex, even though Pastor is preaching his sermon full steam. Let Pastor conclude and then gather in the narthex to be on duty to gather the offering.)*

Rule #7: Restless children are disruptive during the worship service, most likely due to the fact that they rarely attend church and don't have the first idea that parishioners expect them to remain quiet for one full hour. (*Explanation: If your child, whatever their age, makes a lot of noise, take him or her out of the sanctuary so the rest of the worshippers can actually hear what's going on. Have the courtesy to sit in the back pew so it is more convenient to take them out, if necessary. When they calm down, bring them back in.*)

Rule #8: No food or drinks are allowed in the sanctuary. (*Explanation: Bringing takeaway coffee into the sanctuary is just plain inconsiderate. Parishioners get a whiff of your coffee, become jealous, and wish that they had some, too. This impolite behaviour is really spreading around nationwide as more and more people are arriving at church toting along a fancy flavoured coffee, planning to sip on it during the worship service. Tempting coffee aromas circulating around the sanctuary like Chocolate Raspberry, Praline, Cinnamon & Nutmeg, or Hawaiian Hazelnut are alluring, tempting, and almost beguiling to those who are sitting there being completely coffee-less. It is also rude when a person cracks open a can of pop, slurps on its contents which, by the way, may lead to a burp. If it is essential to chew on candy or suck on throat lozenges during the worship service, unwrap them ahead of time, placing them in a small food bag. The action of twisting a cellophane wrapper off of a piece of hard candy or a lozenge is as loud as the person who is guzzling pop.*)

Rule #9: Whatever you do, don't clip your fingernails, file them, or apply fingernail polish while in the sanctuary, or anywhere else at the church. (*Explanation: It's too bad that you wanted to paint your fingernails with your new bottle of Tangerine Kisses before church, but because you ran out of time – you can refer to rule #2. In regard to clipping fingernails during worship, nobody enjoys that noise, and the thought of clipped fingernails falling who-knows-where is downright repulsive.*)

Rule #10: Don't bring items with you to church and pass them around during the worship service. (*Explanation: If you have extra shopping coupons because you subscribe to four or five newspapers, find another way to distribute them, especially not during worship services on Sunday mornings.*)

Clement chuckled at all ten of the etiquette rules that Aia brainstormed, mentioning that she wrote the list in a straightforward manner, but it is too on target and far too harsh, having the potential to hurt parishioners feelings. Aia agreed, but she did tell him just how good it felt to write those things down and get them off of her chest. They both agreed that all they can do is to have proper church etiquette and set a good example that parishioners might notice and imitate. Gretchen piped up by telling them that she knows people who don't obey the rules. They asked her to tell them about that. Clement reread the ten rules out loud, one at a time, and Gretchen responded with her thoughts as follows:

Rule breaker #1: Mrs. Vargas goes to the washroom every Sunday morning during the opening hymn. Gretchen said that she knows this, because when Mrs. Vargas returns to her place she is wearing lots of pinkish lipstick, and she looks much prettier that way than without lipstick. Her time in the washroom makes her look much better.

Rule breaker #2: Mr. & Mrs. Caldwell and their three sons, and one daughter, always arrive late for church. When the family arrives, they all smell like pancakes, syrup, bacon, and coffee. They smell just like the breakfast served at Wood's Wake-Up Wagon, located on the east side of town.

Rule breaker #3: Kennedy and Londyn McCoy are sisters that whisper constantly during church. That is a bad habit, but worse than that is their mother, Mrs. McCoy, who tries to get them to stop whispering by placing her index finder to her lips and sending forth a very loud "shush" to demand silence. That shush is as loud as a wild wind blowing in a cornfield.

Rule breaker #4: Christopher Snyder doesn't wear his Sunday best because he attends the worship service wearing his baseball cap. Gretchen said that he must not wash his hair very often and that the cap covers up his greasy hair, or else he is in a hurry to go play baseball.

Rule breaker #5: Mr. Stevenson socializes during worship and talks about the weather and his hearing aids. Last week he talked about how he nearly got in a car wreck on his way to church.

Rule breaker #6: The ushers don't sit down very long in church because they are in a hurry to stand in the narthex and talk about soccer, hockey, golf, and football.

Rule breaker #7: Mrs. Jewel's new baby Aidan cries a lot in church. Perhaps if she would let him have his pacifier more often he would be quiet. She said Aidan *loves* his pacifier.

Rule breaker #8: Lots of people eat and drink in church, especially suckers from the candy man. Gretchen asked her Daddy if Holy Communion counts as eating and drinking.

Rule breaker #9: Angela Fox painted her nails hot pink in church with a quick dry polish and placed pretty nail stickers on them after they were dry. Gretchen said that Angela showed them to her after church and they were so pretty. Gretchen said she wants to go to Bill's Dollar Bill and get some nail stickers, too, just like Angela's.

Rule breaker #10: Miss Charmaine Reyes passes her coupons around the church every Sunday. Gretchen said that she got to look at the coupons once and found a coupon for yogurt, helped herself to the coupon, and then they purchased the yogurt at Grocer Dan's the next time they went shopping. Now their yogurt is all gone. She asked if she can have permission to look in Miss Charmaine's coupon bag next Sunday to see if she can find another coupon just like the one she got the first time.

Clement and Aia gave Gretchen a hug. It is clear that children notice all kinds of behaviours.

At 11:30 p.m. Ruby and I travelled to the parsonage hoping to snack on morsels of the Osterhagen's dinner that consisted of dill pickle soup, Polish sausages with whole grain mustard, bread and butter, finished off with spiced plum kolaches. Both Clement and Aia remarked that the kolaches had an abundance of filling, that there was no stinginess when it came to the most important kolache ingredient. All we found of their meal was a kolache crumb under Aia's chair. While we ate, we quietly batted around something we heard from the Osterhagen's suppertime conversation. Aia mentioned that she had just finished reading a novel written by Willa Cather, *My Antonia,* and as a result became hungry for a kolache because the Czech pastry was mentioned in the book. While Clement was at his office this afternoon, Ruby noticed that Aia and Gretchen left the house and returned with a white bakery box that was imprinted with the words, Zuzanna's Polish Bakery. Ruby and I will check the church library soon to see if it contains a copy of *My Antonia.* I am under the impression that we might enjoy reading it out loud together, reading responsively paragraph by paragraph, just like a Psalm is read responsively in church each Sunday by Pastor and the congregation.

– F.N.

EARLY THIS MORNING A DISAGREEMENT FLARED UP BETWEEN A COUPLE IN OUR VILLAGE, Bland and Hottie Leblanc. I feel compelled to explain the essence of the Leblanc's argument which led to an emergency meeting. This is how it began: Hottie revealed to Bland that she wanted to name their five-day old twins Blanche and Beige. After that, Bland delivered a two-minute speech dwelling on how dragged down, faded, and washed out those names would be especially combined with the last name Leblanc. Hottie evidently has a hot temper, began using it, after which Bland emulated Hottie, thus turning up the volume of their conversation. Their squeaking and squealing amplified so loudly it nearly became a safety issue for our village. To quiet them down, an emergency village meeting was convened about the two of them being unable to agree on the naming of their twins. The first thing Bland did when he spoke to the mice village was to admit his persisting dislike of his own first name, emphasizing that he does not want their twins to carry that same burden. Bland described his name with the words milquetoast, plain-vanilla, sombre, colourless, and lackluster. Deciding to exercise his freedom and independence, he informed everyone that he is replacing his first name with one far more spirited and lively. When Hottie heard the news she was noticeably supportive and completely in favour of Bland and his desire. She immediately asked him, in front of everyone, what name he had in mind. Without pausing, he announced from now on he will go by the name "Jett." She was so tickled that she began joyfully spinning herself around with a jaw-dropping pirouette. This amazed the entire village as they had no idea of Hottie's ballet abilities. After that, Hottie asked Jett for forgiveness for fighting with him. The village thought it was moving when Hottie looked deeply into Jett's eyes and affectionately said, "Jett, Jett, my pet, please don't fret. Let me bet, Jett, we can forget. On two names we will set. Oh Jett, my Jett, I'm so glad we met!" To finish off her thoughts, Hottie spoke almost breathlessly (due to her spinning pirouette move) while trying to burst out the glad tidings that both of their names have something delightful in common: Jett and Hottie are both spelled with double t's!

After all was quieted, Jett proclaimed that the little ones deserve names with passion, suggesting Pandora and Peyton. Pandora we understood, because she was the curious girl who couldn't help opening up a box of troubles. But we asked

Jett how he came up with the name Peyton. He mentioned that before moving to St. Pete's he lived with his Auntie Adelaide in a home for the elderly. Each evening before bed they would watch as one particular resident would unearth a book from the bottom of her dresser drawer where she stored her nylon stockings. Every time she was through reading this book she placed it back in the same spot, hiding it in a secret place. The title of the book was *Peyton Place*. Jett told Hottie that he suspected the book's contents might have provoked some shame in her and that she would not have displayed it on her nightstand. She just might be mortified and humiliated if anyone knew that she was reading that book. So, the book was permanently kept under her supply of nylon stockings, which were assembled into two sections. One group was labeled with the word "good," while the other one was labeled, "have runs."

At 10:30 p.m. Ruby and I travelled to the parsonage and searched for a snack. Thankfully, because of our whopping hunger tonight, we found two pieces of buttered hominy underneath Gretchen's chair at the dining room table! As we quietly chewed, Ruby thanked me for being her "butter" half. I told her that no one is "butter" than her.

– F.N.

Thursday, June 18

ANSWERING THE DOORBELL THIS AFTERNOON, AIA FOUND HER GOOD FRIEND, ANNETTE, and welcomed her into the parsonage. As they walked through the dining room, Ruby and I noticed that Annette was carrying a fancy cake box from the newest bakery in town, the Sweet Indulgence Bake Shoppe. Our attention was drawn to the artistic flair of the windowed bakery box that Annette held. Printed with royal purple and cobalt blue filigree, and tied up with a sparkling silver ribbon, the bakery box's presentation is far more attractive and stylish than the simple unadorned white boxes from Zuzanna's Polish Bakery. Currently the Sweet Indulgence Bake Shoppe is the buzz around Oswald County. Their newfound popularity is not just about the appearance of their bakery boxes, but how quickly this new business has blossomed into having a first-rate reputation. Most people look forward to trying out the new place, at least once. Ruby and I are no strangers to the fact that Zuzanna's Polish Bakery, the very popular establishment that opened in 1957, is a favourite of the Osterhagens and many of St. Peter's parishioners. We are hopeful that the Sweet Indulgence Bake Shoppe will not permanently lure faithful customers away from Zuzanna's, as we are certain that a town of this size can handle more than one bakery. Ruby whispered to me that she had a design idea about improving the dull look of Zuzanna's white bakery boxes by simply adding eye-catching flourishes: 1) a large white paper doily placed underneath the baked goods, 2) "Zuzanna's Polish Bakery" imprinted on a decorative red sticker, and 3) each box all tied up with red and white ribbon (Poland's national colours). This would manifestly improve the appearance of the boxes. After listening to Ruby's hugely creative suggestion, I told her that she had utterly spoken in Trinitarian fashion, just like Aia. She beamed from head to toe when I gave her that pat on the back, as Ruby has a sky-high opinion of Aia. She said Aia possesses a notable amount of faith, intelligence, and kindness. Once again, I told her that she just spoke Trinitarian, which led to Ruby making another Trinitarian move: She told me that she loves me, planted a peck on my cheek, and embraced me with a warm cuddle.

We listened with fascination to the conversation between Annette and Aia. Together they discussed the new bake shop and how everyone in town is raving about their sweets and handcrafted breads. While they were talking, Annette got out dessert plates, forks, napkins, and a knife, followed by opening up the Osterhagen china cabinet that houses twenty-four English bone china cups and saucers. Ruby and I quietly remembered how just last week we listened as John Roberts, the Osterhagens' insurance agent, stopped at the parsonage to review details of their current life insurance policies. As they sat at the dining room table, Aia served tea. We heard John remark that Aia is the only woman on earth that he knows who uses English cups and saucers instead of common coffee mugs with sayings on them like, "Caffeined," "HEBREWS: Proof from the Bible that men do coffee," or "This coffee hits the spot."

Aia chose a cup and saucer with scalloped edges and gold trim that was embellished with large deep pink roses, while Annette chose to drink tea from a cup and saucer decorated with wild bluebells. After the tea was poured, Annette opened up the bakery box, uncovering a sumptuous jewel of a baked creation called the Ritzy Raspberry-Twirl Coffee Cake. Aia said how impressed she was that this coffee cake is nearly pink in colour due to the abundance of fresh raspberries incorporated into the batter.

Aia told Annette that she was bewildered about the reason for the impromptu tea party. When she asked for an explanation, Annette said that she had a purpose for meeting before the twins are born, as she wanted to voice concern about the words Aia will say when it is time to deliver the twins. Annette mentioned to Aia that since she is a Christian woman, she knows that she will be careful not to take the Lord's name in vain. Since she will carefully choose her words during labour and delivery, Annette suggested a way for Aia to voice pain and tension without ruining her good reputation. She should simply say swear words in other languages, words foreign to everyone on the hospital staff. Being that the two of them are such good friends, Aia listened to Annette's words of wisdom and told her that she might give it a try, but she wondered how she will come up with the swear words. Ruby and I saw Annette hand Aia a recipe card with five foreign words written on it. She told Aia to carry the card with her to the delivery room, and when the pain is beyond bearable, concentrate on the card and call out any one of those words. It won't sound like swearing, as those in the delivery room will not know what they mean, and neither will Aia. Knowing that Aia's words might be heard by three members of St. Peter's, Annette said that they will certainly remember the words that their pastor's wife chooses to say in her time of trial. Aia pointed out to Annette how thankful she is that the anesthesiologist, Dr. Joseph L. Melander, and Samantha Hill and Elizabeth Carson, two delivery room nurses, could be on duty when the twins are born. She added that God will be right with her in the delivery room, the best doctor of all.

As Annette prepared to leave, satisfied that she had helped her friend, she hugged Aia and wished her well. Annette conveyed that she will leave town tomorrow to be with her mother-in-law who is having major bunion surgery on both feet, which is no joking matter. Annette told Aia to enjoy the rest of the Ritzy Raspberry-Twirl Coffee Cake with Pastor and Gretchen, adding that she will be praying for her. As she walked out the door, she handed Aia another index card that contained her in-law's telephone number, asking that Pastor give her a call with the news about the babies.

At 11:30 p.m. Ruby and I travelled to the parsonage and snacked on a tiny crumb of the coffee cake. We decided that we preferred the taste of the spiced plum kolache that we tried last night far more the frou-frou raspberry coffee cake. Ruby and I voted as to which bakery is better. We were in complete accord in choosing Zuzanna's Polish Bakery over the Sweet Indulgence Bake Shoppe.

– F.N.

This afternoon Aia's parents, whom she calls her "folks," Arni and Juliette Nygaard, arrived several days ahead of the twin's due date. They are eager to help, especially before, during, and after Aia is in the hospital. Already they are absorbed in spoiling their sweetheart granddaughter Gretchen, who Juliette often calls "Sunbeam." Juliette appears eager to take on the work of the household chores while Arni is committed to roll up his sleeves and attack the kitchen wallpapering project that Aia earlier became overwhelmed with. Ruby and I are certain that during these next few weeks we will be observing two people in midlife that are happily fired up about their activities. Already Aia has thanked them numerous times for their helpfulness.

Aia doesn't feel like accomplishing anything at this point, so she instead sits down and knits dishcloths. She has knitted plenty to supply her mother, Clement's mother, and herself for years to come. There probably are enough to wash a massive amount of dirty dishes, just as long as the person washing them does not fall into the category of being a "reluctant dishwasher." Reluctant dishwashers favour stacking towers of dirty plates, drinking glasses, and cutlery in the kitchen sink to soak for hours upon hours in a sea of bubbles. When there is an overflow in the sink, the reluctant dishwasher turns to building towers of plates, bowls, and pots and pans on the kitchen counter. Their dishcloths are often left soaking in the dirty dishwater, which makes them not last as long.

Ruby and I wonder if reluctant dishwashers could conquer their behaviour by seeking out a therapist. Perhaps after a couple of sessions they could make a few improvements to change from being a "reluctant dishwasher" to a "diligent dishwasher." But we know that people will only change if they want to. We cannot complain about the Osterhagen family and their dishwashing habits, as they definitely qualify as diligent dishwashers. That must be the reason as to why they seem to go through such a large amount of dish soap.

The Nygaards are attracted very much to the church breezeway that includes many large windows that look out on a breathtakingly manicured courtyard with a variety of trees, shrubbery, and blooming flowers. Positioned centre stage is a towering concrete angel with long-flowing tresses and ringlets. Ruby and I remember many months ago when Gretchen gave the statue the name Angelica.

Since that day the name has stuck. Angelica's arms are outstretched and her face portrays a soothing smile which is of comfort to everyone who gazes her way. Also wonderstruck by the beauty are two mice in our village, Pistachio and Char. (Char's given name is actually Chartreuse, but she is much more partial to the fiery, edgy shortened form of her name.) Hiding behind the breezeway's fiddle leaf fig tree, Pistachio and Char witnessed Arni and Juliette claiming an area for their eight a.m. coffee time and five p.m. cocktail hour. They were in such a rush that it seemed similar to the Oklahoma Land Rush of 1893 when land was there for the taking, except they were on foot instead of on horses. Arni quickly positioned two red plastic deck chairs in the breezeway along with a TV tray. Juliette had her arms full carrying a tray holding two Cuban cocktails, a small bowl of cashews, and one individual pouch of cheese puffs. Pistachio told us that Arni mentioned that cheese puffs are the number one snack that has ever been invented. Juliette is already missing her favourite peppermint hard candy from Montreal, the famous humbugs, so she intends to solve that problem tomorrow by placing an order over the telephone, having them mailed to her at the church address.

There was a lot of Father's Day action at the parsonage today. I'm far too exhausted tonight to cover the details, so I suggest that you use your imagination.

At 7 p.m. Ruby and I travelled to the breezeway and sampled a morsel of a cheese puff and a bit of a broken cashew, which elevated our snack so high that it became a special occasion. Cashews are so delectably scrumptious that we have no problem understanding why people complain that they are so pricey. Even though stir-fry is a once-a-week supper at the parsonage, we have noticed that cashew chicken rarely comes out of their wok pan. Ruby and I concluded that the Osterhagens must not be able to afford cashews. We feel for them. This is simply sad.

– F.N.

Wednesday, June 24

THE LUNCH HOUR FLEW AWAY FROM THE NYGAARDS AND THE OSTERHAGENS TODAY because of the kitchen wallpapering project. Later on though, Juliette was able to navigate her way around the kitchen to prepare a meal. At 3 p.m. everyone at the parsonage was sitting down at the dining room table eating "lupper." On days like today, when lunch is missed, supper is eaten very early. Juliette mentioned that, given the circumstances, it is reasonable to call it "lupper," which takes the first two letters of lunch and combines them with the last four letters of the word supper. She went on to say that it is similar to the first two letters of breakfast when they are combined with the last four letters of lunch, which makes brunch. Ruby and I were terribly confused when we heard this conversation as the word lupper sounds almost identical to the word leper, a description of people who are contagious, have suffered much physically, and had to call out, "Unclean! Unclean!" just as what is written about in Leviticus. We know that Juliette frequently washed her hands as she prepared lupper, as we often heard the water running in the kitchen faucet. Juliette is such a clean woman that we could never refer to her as a leper who prepares lupper.

At 3:30 p.m. Ruby and I were discouraged as we tried to figure out the exact meaning of these two words, lupper and leper, in the English language. We travelled to the church nursery and were thankful to find a few crumbs from a teething biscuit which we ate for our lupper.

– F.N.

TODAY IS THE FEAST OF ST. PETER AND ST. PAUL. IT IS ALSO THE DAY AIA'S LABOUR began. Having awakened at 1:30 a.m. with the first labour pain, she woke Clement and told him the news. We heard her say to Clement words of thankfulness that her folks arrived last week and will take over at home during this time. After that, Aia got up from bed and Ruby and I could see her sitting on the sofa. Each time a labour pain started up, she stood up and took a brisk walk around the dining room table until it passed. Two hours later she reawakened Clement and told him that they'd better get ready and head to the hospital. Aia tried to get ready, but each time a labour pain interrupted what she was doing, she went for a little walk around and around the dining room table while breathing deeply. That eased some of the pain. Clement woke up his in-laws and told them they were off to the hospital. Both of Aia's folks hugged them goodbye and said they would pray for all to go well. Their last words to them were to say that Gretchen will be fine while they are away and that they look forward to hearing news about the twins.

After Aia and Clement arrived at Our Lady of Lourdes Hospital, Aia was admitted. All of the details about the birth spread like wildfire in our village, as one of the mice, Purity, arrived at the hospital in one of Aia's sneakers. Aia's feet were so puffy and swollen that she has not been able to wear shoes these last days, so she arrived at the hospital pregnant and barefoot. Clement carried a workout bag that contained Aia's clothing and her sneakers. Purity was able to sneak into the labour and delivery room and firsthand keep an eye on the event, finding it easy to hide behind the many gizmos and whatchamacallit machines. She said that Aia kept a firm grip on the index card given to her by Annette. That way the card was near and ready to be used, if necessary. Aia seemed to find it to be of psychological comfort, especially as the labour pains grew in intensity. Ruby and I could just imagine that each time one started up she walked up and down the hospital hallway quietly repeating the words on her index card. Purity said that the foreign swear words helped her, just as much as the breathing techniques. Purity added that when the pain was unbearable, Aia would freely call out her secret swear words, having no fear of anyone understanding their true meaning. Continuing on like that for hours, Purity said that Aia was finally ordered by the doctor to stay in bed and to stop walking around, which meant total confinement to the hospital bed. Throughout all of her labour that was the only time that Aia cried. Purity said that Aia made herself stop crying by becoming fully focussed on her index card.

Six hours after arriving at the hospital, the two very precious and perfect babies arrived, identical healthy twin boys. Purity noticed that Aia and Clement were both delighted and exhausted beyond words. The hospital staff immediately inquired what the boys were to be named, but Clement and Aia weren't ready to give an answer. They mentioned that they would make a decision tomorrow, as they wanted to take a little time with the babies before deciding what their names would be. After Aia was taken to her hospital room, she and Clement held hands and prayed words of thankfulness and praise to Almighty God for the gift of two healthy little ones. After that, Clement told Aia that it was time for him to go home. She asked him to take her sneakers back home, saying that she would prefer to wear her slippers. As they were kissing goodbye with their eyes closed, Purity found her chance to hide, once again, in Aia's sneakers in order to get back home to St. Pete's. Clement also returned home carrying great news to share with his in-laws and Gretchen, expressing how proud he was of Aia. He told them all about the baby boys, describing what they look like and saying how healthy they are. The words he used to describe the babies could only come from a complete-ly loving husband and father. At that moment, Clement simultaneously was the happiest father in the world and also the most tired man on earth.

Clement mentioned to Arni and Juliette that Aia frequently spoke in another language during labour and delivery. Aia is fluent in French, but Clement said it wasn't the French language, and it definitely wasn't German, because Clement would have understood German. He guessed the language might have been Rus-sian or Polish, and asked Arni and Juliette if Aia had ever taken any other language classes at some point in her education. Aia's folks weren't sure if she had taken either Russian or Polish, but told him that Aia has always been a girl with so many interests that she might have taken one of those classes. Arni and Juliette said they would not be surprised if she had studied another language as Aia certainly has the brain power to learn anything she sets her mind to.

Ruby and I stayed very close to the crack in the dining room wall so we would not miss a single word of the conversation that was going on in the Os-terhagen home. The Osterhagen home is a happy home, with a happy family, where every person is a blessing from God. I looked at my Ruby when Clement was telling about the precious twins and saw that she was happy about Pastor's news, too, as two tears fell from her eyes, one for each baby. We agreed that there is nothing on earth more beautiful than a new baby or two new babies, whether it is mice or men.

At 11:30 p.m. Ruby and I travelled to the breezeway and snacked on a small piece of homemade peanut brittle and a tiny droplet of a lemon drop martini that was on the breezeway floor from the Nygaard cocktail hour today.

– F.N.

Tuesday, June 30

In time for tonight's supper, Clement arrived home from Our Lady of Lourdes Hospital. Over chicken fried steak, green beans, and garden salad, Clement shared many extra-special details about the twins, including announcing the selection of their names. Since the twins were born on June 29, The Feast of St. Peter and St. Paul, Clement said that he and Aia briefly contemplated naming the boys Peter and Paul. Finally deciding to use those names as middle names, they chose the first names Marc and Luc. Juliette was especially thrilled to hear this news as her twin older brothers, Marc and Luc Barteau, residents of the small historical village of Saint-Antoine-de-Tilly, Quebec, share the same first names as her grandsons. Juliette expressed several times tonight that she is so happy that they are here to receive a healthy dose of Vitamin G. (Note: Vitamin G means Grandpa and Granny spending time with their grandchildren.)

At 8:30 p.m. Ruby and I travelled to the breezeway and snacked on a morsel of a shrimp chip we found on the floor. We also came upon a droplet of something the Nygaards called a gin gimlet. We found the beverage to be extremely refreshing. After that, Ruby put forth an idea to use at the upcoming potluck in Woolcox Hall. The hosts of the potluck could fill the church's big punch bowl with the gin gimlet mixture. To dress up the presentation, an ice-ring containing lime slices could be added, which would keep the beverage cold throughout the entire potluck. Ruby was confident that everyone would so enjoy a cup or two of this citrusy and thirst-quenching beverage served alongside the variety of flavourful hotdishes, salads, pickles, and buttered fluffy buns. After a lengthy discussion we let go of the idea, as we are beginning to suspect that gin gimlets are meant to be served in very small portions and in moderation. Certainly they are not to be served in punch bowls where people might drink too much. Anyway, lemonade is what is usually served at potlucks, always being a big hit, and it is cheaper. We concluded that some changes are simply not worth making when thought about logically.

– F.N.

JULLIETTE WOKE UP THIS MORNING AND STRAIGHTAWAY BECAME EXTRA ENGAGED IN THE parsonage kitchen by preparing a special breakfast of homemade crepes served with pure maple syrup, browned sausage patties, fresh blueberries, and strong coffee. Everyone except for Clement and Aia enjoyed beginning the day at the dining room table dressed in their pajamas, ready to feast on a hearty breakfast. While they ate, Juliette announced to Arni and Gretchen that she had planned the day's activities. Speaking with such confidence, emphasis, and promise, Ruby and I noticed that Juliette's speech possessed similarities to that of a high ranking political official declaring something of worldwide importance. Telling Arni and Gretchen that she will be in charge of today's food, festivities, and the fun, she emphasized the spirit of this special day, Canada Day. She also told them that there will be a fun-loving outing today, saying that it is a day to wear something red and white. When breakfast was finished, the three of them stood up at their places and sang the national anthem of Canada, "O Canada," especially emphasizing the meaningful words included in the text, "God keep our land, glorious and free!" The anthem was sung once again, but this time it was sung in French. Gretchen kept a close eye on her Granny Juliette and tried her best to sing along with her. When it came to "*Et ta valeur, de foi trempée,*" Juliette, once again, especially highlighted those moving words. The original plans were to leave at nine o'clock, but that decision got a bit slowed down. Since Gretchen's face was covered with maple syrup and blueberry juice, the only solution was to give her a bath. By ten o'clock the three of them were ready for the day, so they hopped in their station wagon, headed west, and did not return home until eight o'clock tonight.

At 5 p.m. Ruby and I travelled to the parsonage and snacked on a morsel of a crepe. We took the risk of being caught in the parsonage at this time of day, but no one was there. It was wonderful to have our supper early in the evening. We usually have to eat so late, after the Osterhagens have all gone to bed. Ruby and I were puzzled about which places Arni, Juliette, and Gretchen visited on their outing today. We guessed that part of the day was spent at Our Lady of Lourdes Hospital to see the babies. Hopefully we will glean details about their day trip excursion sometime tomorrow.

    – F.N.

Independence Day ~ Saturday, July 4

On Thursday, July 2, Aia, Marc, and Luc came home from the hospital. Today is the first day since the births that Aia has felt up to showering, getting dressed, and fixing her hair, instead of wearing her bathrobe and slippers nonstop. There is so much love in the parsonage evidenced by the family wanting to hold wee Marc and wee Luc. Even Gretchen, who no longer appears little, is able to quietly hold one of them at a time with just a little bit of guidance. She covers her brother's cheeks and foreheads with precious kisses dozens of times a day.

Clement is taking a few days off from work. He and Arni have collaborated on the task of transforming the kitchen walls. They estimate the project being completed today. Juliette works around them preparing meals. Some are cooked outside on the charcoal grill. Aia is noticeably happy for all the help her folks are giving them.

Juliette excelled at today's menu as she whipped up classic Fourth of July food, a menu consisting of hamburgers with various toppers, potato salad, Bygone Homesteader's Baked Beans (a new recipe published last Tuesday in the Oswald County Gazette), and fresh fruit nestled in a carved watermelon boat that she and Gretchen prepared this morning. Clement is continually amazed at the flexibility of his mother-in-law's cooking. Most of Juliette's daily cuisine is French-style, using only the best ingredients, but Clement seems disappointed with the small portions. That didn't hold true today as everyone enjoyed the celebration, one-hundred percent American-style. We noticed the most popular item on the makeshift burger bar was the thickly sliced hickory smoked bacon. The men were tired out from all of their work today, so Clement and Arni said that they deserved the reward of eating several strips of bacon. We have noticed that many humans seem to be lovers of bacon. Bacon lovers appear to have gone to hog heaven, pig heaven, or maybe seventh heaven while they are chewing on a strip of bacon. Ruby and I are not certain which one of the heavens happens to be the appropriate description of their bacon gratification, but are convinced that perfectly fried bacon must be a real taste of paradise.

Tonight Clement, Arni, Juliette, and Gretchen watched the fireworks display held at the Oswald County Fairgrounds from their back yard. Aia stayed inside with Marc and Luc and watched a different fireworks display on television.

After everyone came inside and headed to bed, Aia revealed to Clement her disappointment in having a chubby tummy. He told her not to dwell on it, or to lose any sleep because those few chubs provide a nice soft holding platform for the babies to rest on. Finally, he added that he likes her the way she is, well-rounded and super curvaceous.

They also discussed how awkward and perhaps problematic it is that Aia's folks set up daily cocktail hour in the breezeway, knowing that it might bother some parishioners. Those members might get on their case about it and take it to someone on the church council, anxious for it to become a thumbs-down discussion topic at the next meeting. Most of the parishioners at St. Pete's would think it's cute that Aia's sixty-plus parents enjoy their cocktails and appetizers in the breezeway each day, but some of the uptight ones would not appreciate that cosmos, beer, martinis, stingrays, wine, or mimosas are being consumed on the church property. Aia and Clement don't mind, but they tell each other that they are afraid of repercussions. One strong point that Clement brought up is that cocktail hour in the breezeway will only last for a limited amount of time, just like a puff of air coming to an end.

After that, they returned to Aia's chubby tummy concern. Clement did not stay awake much longer, as we soon heard him snoring while Aia was softly crying. We felt sorry for her and wished that Clement could have stayed awake a tad bit longer to help her work through her troubles. Ruby was so overcome with compassion for Aia that she broke one of our rules by travelling to the parsonage, going beyond the kitchen and dining room to rest just outside their bedroom door. At first I treaded on Ruby's heels for safety reasons, but then I put effort into memorizing the creative poetry that Aia said quietly to herself. She said, "Clement came through the door. Heading down the corridor, to our boudoir, into the bed he did soar, which was not a chore. In double-quick time he began to snore, just as loudly as a wild boar, or a singing troubadour, on a ship where the commodore has dreams of the seashore. But, he might as well have been in Ecuador, Singapore, or El Salvador." Aia's words were a million miles away from our understanding, but we noted that she finished off her tearful lamentations in true Aia fashion, in Trinitarian-style, so we were confident she still is just as brave as before.

Many adult mice in our village gathered in the bell tower of Historic St. Peter's tonight for some homespun fun. Being that we were so high up in the air, we had a matchless view of the fireworks. We called our outing "Let Freedom Ring." With gusto we sang the Mouse National Anthem, *"Hgpoinq Wbpoit*

Oovpij," which means, "Our Evensong of Freedom." Following that, we sang it in the English language thanks to Dr. Theodore Simonsen, our head librarian, who translated it just for this special event. Our mice village usually sings our songs in an ancient, distinctive polyphonic folk-style, much like the way singing was done during the time of the Renaissance. I guess it is a bit similar to how the Amish treasure their distinctive type of singing songs from their *Ausbund* hymnals: slow, drawn-out, deliberate. This tradition gives us a connection to the past, the present, and also to the future. No one heard us sing because we were so high up in the bell tower that only the birds listened. They enjoyed it, because when we started singing, they became quiet and attentive. When we finished singing, they reciprocated by singing us a song. We were hushed as we listened to their birdsong. It sounded a little bit like "I'm a Yankee Doodle Dandy," but I'm not certain it was that particular song. It might have been another patriotic tune. Anyway, it was a song which brought out feelings of being devoted and loyal to our country. "Let Freedom Ring" was a firecracker of a bell tower excursion!

At 11:30 p.m. Ruby and I travelled to the breezeway and came upon a salted peanut along with one drop of a red, white, and blue cocktail. We took a hazard guess that it must be a special Fourth of July cocktail that might have been invented by George Washington or Betsy Ross. I guess we will never know the answer to who invented it, but we are okey-dokey with that as we don't wish in any way to become wise apples.

    – F.N.

THIS MORNING PASTOR OSTERHAGEN SPOKE WITH JOSIE, THE ORGANIST, BEFORE THE worship service. Because she continues to speak with a tissue over her mouth, he asked her if she was feeling any better, noticing that a tiny cough has been hanging on for weeks. He said that perhaps he could help her.

While Black Walnut was hiding out in the choir loft, he heard this morning's discussion between Pastor and Josie as they went over details of the upcoming worship service. Josie, once again, spoke with a tissue covering her mouth so that Pastor would not catch her relentless common cold. Pastor revealed to Josie that after finishing university he was accepted to medical school but only stayed there one year because he felt a calling from God to enter the Holy Ministry. While he was there he did learn a lot about the common cold, suggesting that it might be best to make a doctor's appointment. As Josie was speaking with him, she accidently dropped her tissue and it landed on the organ pedals. As she got off of the organ bench to retrieve her tissue, a huge blast of whisky breath came out of her mouth. It was so potent and excessive that Black Walnut said he even got a colossal whiff of her moonshine from a distance of five feet. Pastor evidently realized that this is at the core of why she speaks with a tissue placed over her mouth. Josie admitted to him that she gets so jumpy when she plays the organ that a few shots of whisky beforehand helps to calm her down. Black Walnut said that Pastor Osterhagen backed off from this revelation, as it was time for Josie to play the prelude. Being kind to her, Pastor told her to do the best job that she could, and that it would be good enough for today. Josie told him he is the kindest pastor she has ever worked with and thanked him by giving him a big hug.

At 11:15 p.m. Ruby and I travelled to the parsonage and split a shred of cabbage that must have fallen out of a crispy egg roll. We wished that we could find more, so we spent a few minutes searching, but our efforts were fruitless. We are not disheartened. We are confident that Aia will prepare another batch of egg rolls soon, when she feels better, since stir-fry is a weekly meal at the Osterhagen's.

    – F.N.

ARRANGEMENTS WERE MADE BY THE LOCAL "SERVES YOU RIGHT SUMMER VOLLEYBALL Club" to use St. Peter's outdoor volleyball court every Tuesday evening during June, July, and August. A contract was drawn up by the church council and was signed last May for permission to use the court from 7 to 9:30 every Tuesday evening. The church building itself will not be used by the club, except for the washrooms. The leader of the club, Ben Atkinson, was given a key for the building. That way he would be able to unlock the back door of the church at 7 p.m. and lock it up at 9:30 p.m. There have been no problems, no damage, and absolutely no mess. The mice village thinks the volleyball group is not only neat as a pin, but athletically incredible.

Ruby and I know that Clement and Aia are aware that there is a brief tailgate party in the church parking lot after their volleyball games, with some simple snacks and beer. Because this has not been a problem, they are not against it. They are glad that this group of young adults enjoy their time together at the church property on these long summer evenings.

All has gone satisfactorily with the SYRSVC until today. Catch-a-Wink-Dink, an older mouse in our village, was sound asleep underneath the kitchen stove when Viola Worthee showed up, as she often does, and began her weekly patrolling. As she rooted around the room, she soon discovered empty beer cans deposited in the blue recycle bucket located in one corner. Catch-a-Wink-Dink watched as Viola picked up one of the beer cans and headed towards Pastor Osterhagen's office. Catch-a-Wink-Dink quickly got a wiggle on and followed her. It was there that he heard Viola demand an explanation as to why beer cans are on the church premises. He began to explain, but when Viola heard the two words, "volleyball club," she interrupted him by referring to the club with a string of roughneck words that included scrappy, ignoramuses, trashy, and low caliber. Viola told Pastor that he had better step on the gas and take care of this problem faster than ASAP or she will tell the whole church.

After Viola left, Clement went home and talked with Aia about the empty beer can discovery. Together they agreed that it would have been better if one member of the volleyball club had simply gathered up the empty cans and placed them in the trunk of their car to be taken home to their own recycle bin. That way

Viola would not have spotted the beer cans. If that had happened, the volleyball club and Pastor wouldn't be in trouble with her. Perhaps it was others who had a beer drinking party in the middle of the night in the church parking lot. Aia said that it actually would have been better if the volleyball players had thrown the empty beer cans all over the church parking lot rather than bringing them into the church. Clement wondered if somebody not connected to the volleyball club, but one of the parishioners, had just kindly picked up the littered beer cans in the parking lot and brought them into church, dropping them in the recycle bin. Viola might not be aware of it, but there are many instances of "scrappy ignoramuses," to use two of her mean-spirited words, depositing rubbish on church properties everywhere throughout the nation, especially on Saturday nights.

Hopefully, the SYRSVC won't lose their contract to play volleyball on HSP's property. Clement and Aia have seen how much fun the team members have on Tuesday evenings. They know the players will be very disappointed if their contract is cancelled, as they are expecting the seven remaining Tuesday evenings of the summer to be full of volleyball fun.

Clement spent a few minutes talking about how recycling related to Viola. He wondered just how long Viola Worthee has been interested in the subject. Up until this point, he has noticed that she doesn't care a hoot about recycling. It was Viola who threw all of the empty dill pickle jars, the empty plastic chip dip containers, and even an empty coffee can into the kitchen garbage can the day of the church picnic last month. Instead of placing those items in the blue recycle bin, she threw them in the garbage can. When Clement saw her do that, he reached into the garbage can and pulled those items out, placing them instead in the recycle bin. Clement said that Viola's interest in recycling is so new that it couldn't be more than a few minutes old. It is definitely more about Viola's long-standing intolerance of any alcohol. Clement and Aia feel for her as they think back and remember her late husband, Henry, who had a lot of similarities with Otis Campbell on "The Andy Griffith Show." They were two of a kind.

Clement shared with Aia one of his favourite quotes from Mr. Rogers, which goes like this: "When I was a boy and I would see scary things in the news, my mother would say to me, 'Look for the helpers. You will always find people who are helping.' To this day, especially in times of 'disaster,' I remember my mother's words and I am always comforted by realizing that there are still so many helpers – so many caring people in this world." Clement concluded his discussion with Aia by adding that whoever brought the empty beer cans into the blue recycling bin was one of the helpers. He said that Viola did not recognize that, as she only looked at what she considered was a disaster.

At 9 p.m. Ruby and I travelled to the church kitchen and snacked on a morsel of a tortilla chip and a tiny droplet of beer. We like the "Serves You Right Summer Volleyball Club" and maybe, if the church people are kind to them, some of them might start attending church on Sundays at Historic St. Peter's.

– F.N.

ONE OF THE HYMNS SUNG IN CHURCH TODAY WAS "SIMPLE GIFTS," A WIDELY popular Shaker dance song that was made famous by Aaron Copland's composition, "Appalachian Spring." Because the hymn is not included in Historic St. Peter's hymnal, the words were inserted in today's bulletin. After the parishioners left St. Peter's, a few mice found a dropped bulletin on the sanctuary floor and dragged it to the village meeting room for safekeeping. Some in our village heard the parishioners sing the hymn and thought that everyone would enjoy singing "Simple Gifts." Perhaps with some work the simple Shaker dance steps could be learned by all of the mice, steps that we could synchronize with the music, just like the Shaker Communities used to do in the mid-nineteenth century. The "turn, turn... turning, turning" part sounds simple enough to learn.

While changing from church clothes into old clothes, Aia told Clement how she had not slept well last night. She was weary from being up with the twins during the night, but also weary from worry and completely unable to rest. She told Clement that she had a premonition that something was going to happen this week to them involving the police, something unpredictable and surprising, and not necessarily good.

Aia had decided to keep her scary thoughts to herself, but after she heard the words "'Tis the gift to be simple, 'tis the gift to be free" she couldn't contain those thoughts any longer. She told Clement that she doesn't think she has received the gift to be simple or free like the Shaker song suggests. She said that she will try to forget about her premonition, but she has a strong feeling inside her, right down to her bones, that something foreboding is going to happen soon.

At 11:30 p.m. Ruby and I travelled to the parsonage. All afternoon we looked forward to snacking on morsels of a homemade classic Shaker meal, but couldn't find even a crumb. It appears that the Osterhagens' "Shakered their plates" today, which means to eat every single crumb that is on their plates. This resembled the actions of the thousands of members of the Shaker Community long ago, and also the actions of the Shakers that remain alive today. If the Osterhagens continue to "Shaker their plates," Ruby and I will have to travel elsewhere to find our snacks, as there won't even be a crumb to be found at the parsonage.

– F.N.

Monday, July 13

AT TEN O'CLOCK THIS MORNING PETER "ROCKY" COLLINSWORTH MET WITH PASTOR Osterhagen, asking to become a baptized and confirmed member of Historic St. Peter's. This conversation was overheard by Little Bluegrass, son of Bamboo and Belladonna. Today is the first day that Little Bluegrass has been allowed to go out and about all alone. Finding a safe place to hide behind a filing cabinet in Pastor's office, Little Bluegrass was full of anticipation about his first outing. After all was clear and safe, he found his way home and revealed all that he had heard and seen to his parents, who then communicated it to everyone at tonight's mouse village meeting.

Peter is a newer attendee at Historic St. Peter's, having come from a non-church upbringing. Little Bluegrass overheard Peter tell Pastor Osterhagen that one day, simply out of the blue, he pulled into St. Peter's parking lot finding himself to be deep in thought. He was certain that something was stirring inside him, calling him to visit St. Peter's the next Sunday. Peter chose Historic St. Peter's simply because it matches his first name.

Since that first Sunday, Peter is one of the most frequent attendees. Arriving early each Sunday while whistling, "Carolina in the Morning," he finds many jobs to do at church before the worship service begins. He races to put the hymn numbers on the hymn boards, turns on the switch for the sound system, passes out bulletins to those attending the coffee hour even before the ushers arrive, is a pre-greeter by standing in the greeter spot before the greeters arrive, and all morning is on standby, ready to be on duty in case the person who is scheduled to read the Scripture lessons does not show up that particular day.

Peter has changed his tune in two other ways: 1) He prefers to be called Rocky instead of Peter because, according to Matthew 16:18, Jesus Christ said, "And I tell you that you are Peter, and on this rock I will build my church, and the gates of Hades will not overcome it." 2) Upon entering the building, Rocky now prefers to whistle "Rocky Top" instead of "Carolina in the Morning."

Pastor spoke with Rocky about the sacraments, Holy Baptism and Holy Communion. They agreed to meet several more times for adult instruction, but the baptism took place as soon as their meeting was over with. Two mice from our village, Matins and Vespers, hid behind the communion rail and watched Rocky being baptized. Matins told Vespers that Rocky is now God's own child.

At 9:50 p.m. Ruby and I travelled to the church kitchen where we happened upon a single butterscotch chip that had fallen to the floor from yesterday's coffee hour cookie plate. We discussed and agreed that the invention of butterscotch chip cookies is superior to any other invention ever made, as the chips absolutely melt in your mouth, which brings about an abundance of joy and delight!

    – F.N.

SEVERAL WORKERS EMPLOYED BY CADWALLER'S CONCRETE CONTRACTORS ARRIVED AT Historic St. Peter's this morning wearing dust masks, safety goggles, heavy-duty work boots, and work gloves. St. Pete's Board of Property finalized their decision several weeks ago to improve the sidewalk area leading up to the front steps of the church. The decrepit and rickety sidewalk has become a safety issue, especially for older members who are not as sure-footed as they once were. Because the old sidewalk is so deteriorated and dilapidated, it was decided it was best to remove it completely and have new concrete poured to produce a brand new sidewalk. This upgrade will provide a smooth path for everyone to walk on, putting safety first. Many members of the church have responded by saying they are thankful about this needed improvement.

All summer long one of the families in our mice village, the Lavenders, have been spending most of their time in the fragrant herb garden at St. Pete's. There are five members in their family. Parsley and Sage are the father and mother of Rosemary, Thyme, and Little-Herb. They like to hide and keep safe under the growing herbs. That way they stay cool by avoiding direct sunlight. The herb garden also adds to their well-being by providing completely natural herbal aromatherapy; they also clearly benefit from munching on oregano, curly parsley, German thyme, mint, sage, rosemary, dill, and chives. Because of their high chlorophyll consumption, Ruby and I surmise that they must be the healthiest family in our entire mice village, all five of them in fine fettle.

The workmen from Cadwaller's Concrete completed their undertaking at Historic St. Peter's late this afternoon. Prior to leaving the property, they cordoned off the wet cement with a barricade of colourful tape that was meant to caution everyone to stay away from the sidewalk until the concrete had hardened.

Our mice village meetings are held on Sunday evenings, unless there is an emergency. There was an emergency late this afternoon, so a meeting was immediately called to see if we could solve our problem, which involved the youngest member of the Lavender Family, namely Little-Herb. While Parsley and Sage were taking a siesta under the dill plants, Rosemary and Thyme were practicing their coordination skills by spinning and twisting. They had spent the better part of the morning stripping the leaves from two rosemary sticks in order to fashion their own homemade twirling batons. They were supposed to be watching Little-Herb while their folks were napping, but were so wrapped up in twirling their batons that they didn't see Little-Herb get away from them. When they discovered that he was gone, they frantically went in pursuit of him. Rosemary and Thyme found him having the time of his life running around in the newly poured concrete, leaving his footprints everywhere. The villagers decided that there was nothing that they could do about the damage done to the concrete. It was mentioned that Little-Herb was, well, so little, that he was not aware that he was doing any harm. We closed the meeting tonight by saying it could have been much worse, as it was just some cosmetic damage done to the new sidewalk. Barker, our most ornery mouse, had the nerve to say that it would have been much more destructive, for instance, if Gretchen had gone out there and decided to lie down flat on the concrete and make a snow angel. When I heard that comment about Gretchen, I got upset at Barker because Gretchen would never, ever do anything like that. I stood up, walked to the front of the assembly, and corrected Barker. I let everyone know that Gretchen is an adorable, intelligent, and thoughtful girl that has way more common sense than Barker.

At 11:45 p.m. Ruby and I skipped a snack and flopped into bed. The village meeting lasted an awfully long time tonight. Everyone felt sorry for the Lavender Family. Parsley, Sage, Rosemary, Thyme, and Little-Herb all shed tears, but everyone gathered around them and sang, "All are Welcome Here." No one wanted them to feel rejected, like they were outcasts, *persona non grata,* or lepers. Some of the mice did not know what the word leper meant, so Dr. Theodore Simonsen, our head librarian explained it very well. He said leprosy is written about in the Bible. It is a terminal skin disease easily passed on, so those who get it have to be quarantined from the whole community – how awful. (It has nothing to do with the mid-afternoon meal "lupper," by the way.)

– F.N.

Thursday, July 16

Aia answered a knock on the parsonage front door today. There stood a couple that she did not know, who politely inquired if they could speak with Pastor Osterhagen. Aia told them that he was studying in his office at the moment, but perhaps he would be able to take time to see them. She invited them into the parsonage living room and offered them a place to sit on the sofa. Aia then called the church office and asked Clement to come home. He arrived at the parsonage within two minutes.

The couple introduced themselves to Pastor Osterhagen as Isaac and Hannah Suderman, noting that they are Mennonites who own a heritage farm several miles west of Historic St. Peter's. They revealed that they were bewildered and baffled about something, not knowing what to do. Isaac was clear that they were seeking Pastor Osterhagen's advice, adding that they have feared asking anyone's help within the conservative Mennonite community. They would feel ashamed for lacking foresight and might be judged unfairly for the predicament they are in. They were advised by their good neighbours, Mike and Helen Linden, faithful members of Historic St. Peter's, to consult Pastor Osterhagen. The Lindens have told the Sudermans numerous times that Pastor is of great help to people when they need guidance, advice, and prayers. Isaac and Hannah said that they need all three, hopeful that Pastor can assist them. They wondered if Pastor Osterhagen would be so kind to take his time to listen to their situation, noting that their understanding of pastors is that they keep things confidential. They said they hope that he can do that in their case. Maybe later the story will come out, but for now it needs to be kept private. Pastor agreed to hear their story and to keep quiet about it.

Isaac began by explaining that something random and odd happened at their farmstead two weeks ago. While the two of them were outside working, a black pickup truck pulled into their driveway and a clean-cut looking man in his mid-thirties got out of the truck and walked up to them. The first thing he did was to introduce himself as John Becker. They introduced themselves to him and John commented that he was surprised that they had never met before. He told them that it was about time that they got to know each other, being they lived in the same area. John talked about how busy everyone seems to be nowadays and how difficult it is to become acquainted with everybody in town. Despite his work and family activities, he is trying to get to know others in the community.

John continued the conversation by telling them that he was scheduled to have some repairs done on his truck today at Field's Filler-Upper. Being that the repair is minor, he said that it would be as good as new later this afternoon. He wondered if they would be kind enough to help him out with something. John explained that he had just attended an estate sale in nearby Beeker County and had purchased an exquisite oil painting. He said that it was a blessing from God that he was able to purchase it and was planning on hanging it in a place of honour in his home.

John kindly inquired if they could store the painting in their garage for just a few hours, as he'd be back to pick it up after his truck was repaired. Explaining that he did not want to leave the painting in the back of his pickup truck because he was afraid it might get damaged, or that someone with sticky fingers might steal it, he was certain that it would be very safe in their garage. John further explained that he had several other things to do in town today, including a dreaded dental appointment and also an appointment with an attorney regarding his grandmother's estate. John told them that she was such a precious person that it feels far too soon to discuss her estate, but he knows it is best to get it settled. His final words were simply about not being able to carry a large painting throughout town today as he would be travelling on foot.

It was at this point that the Sudermans made their mistake. Isaac and Hannah agreed that John could store the painting in their garage for a few hours. He made a promise to be back before suppertime to pick up his painting. That happened to be thirteen days ago. They have not seen or heard a peep from him since that day. It was obvious to Ruby and me that they are full of worry because both voiced an intuition that something is crooked, adding that they suspect there might be a crime of some sort involved with this so-called John Becker and his painting.

Yesterday, without any more delay, John unfastened a corner of the painting's wrapping. He hoped to find out if, by any chance, there was some documentation inside: a telephone number, address, or even the name of the place where the estate sale took place. When Isaac loosened some of the outer wrapping, he did not uncover any paperwork. What he did encounter was an oil painting of a nude woman. If any of their community were to know of this painting on their property, it might harm the Sudermans' reputation, which would take a long time to restore. Isaac and Hannah are more than desperate to get this painting off of their property.

Hannah told Pastor that the talk in their community is that the Osterhagens are very knowledgeable about fine art, as she heard that he studied art in Europe during his university days. Hannah also heard that Mrs. Osterhagen was a dual major at her college having received both a degree in art and in music, which led her to obtaining a master's degree in art education. Hannah said that no one in town is more qualified to help them out than the Osterhagen's. The Sudermans meekly asked Pastor if he and his wife would be willing to drive out to their farm and take a look at the painting to see it if might be a valuable work of art. They have begun to wonder if this so-called John Becker might be an art thief. The Sudermans told Pastor that they are certain he and his wife, because of their qualifications, will be able to immediately decipher whether it is a valuable original or just a risqué wall hanging.

Clement, Aia, and Gretchen left the twins at home with Arni and Juliette and followed Isaac and Hannah to the Suderman Farm. They were quite unaware that Lewis and Clark, our expert mouse village explorers, had hitched a ride to the farm with them. After entering the garage, Isaac uncovered the painting. Lewis remarked that Aia's face fell in disbelief, becoming completely pale in colour. She suggested that this painting might be worth a fortune. Because of Aia's art studies at Trinity College, she recognized it as a work painted by Frederick Arthur Bridgman, "Nude at the Tableside," perhaps a hundred years old. If not the original, it was a very good forgery. She said that either way it looks like a crime has been committed. Clement straightaway advised Isaac to call the police, as it was best to get the painting into the hands of the authorities. Aia was certain John Becker had no intention of displaying the masterpiece in his home, but would find the most lucrative way of all to sell it. With the painting in their possession, the Sudermans' safety was at risk.

When the police arrived at the farm, Isaac revealed relevant facts about the situation they were in, after which Clement made clear that the painting, if an original, is of great value. If it is a forgery, then it is a very good one. After listening to Isaac and Clement, one of the police officers radioed the Oswald County Sheriff. The sheriff told the officers to place the painting in the trunk of the cruiser and that he would be over soon. The officers very carefully wrapped up the painting and placed it gingerly in the trunk of the cruiser. Aia later commented that it was as though they were handling the Crown Jewels. After placing the painting safely in the trunk, one officer did not move, but stood at attention as if he was a Beefeater guarding something priceless, a national treasure.

After the authorities drove away from the Suderman Farm with the painting, Hannah invited the Osterhagens into their home for coffee so that they could process what had just happened. Over their cups of coffee and Russian sour cream coffee cake they talked about how thankful they were that this painting was off of their hands, off their property, and out of sight. The two couples talked for a long time about the ramifications of this painting while Gretchen had so much fun playing with Jewel Bethany, the youngest child of the Sudermans.

Isaac shared with them that on his last trip into town he had been doing a little research on John Becker. He told Pastor and Aia that he had spoken to several people, inquiring if they knew him. It seemed that no one had ever heard of anyone named John Becker, almost as if he didn't exist. Isaac stopped by the dental office, asking Dr. Cooper if he knew of a man by that name. He, too, said that he didn't know him. After that, Isaac stopped into the law office and asked Attorney Lance Ramsey the same question he asked Dr. Cooper, and again the answer was negative. Lastly, he stopped into Field's Filler-Upper and spoke with the owner, Franklin Field, who told him that he did not know anyone named John Becker, nor had he worked on a black pickup that day.

Hannah, too, did a little research of her own. She inquired at the gift store, the antique shop, and at the drug store. Not one of them had heard of a resident by the name of John Becker. The clerk at the drug store helped out by asking the other employees, including the newly hired pharmacist, Zachary Zimmermann. It was understandable why Zachary hadn't heard of him because he is new in town, but none of the other employees at the drug store had heard of John Becker either, and they are deep-rooted lifelong locals.

No one knew him. No one had heard of him. Isaac said that there must be thousands of men in the United States by the name of John Becker, but no one in Oswald County seems to have heard of this particular John Becker.

As all were visiting over coffee, both of the Sudermans began to imagine that they might be in a potentially dangerous situation now that the painting is gone. Pastor did not want to frighten them, but agreed that it might be a possibility, especially because John Becker knows exactly where they live. Hannah admitted to Pastor and Aia that she has been having panic attacks because of this. She went on to say that she cannot calm down her jittery nerves because her gut tells her that something must be wrong. This has led her to start smoking cigarettes, which she has never done in her life. The other day she was hiding in the alley behind the drug store in order to sneak in a cigarette, when a lady with a camera took her photograph. The lady appeared shocked that she, a Mennonite woman, dressed in a dark printed floral dress, a kerchief on her head, and black tennis shoes was smoking a cigarette. The stranger obviously couldn't resist taking a photo. Hannah explained that smoking generally is not permitted in conservative Mennonite circles as one's body is considered God's temple, but that her nerves are so shot, every once in a while she needs three or four minutes off from her worries, which is accomplished by smoking a cigarette. Hannah revealed that she fears John Becker might bring harm to their family, adding that he might want revenge because he lost out on a lot of money that he could have made from selling the painting to someone in the illegal art market. She said that her imagination is leading her to surmise that it might even be connected to a big drug deal.

Clement advised Isaac and Hannah to watch their backs, change up their schedules, keep their doors and windows locked, and to make an appointment right away with the sheriff. He said to talk to the sheriff and tell him about the danger that they feel they are in. Clement gave them his telephone number but reinforced the fact that, if something happens, they should call 911 immediately.

When Pastor, Aia, and Gretchen were saying goodbye to the Sudermans, Hannah gave Aia a carton of eighteen healthy, free-range, farm fresh brown eggs. Aia was delighted to receive the eggs and told Hannah that she can't wait for breakfast tomorrow as she'll use some of the eggs to make a farmer's omelette. Hannah told her the German word for a farmer's omelette is *Bauernomelette,* being made with cooked potatoes, onions, peppers, ham, parsley, and eggs. Aia told her that she likes to try new recipes, so she will try to make a *Bauernomelette* tomorrow. They hugged each other goodbye and both of them said to each other that they made a new friend today.

At 11:30 p.m. Ruby and I travelled to the parsonage kitchen and came upon a drop of potato leek bisque that must have dropped to the floor while Juliette ladled tonight's soup into a large earthenware tureen. Earlier in the evening the mice village called a meeting to hear Lewis and Clark present their observations at the Suderman Farm. They explained thoroughly the details of what they saw and heard. The mice village decided to meet again tomorrow evening to discuss if the Osterhagens might also be in danger, not just the Sudermans.

Ruby and I can hardly wait until Aia makes a *Bauernomelette* tomorrow morning. We might be able to find a morsel of the German or Austrian egg concoction. We like to sample new recipes, too.

Ruby shared with me the description of a painting of a field mouse eating raspberries that she noticed in one of the children's books in the nursery. She is certain it would be dreadful if it were stolen, as children would not be able to see that delightful work of art. Our conversation shifted to finding out who exactly was the artist of that painting. Ruby suggested that it might have been Wyatt Earp, as his full name was Wyatt Berry Stapp Earp, noting that he was a talented man who might have possessed a painter's finger, even though he is famously remembered for his trigger finger. We wondered, too, if growing up on a farm in Pella, Iowa, Wyatt might have often seen field mice in the raspberry patches, drawing inspiration to paint from his observations. We ended our conversation with a strange thought after the town of Pella was mentioned. Ruby is convinced that if she ever has a baby and it is female, she hopes to name her Pella, which means, "Marvel of God." As she is getting older each day, Ruby is aware that it would be a true wonder if she could at last get pregnant as her "wheel of life" is quickly rolling along. I did not know what to say to comfort her about not having any babies, so I just said *"Mqvw plv xxat,"* which means "I love you" in the mouse language.

    – F.N.

CLEMENT'S FOLKS, FRED AND NANCY OSTERHAGEN, HAVE DRIVEN EIGHTY MILES THIS morning to Historic St. Peter's for the baptism of their new grandsons, Marc and Luc. This is the first time that they have seen the twins and their delight was way beyond what words can express. Both babies were dressed in white baptismal outfits purchased at the Olden T'ings Antique Shop, Aia's favourite place to roam around for treasures. When Gretchen saw her brother's baptismal outfits several days ago, she immediately asked if she could have a new outfit, too. When Juliette heard that, she wanted to know what Aia would be wearing, offering to sew a similar dress for Gretchen, making their outfits a mother-daughter match. Aia loved the idea, so Juliette drove over to Messmer's Fabrics and purchased a child dress pattern and fabric to sew Gretchen a dress using Aia's sewing machine. She claimed that she could sew it in no time as it isn't much larger than a doll outfit. She began the sewing project one evening, and by putting in some midnight oil, the dress was completed by 1:45 a.m. When Gretchen saw her dress the next day, she thought it was beautiful. In a hurry to try it on, she kept talking about the fancy flower patch on the front of her dress. Juliette told Gretchen and Aia that she could not resist purchasing the decorative pink and red rose flower embroidered appliqué from Messmer's. Gretchen wanted to wear the dress all day, but she understood that it needed to stay in the closet to be kept clean and spotless for her brother's baptismal day. Every morning since that day she has asked if it was the day to wear her beautiful dress. Gretchen was elated that today was finally the day.

Juliette has outdone herself in cooking, as the refrigerator, oven, and one slow-cooker are filled with special German foods for the baptismal dinner, which everyone enjoyed after church. Fred and Nancy will stay at the parsonage until Gretchen's birthday on Thursday, July 24, leaving on Friday. Both Aia's and Clement's folks enjoy each other's company, are keen on cocktail hour in the breezeway every day at 5 o'clock, and spend time before bed playing cards. Ruby has noticed that Juliette and Nancy are true card teammates and take their husbands to the cleaners regularly.

The baptism of Marc and Luc went beautifully this morning. Clement, Aia, Gretchen, and the rest of the relatives were beaming and in good spirits. All went well until Carole Browne cornered Pastor and Aia. One of our village's most dainty member, Dotted Swiss, had posted herself in the narthex behind a portable floor display board that contained photographs of the recent youth trip to Riverson's Outdoor Fun Park. Dotted Swiss, who prefers to go by Dotty, heard Carole tell Pastor and Aia that there were two typos in today's bulletin where the names Mark and Luke were spelled incorrectly. Aia explained to Carole that her mother's side of the family is French-Canadian, kindly educating Carole that Marc and Luc are spelled correctly in today's bulletin and in the French language. Carole barked at both of them, telling them that the boys should have been named Matthew and Mark, instead of Marc and Luc. Dotty was proud to tell us that, even though Aia almost lost control, she took the high road, breathed deeply, and kept her negative thoughts about Carole's so-called wisdom to herself. Aia also kept to herself that she does not care for the name Matthew because of the overused nickname Matt, which is something people wipe their feet on.

Aia also refrained from asking Carole if her first name is misspelled, because off the top of her head she could think of at least eight ways to spell the name Carole. Before bed tonight Ruby saw Aia's "Carole List" that accidently missed the kitchen wastebasket, which included the following spellings: Carol, Cariel, Carrill, Carrole, Karell, Karel, Caril, Carrel, Carrell, Carriel, Carril, Carrol, Caryl, Carryl, Kerril, or maybe even Kerrol.

Since Gretchen's birthday is on Thursday, her two grannies, Juliette and Nancy, are preparing a very special birthday party. Putting their heads together, they planned on a Hawaiian luau. Juliette said that she will ask Aia to teach "The Hukilau Song" and accompanying actions to everyone during cocktail hour, which will be great entertainment. Juliette told Nancy that the grownups can enjoy Mai Tais and petite Waikiki meatball appetizers. The island meal will consist of sweet and saucy slow-cooker chicken, grilled pork kabobs with chunks of peppers, Hawaiian rice, fresh fruit with pineapple dip, ending with a birthday cake topped with a small hula girl plastic decoration. Tomorrow morning they will make a quick trip to Grocer Dan's for the ingredients, and then head over to Bill's Dollar Bill for plastic leis, a hula cake topper, and tropical party decorations. Before returning to the parsonage, they will stop at Zuzanna's Polish Bakery, place an order for a sweet butter cake layered with lemon curd, topped with white frosting, and then covered in snowy white coconut flakes. They will take a coffee break at Zuzanna's tomorrow and have a cup of coffee and split a sweet. Both agreed that the birthday cake will be expensive, but decided they will divide the cost of all of the supplies, assuring each other that it will be well worth it.

Juliette was inquisitive about Nancy's pineapple dip recipe. Nancy has prepared it so many times she has it memorized. Our village has noticed that church people somehow have memorized the most important things in life, like the Ten Commandments, the Twenty-third Psalm, the Apostles' Creed, the Nicene Creed, the Lord's Prayer, several parts of the Catechism, the hymns "Amazing Grace," "How Great Thou Art," and "Just as I Am," as well as the phrase, "and also with you." Hearing that Nancy had the pineapple dip memorized, I quickly wrote down the recipe as it must be very important. This is what she said from memory:

Pineapple Dip for Fresh Fruit

2 ½ cups pineapple juice
1 T. butter, softened
2 eggs
2/3 cup sugar
2 tsp. flour

Heat the pineapple juice on the stove. In a bowl, combine butter, flour, and sugar. In another kettle, whisk the eggs and then add the butter, flour, and sugar mixture, beating until smooth. In a thin stream add the heated pineapple juice, stirring fast and constantly. Place on the stove and heat until thick. Remove from heat. Cool and refrigerate. Serve dip with fresh fruit.

Many comments were made by the parishioners today in praise of the new sidewalk at St. Pete's. The artistic designs are in no particular pattern, just random, but delicate, intricate, and anything but humdrum. At tonight's mouse village meeting I was the first one to speak to the assembly regarding the new designer sidewalk that has been positively praised by the parishioners. The Lavender Family has been keeping a very low profile since Little-Herb had the time of his life randomly running around in the fresh concrete. This good news helped them lift their heads high and to not feel ashamed any longer.

At 11:30 p.m. Ruby and I travelled to the parsonage hoping to find spillage from today's baptismal dinner. All we found was a tiny shred of roast pork. This afternoon we stayed near the crack in the dining room wall and listened to the fascinating conversations. We breathed in the savory aroma of their scrumptious dinner:

roasted pork tenderloin with sauerkraut, hot potato salad, asparagus, homemade pretzels, and pickled cucumbers. For dessert they enjoyed a decadent Black Forest Cake. This family knows a thing or two about celebrating important occasions.

    − F.N.

Thursday, July 23

Today was Gretchen's birthday. She was completely ecstatic after breakfast when she got to open two birthday gifts from her Nygaard grandparents. But before that, she opened the birthday card, asking her daddy to read the contents. It said, "You are as sweet as flowers blooming in a beautiful garden. Your precious smile and loving heart brings joy to everyone around you." It was signed by Grandpa Arni and Granny Juliette. On the inside of one box was a pair of red round-toe cowgirl boots. In another box was a red cowgirl hat along with a red gingham bandana scarf. Gretchen thanked them profusely by throwing her arms around them, followed by speed walking with her gifts to her bedroom to dress in a cowgirl ensemble. After she was dressed, she walked down the hallway, calling out to everyone to close their eyes. When Gretchen entered the living room, she told them to open their eyes. Ruby and I enjoyed watching her perform a one-girl fashion show as she was decked out in blue jeans, a white blouse accentuated with the bandana scarf wrapped around her neck, and sporting a big smile. Often she pointed to her boots and tipped her cowgirl hat as she sang "Home on the Range." After everyone clapped, the Nygaards told Gretchen that they were going to take her for a pony ride at Bracken's Riding Stable.

When the three of them returned home, the family enjoyed eating Sloppy Joes, Gretchen's favourite meal. Gretchen talked all about Bonehead, the really gentle pony that she rode. After lunch Clement and Aia took Gretchen for a fast wheelchair ride around Woolcox Hall, providing a small way for Clement and Aia to get in some exercise. At two o'clock in the afternoon, Gretchen's three friends from church came over for a birthday party, wore princess hats, played a game, and enjoyed birthday cupcakes. The party was over by three-thirty. At four o'clock Grandpa Fred and Granny Nancy took Gretchen to the city swimming pool, planning to be back home in time for cocktail hour. Their gift to Gretchen was a Hawaiian print swimming suit, fancy flower flip flops, a Hawaiian beach towel, and a child's inflatable dolphin. At the pool Gretchen saw Amanda, her new babysitter, who now works part time as a lifeguard. Amanda became Gretchen's new babysitter a while ago because she is far more available than Christine who is currently car-hopping at the drive-in.

Gretchen received one more present, a birthday gift that she had asked her parents to give her. She wanted a doll that sits in a wheelchair so she can give her rides, just like they give her rides in the church wheelchair. Aia purchased a soft girl doll with red hair and a blue outfit that comes with a sporty, splashy wheelchair. Gretchen was delighted with the doll, not just because of the wheelchair, but that she has stunningly red hair. Immediately she named her doll Bettie. Very importantly, Aia had added to the gift a foot of cotton cord, which she said is intended to band around the doll's waist like a seat belt, just as Gretchen is girdled (to use a church word) in the church wheelchair with her daddy's clergy cincture. We found the word girdle confusing until we had Dr. Theodore Simonsen research it after we heard the news that John the Baptist wore a leather girdle. Dr. Simonsen revealed that there is also another type of girdle that is made of a stretchy, tight-fitting fabric, and is an undergarment sometimes worn by women. A modern girdle encircles the persons Southern Hemisphere for the purpose of sucking in plumpness. Definitely modern day girdles and John the Baptist's leather girdle cannot be anything the same. John must have been extremely fit and trim from consuming only locusts and wild honey, unlike some women nowadays who consume too many profiteroles, the decadent fluffy and sweet cream puffs with custard filling. I admit that I am apprehensive to admit that I have only recorded this particular girdle information as it might somehow be of grand importance in the scheme of things, although I cannot imagine why.

At 8:30 p.m. Ruby and I travelled to the breezeway and snacked on minuscule morsels of a butter-flavoured cracker. All day long we have not been able to get Gretchen's birthday song out of our heads. Ruby and I especially were keen on memorizing and singing, "Where seldom is heard a discouraging word, and the skies are not cloudy all day." When we were singing it today we somehow felt we were visiting the majestic State of Montana. We are of the opinion that the VIP who wrote the celebratory birthday song, "Home on the Range," must have gushed out their heart and soul into the text and the tune. We thought it might be a grand idea if it were to be included in future hymnals, probably the next one published twenty-plus years from now. We won't be around by then, as we will have gone to our final resting place. But we are forward-thinkers, being certain that future generations would enjoy this birthday song. Knowing that contents of the hymnals at St. Peter's are arranged according to the church liturgical year, we think there should be an additional section dedicated for birthday songs. The last thing that Ruby said to me tonight was to ask me if butter-flavoured crackers are higher in calories than locusts or wild honey.

– F.N.

AFTER SPENDING THE MORNING IN HIS OFFICE, CLEMENT RETURNED HOME FOR A QUICK lunch. Throughout the meal Arni, Juliette, Fred, and Nancy spoke with elation about their plans for the evening. The two couples had made reservations to attend a special summer event on Lake Harvey, hosted annually by the Elkridge Mansion. The annual "Wine-Athalon" begins with a late afternoon boat ride touring Lake Harvey's spectacular scenery, all the while nibbling on hors d'oeuvres and sipping wine produced by the local winery, The Bluebell Vineyard. After the boat tour, plans were to savour a memorable dinner at the famous Elkridge Mansion, prepared by Chef Axel O'Gara, with another glass of wine from The Bluebell Vineyard. The third and final portion of the "Wine-Athalon" was to be shuttled to the nearby nature trail on the Elkridge Estate, where they will take a scenic outdoor walk. When they reach the end of the nature trail, they will receive a very petite glass of dessert wine, also from The Bluebell Vineyard, along with chocolate dipped Bing cherries.

Aia has made plans with her friend, Annette, to be a guest at Annette's exercise studio, where free babysitting is provided on Friday evenings. After Clement heard that he and Gretchen would be on their own tonight, he promised Aia that they will have an evening full of fun, too.

Even though the two couples, Arni and Juliette and Fred and Nancy, were very excited about their Friday night activity, they assured Clement and Aia that if there are any problems, they will be happy to return home to be of help. Both Clement and Aia were given a slip of paper with the Elkridge Mansion's telephone number, in case of an emergency. The four of them will be leaving at 3:30 p.m. and won't arrive home until after dark. In all likelihood it will be well before midnight.

After lunch Clement drove out to the Swanson farm to call on Roscoe and Rose, elderly members of St. Peter's. Two mice from our village, Canoe and Paddle, sometimes hang out in the parsonage garage. (Recently they told me that seizing opportunities to travel is their top aspiration. They mentioned how thrilling it would be to secretly stowaway on a canoe ride down the mighty Cedar River.) After Pastor opened the van door, he must have realized that he had forgotten something, so he turned around and returned to the parsonage, leaving the van door wide open. During this brief time Canoe and Paddle propelled themselves faster than a slingshot into the vehicle, hiding quietly under the driver's seat. When Pastor returned to the garage, he was holding his home communion kit. When he backed the van out of the garage, Pastor, Canoe, and Paddle were on their way to the Swanson's. Shortly after today's excursion Canoe and Paddle came to our dwelling and revealed all they had seen and heard. Since most of the village is aware that I am writing a journal, many of them want to be included in my writings. I am happy to find out so much information, but Ruby notices that I am beginning to suffer with the presence of too much information, suggesting that I should cut back on recording so many details. I am taking her recommendation to heart, as her top priority, besides safety, is my personal well-being.

Since it was pleasant weather today, Canoe and Paddle were able to get out of the van at the Swanson's. After opening the front screen door, Roscoe welcomed Pastor into their home. Canoe and Paddle held back for a few moments, but then rested on the stoop where they were privy to the conversation going on in the living room. The room was clean, full of sunlight, and set up with two matching recliners, a sofa, end tables and a coffee table. They thought that they smelled chocolate chip cookies baking. The unusual part of the decor was that there were four TV trays in the living room, each covered with some type of home project or frequently needed supplies. On one tray was Rose's yarn for her current knitting and crocheting projects. On a second tray there was a tissue box, prescription pill bottles and a tube of a sore muscle rub. Another TV tray held books of large print crossword, mind puzzles, word search, and several pens and pencils. The fourth and last tray contained a soda cracker box, a can of cookies, and a crystal candy dish that was filled to the brim with hard candy. One half of the sofa was home to two crocheted afghan throws. The coffee table held several books and a big Bible. Since every surface was covered with something, Pastor appeared to have a little bit of trouble finding an uncluttered place for his home communion kit.

Canoe and Paddle watched as Pastor opened up the communion kit and poured tiny mouse-sized glasses of wine, said a prayer, and told the Swanson's to "take and eat" a small wafer of bread with a cross mark on it. He also told them to "take and drink the true blood of Christ shed for the remission of their sins." As they watched, it was all a bit strange to them, but they reported that the tiny bit of bread and wine left a very satisfied look on the Swanson's faces.

Before Clement left the Swanson's farm, Rose talked about how they are not able to tend a garden like they used to. But with the help of their grandson Kyle, they were able to plant a large garden once again. Just this morning Kyle was at the farm and harvested a big box of small cucumbers. Rose offered Pastor the box of cucumbers and her pickle recipe, along with canning jars and a large canner. She told him that this is the first year she is not able to put up pickles, hoping that he and Mrs. Osterhagen would enjoy canning enough to last all year. Clement was really happy about the gift, thanked Rose, and then put everything in the van, returning to the house to say goodbye to the Swanson's. Pastor arrived home at 3 p.m. and shared with Aia and Gretchen his excitement about tonight's pickle plans. Canoe and Paddle told me that they had no problem getting back into the van to return to St. Peter's as Pastor had all the doors flung wide open when he was loading the pickle paraphernalia. Upon hearing about the doors being flung open, it made me recall a hymn that was sung in Advent called "Fling Wide the Door." Now that tune is in my head and I can't get it to stop. Dr. Theodore Simonsen, our head librarian, once told me that there is a cure for this, which is simply to chew gum. Unfortunately, because I suffer with music repeating itself over and over, I find that the cure does not work. Maybe it does for people, not mice.

Canoe and Paddle's only safety issue that arose at the farm happened at the tail end of their outing. It was when Rose stepped outside and called the Swanson's cat, Radcliffe, and their dog, Jackson, who came running when she belted out their names. Thankfully, Canoe and Paddle were already in the van before safety was a concern.

After Aia, Marc, and Luc left the house, Clement put on his apron, the black one that says, "Let's Get Cooking," and Gretchen put on her little pink apron that says, "I'll Help!" They began the pickling process by giving the small cucumbers a bath to rub away the sand, dirt, and grime. It took an unusually long time before the cucumbers were clean and ready to begin their journey down pickle path.

When Clement proceeded with Rose's recipe, he realized that he might be in over his head and another adult would be helpful. He talked to Gretchen about this and she suggested that they call Aunt Bee and invite her to come over and help them. Clement didn't know who she meant, so he asked Gretchen many times who she is and what she looks like. After getting nowhere, Clement found out that Gretchen knows Aunt Bee from church, as she looks just like Aunt Bee from The Andy Griffith Show. (Gretchen has watched a few Andy Griffith reruns while her mother is on the sofa nursing the twins.) Clement pulled out a church pictorial directory and sat on the sofa with Gretchen, asking her to point out Aunt Bee's photograph. Within a few moments Gretchen pointed to Aunt Bee, who is really Aggie Cox.

Gretchen told Clement that on the Andy Griffith Show Aunt Bee is not very good at making pickles and that Andy, Opie, and Barney can't even swallow them. Clara is the one who excels at pickles and wins the blue ribbon at the county fair each year. Gretchen told Clement that they can't call Clara for help because she doesn't go to their church. Gretchen asked if she could call Aunt Bee and talk to her on the telephone, adding that since he doesn't even know her, she should be the one inviting her to come over and help them. Clement dialed Aunt Bee's phone number and Gretchen did all of the talking. Within fifteen minutes Aggie Cox arrived at the front door of the parsonage wearing her strawberry print apron – ready, willing, and excited to help them with their pickle production.

Clement explained to Aggie that he hoped they could make three varieties of pickles: old-fashioned regular dills, horseradish dills, and garlic dills. Aggie firmly tightened her apron strings after she heard the plan and said that they had better get busy. By 10 p.m. the pickles were all canned and cooling. In fun, we heard Clement mention to Aggie that Queen Cleopatra consumed a diet full of pickles which has been attributed to her exquisite beauty. Aggie laughed at that goofiness. When it was time to leave, Aggie told them that she had so much fun that if they ever need any more pickle help, just have Gretchen give her a call. She said that she will see them on Sunday morning. "Aunt Bee" kissed Gretchen good night and then headed to her car. Clement followed her and carried along a box containing a dozen jars (four of each variety) of newly made pickles, placing them in the trunk of her car.

Aia arrived home shortly before the pickles were finished. She nursed the twins and put them to bed. After Aggie left, Aia fell asleep as she was reading the story "Little Red Riding Hood" to Gretchen. It was 11 p.m. when the Wine-Ath-alon attendees arrived home, just as Clement was finishing cleaning up the pickle project. He was proud of all the pickle jars lined up and cooling on the dining room table. After Clement crawled into bed, Aia was awakened when he turned on his flashlight. He told Aia that he needed to write something down before he could settle down for the night. His reminder was to look up two Bible verses, Numbers 11:5 and Isaiah 1:8, in his Hebrew Bible, as he read somewhere that pickles are actually mentioned in those two verses. Then he fell fast asleep.

At midnight Ruby and I travelled to the parsonage to satisfy our snack craving. In our search we came up empty handed except for a tiny sprig of fresh dill weed and one piece of minced garlic. Neither one tasted good to us, so we left there and ran full steam ahead to the church nursery where we found a little bit of an animal cracker which we think might have once been a sheep.

– F.N.

AT 10:30 P.M. BEACON, ONE OF THE BRIGHTEST MICE IN OUR VILLAGE, WAS RELAXING inside the back door of the church. He enjoys spending time in this spot because of the soothing light shining from the ceiling exit sign. In the past, he has mentioned to me that the antique sign's milk-white glass, with bright red letters, is the most artistic ornamentation in all of St. Pete's. When the door unexpectedly opened, without delay Beacon hid behind the ages-old oak umbrella stand, peeking out to see an unidentified person entering Historic St. Peter's wearing a black hooded sweatshirt and sunglasses. This person was carrying with him a plastic shopping bag that was stuffed with items. The individual did not turn on the top light switch as he was using a flashlight. Beacon wondered if it might be Griffin the Gremlin.

In great detail, Beacon described to Ruby and me the prank that Griffin did this time. Beacon watched as Griffin the Gremlin placed all twenty-five whoopee cushions directly under the church pew cushions, completely hidden and out of sight. Griffin must have shopped at Bill's Dollar Bill and purchased their entire supply of whoopee cushions, the ones that make that flatulent noise that everyone gets embarrassed of. He must have travelled throughout Oswald County to the other Bill's Dollar Bill stores to come up with that many whoopee cushions. We know that whoopee cushions are a Canadian invention used to play practical jokes on people by giving off loud farting sounds when the victim innocently sits down on one. We mice wonder how in the world the country of Canada could possibly be proud of this invention which results in something that is anything but dignified.

After finishing his work, he exited the building and locked the door. At that point Beacon hurried to our dwelling and enlightened us to all he had seen and heard. Ruby, Beacon, and I are certain that Griffin the Gremlin will be in attendance at the worship service tomorrow morning as he won't want to miss out on the whoopee cushions' performance.

At 11:20 p.m. Ruby and I travelled to the parsonage and split a dropped morsel of a green bean with bacon, or is it beacon? A short conversation ensued between us about the two words. We noticed that they are almost spelled identically, except for one little letter. We know that a beacon is a guiding light and that bacon is served after the sun comes up. However, we are confused as bacon is no longer just a breakfast food, but has found its way into recipes to be enjoyed at other meals, creations ranging from savoury to sweet. Even more confusing is wondering if the English gent, Francis Bacon, was really Francis Beacon. Soon we will seek out Dr. Theodore Simonsen, our village head librarian, for clarification on this bacon/beacon topic.

— F.N.

When parishioners arrived for worship this morning, found their favourite spot, and sat down on the pew cushion, twenty-five of them were completely unaware that another type of cushion was underneath it. One at a time sounds blasted forth. At first others in the sanctuary tried not to show their reaction, but the mice could tell from their faces their great astonishment as they heard the loud explosions. Long before the last whoopee cushion had gone off, everyone realized that a nasty prank had been played at St. Pete's. The twenty-five unfortunate victims who sat on a whoopee cushion all remained seated throughout the worship service, full of anxiety, as they must have feared that these cushions might very well be the self-inflating type. The fear was that if they moved it might send out another loud passer gasser. Will Anderly, Board of Property Chairperson, was clearly upset throughout the worship service due to this prank. After church was over, he quickly gathered up the cushions and dumped them in Pastor's office on top of his shiny walnut desk. During the postlude Gretchen walked into her daddy's office, helped herself to five whoopee cushions, and tucked them into her church activity bag. After today's potluck Gretchen took the whoopee cushions out and placed three of them under the living room sofa cushions and one under the seat of each arm chair. Every time her folks or her grandparents sat down, the whoopee cushions went off. Gretchen plugged her nose and delivered each victim one of her homemade "P.U." notes.

No risks were taken as to the specific food items that were contributed to today's potluck, due to the efforts of one parishioner, Ellie Crowley. Several weeks ago Ellie posted a sign-up sheet in the narthex asking parishioners to record their name and what type of salad, entrée, or dessert item they plan to contribute to the dinner. Ellie's plan was two-fold: 1) to make certain that no recipes would be repeated, thus eliminating double or triple casseroles of cheesy potato bake, and 2) that only summertime foods would be contributed, thus excluding hearty beef stew or shepherd's pie, foods that are warm and satisfying but mostly popular during winter months.

Before worship this morning Pastor listened to Ellie making known her frustration regarding the sign-up sheet, telling him that several parishioners changed their minds as to what food they will contribute to the potluck. Ellie said that the sign-up sheet went from thriving to surviving since parishioners have changed their minds and crossed off their original contribution, substituting it with something else. Ellie showed Pastor how scribbled and illegible the sign-up sheet was while pointing out that today's dinner will be anything but a perfectly well-planned potluck.

Later today Clement communicated to Aia several details about Ellie's discontentment with her highly unsuccessful sign-up sheet. Aia pointed out how different Ellie is than the tomato lady. Somehow Clement had not heard about the tomato lady, so Aia filled him in. She said that last August, she and Gretchen shopped at the Salvation Army Thrift Store. Upon leaving the store, the tomato lady was standing at the exit with the trunk of her car open. She handed Aia and Gretchen each a plastic food baggie that contained seven luscious, homegrown tomatoes. Gretchen and Aia peered in the trunk and saw bags and bags of tomatoes. The tomato lady said that she waits for customers to leave the store, hands them a bag of tomatoes, and returns home when they are all gone. She revealed to Aia that she enjoys tending a large garden of tomatoes, but she cannot begin to use them up, so she joyfully gives them away. At that point, Aia asked Clement if he happened to remember a rustic tomato soup that she made last summer, the perfect soup for grilled cheese sandwich dunking. He said that he clearly remembered that soup. Aia said that those tomatoes were all from the tomato lady. Aia suggested that if "Potluck Patrol Ellie" were to give away tomatoes, she would first have to prepare a sign-up sheet because she would need to know how the recipients intended to use the tomatoes, whether it be on hamburgers, in spaghetti sauce, on BLT's, or perhaps ending up in a batch of homemade ketchup.

For several weeks Oaken, a brawny mouse in our village, has kept Ellie under surveillance as she enters the sanctuary. Oaken reports that Ellie touches the back pew on the right hand side, then moves forward touching the next seven, counting up to the number eight. When she arrives at pew number eight, she sits down, unless there is someone already parked in her spot. Oaken reported to our village that on those unfortunate occasions, Ellie politely tells the stranger to move to another pew as this is her place to sit. Ellie is a work of art herself in a strange sort of way, as her fashion sense is eccentric. Today she was wearing a lightweight fitness running jacket on her Northern Hemisphere (upper body) with a full floral skirt on her Southern Hemisphere (lower body). This was accented by a rhinestone-studded leather belt at the Equator (waist), along with a pair of purple beaded moccasins. Ellie's total look is fun to look at, a hodgepodge of uncoordinated fashion. Oaken speculated that Ellie is not concerned with her clothing fashion being matchy-matchy. Odd, he noted, that when it comes to potluck contributions they had better fully coordinate.

The number one thing we learned from today's adventures came from the words of Jesus we heard read in church from Acts 20:35, "It is more blessed to give than to receive." Ruby said that the tomato lady certainly puts those precious words into action. Oaken was on to something similar when he reported to the village, "It proves to be exceptionally gratifying to bless and provide for others rather than acquiring abundant riches and prosperity." He did a fine job with his report at the village meeting tonight, but the words in Acts 20:35 are much better.

It was an easy decision for Ruby and me to travel to Woolcox Hall at 6:45 p.m. to nibble on a few gleanings from today's potluck. My favourite find was a honeydew melon ball that had dropped to the floor from a fresh fruit tray, while Ruby's was a potato gnocchi smothered in fresh tomato sauce seasoned with oregano. It has been quite a day.

    – F.N.

SUMMER RECESS HAS NEARLY PASSED FOR SCHOOL TEACHERS ARNI AND JULIETTE. IT IS time for them to return to their home and get back to work. On Wednesday morning they will walk into their classrooms to prepare for their teaching positions for the upcoming year. Arni is looking forward to teaching Medieval Latin Literature of the Twelfth Century at the university and Juliette will continue teaching French at the high school. She told everyone that the French language is always in vogue – it's chic, full of beauty, and useful. Aia told Clement that her mother's opening remark to a new classroom of students each year begins with her reciting a memorized quote from Barry Farber which goes like this: "No matter your other language achievement, you will be judged by your French." Barry is the author of *How to Learn Any Language* and speaks over twenty-five languages, even Chinese, Russian, and Finnish.

The goodbyes were tearful, especially for Gretchen and Juliette. Gretchen ran back to her room to get Bettie and her wheelchair and cincture, asking if she could go with them to their house. Granny Juliette said that it would not work out this time, but she promised Gretchen that they would see her soon. Gretchen settled down and blew them goodbye kisses as they drove down the street. Arni beeped the car horn twice, which has deep meaning in the Nygaard family. The first beep of the car horn at departure time means a final goodbye kiss and the second beep means a final goodbye hug.

Clement and Aia are now fully responsible for their three children. They are thankful for all the help they have been given. Aia expressed to Clement that she lacks confidence that she'll be able to keep up with Gretchen, the twins, breast-feeding, cooking, laundry, let alone finding an opportunity to take a shower. She mentioned to Clement that nursing the twins every day takes so much of her time, she has become nothing other than a couch potato. After hearing that, Clement didn't choose his words very carefully and told Aia that she is a strong and healthy woman who can handle just about anything, suggesting that she just get back in the saddle.

Aia got upset at Clement and responded by telling him that he hurt her feelings. She told him that she is a strong woman, but not a classic pioneer woman who can work her ten fingers to the bone day-in and day-out, year-in and year-out, wearing out completely and dying by the time she is thirty-five years old. She communicated to him that she simply doesn't have the strength of a sturdy American pioneer woman. Those women could lug a baby on their back, weed and hoe the garden by hand, enter into the corn field and weed that, too, all the while watching in case they needed to kill a snake. For entertainment they collected big buffalo chips, one after another, and placed them in their roomy burlap apron pockets to be used for fuel. Those early American pioneer women did all of that while living in fear of a prairie fire coming upon them or their dugout being trampled by a heard of buffalo. After Aia said all of this, Ruby and I finally heard her take a breath.

Clement looked at her and realized that inside his wife's head there is a deep, deep ocean, and he told her that. He communicated his confidence in her, and Aia calmed down. He said that he really needed to go to his office because he's had so many days staying home with everyone that his work at church is sunk in a deep, deep ocean right now. His only hope is to sail HSP's ship on a great big sea of grace. Ruby and I saw them lovingly kiss on the lips before Clement left for the office, so we assume everything is once again copacetic between them.

At 11:30 p.m. Ruby and I travelled to the parsonage and snacked on a fallen morsel of a sausage, mushroom, and broccoli quiche. We just love it when Aia cooks French-style.

— F.N.

ANOTHER VERY EARLY SUNDAY BEGAN AT 5:30 A.M. AT THE OSTERHAGEN HOUSEHOLD. Clement headed to the washroom for a shower. Aia badly needed to make use of the washroom at exactly the same time, but instead of interrupting Clement, she sprinted over to the church washroom in her yellow daisy bathrobe, being fully confident that no one was in the building. We have heard Clement and Aia vent many times about the parsonage's horse-and-buggy plumbing system. If the shower is running while the toilet is flushed, a full sixty seconds of scalding water pours out of the shower head before it is restored to an acceptable temperature. From personal experience the Osterhagens have figured out if there ever was one handy thing about living in St. Peter's parsonage, it is that there are extra washrooms nearby for emergencies.

Speckle, one mouse in our village, was hiding behind a wastebasket when she peered out and saw John Overby enter the ladies washroom. When Aia opened the door, she encountered John carrying out the most outlandish caper. He was holding a clear plastic garbage bag that contained several packages of mini marshmallows. Already he had emptied a bag in each toilet bowl, but was now in the last stall depositing marshmallows. She quickly scanned the other three toilets and saw miniature marshmallows floating in each toilet. Spackle told us that Aia called John "Griffin the Gremlin," and he appeared scared that he got nabbed doing a prank at church. Aia sternly told John to follow her to the parsonage, as he will need to explain his actions to Pastor.

Clement was in his bathrobe when Aia and John walked into the parsonage. Aia's words to Clement came out of her mouth at top speed. For a moment Ruby and I thought that she sounded exactly like she was mimicking an auctioneer. Even though she was in such a hurry to tell Clement about the marshmallow prank, she quit mid-sentence, threw up her arms, and walked out of the room leaving Clement and John alone to talk. It was clear to Clement, because of Aia's body language and speaking voice, that she didn't want anything to do with this problem, telling him that this was his circus and his monkeys, not hers, and that it was up to him to solve it. Clement knows her well enough to recognize when she wants to wash her hands of something and withdraw. Or, he thought, she really must need to use the washroom.

Pastor asked John to sit down and start at the beginning by telling him what had happened. John began by speaking not about the marshmallow prank, but by explaining some of his life history to Pastor. It was extremely interesting, so Pastor poured two cups of coffee, handed one to John, and just sat there listening to his every word.

We heard him explain that in 1961 his father, also named John Overby, was in his junior year of college. His concert choir travelled to Norway on a choir tour, which included singing concerts at a Norwegian cathedral, at one of the few remaining stave churches, and at many country churches and town halls. At the end of the two-week tour, the choir spent a few days sightseeing in Norway. One fascinating part of the trip was travelling by boat to northern Norway, to the Nordkapp, where on Midsummer's Day they could witness the magnificent Midnight Sun, a sight that is never to be forgotten.

As the choir enjoyed a casual supper at Redvald's, the local eatery, his father was captivated by an amazingly beautiful young woman. Throughout supper John's eyes caught hers and hers caught John's. After the end of the meal, most choir members ordered a blue nightcap that they had heard so much about, a favourite of old Redvald himself. It was unique because it was not served in a regular glass, but in one made of ice carved from an iceberg. After that, most choir members retired to the guesthouse. John decided to stay behind, hoping to have a chance to meet the beautiful one he had laid his eyes on.

Later on John garnered enough courage to introduce himself to the girl. They sat down at a table for two and ordered coffee. She introduced herself as Marit Ellingson, telling John that she has lived in Nordkapp all her life. Her family home is isolated in the forest where she lives with her parents and her younger sister. She recently got a job at Redvald's and comes in several times a week to work as a hostess just during the supper hour. Since she was finished with her shift, she and John visited with each other for a long time. Before saying goodbye they exchanged addresses. That became the beginning of a two-year correspondence, in which time they came to fall in love with each other. After writing letters back and forth, John invited Marit for a visit, and after one month of courtship they were married at Emmaus Church, a small country parish on the western side of Oswald County. One year later Marit was expecting a baby. On March 28, 1965, a baby boy, John, was born and named after his father. John Overby, Sr. was twenty-five years old and Marit Ellingson Overby was twenty-three years old.

John explained that he was very loved by both his parents, but he noticed oddities throughout his upbringing, mostly coming from his mother. Some of those eccentric peculiarities must have come from her upbringing. She came from an isolated region in the deep northern woods, living in a traditional cottage, where a corner fireplace was used for both warmth and cooking. Many of the older customs, strange myths, dark legends, and beliefs of Norwegian folklore were very alive in her family's everyday experience. Most children at that time who grew up in cities like Oslo or Bergen would not be daily exposed to those older customs. But his mother was. Her memories included dozens of stories about trolls, telling John that she has seen them several times near a waterfall. Marit usually referred to them in a negative way, distinguishing them as slow in intelligence because they must be without brains. She mostly talked about their ugly features, their one eye, or sometimes two or three heads, noses dripping with snot, hideous feet, and how exceedingly hairy they were. John especially enjoyed the few stories she told him about dragons, but mostly she talked about trolls, as though they were real creatures. Describing her childhood home, there were three colourful witches' balls that hung in the main window, while three kitchen witches guarded the kitchen. There were three Norwegian forest cats that lived with them named Agnar, Vor, and Sindri that were considered family members. There was something odd about the number three as it was used frequently by the Ellingson family.

Marit taught John, Jr. how to outwit anyone, how to cause trouble, and how to play pranks on people without getting into trouble. He admitted that his background has caused him to do many foolish things at church, like the handbell glove disappearance, the whoopee cushion Sunday, the spreading of confetti, other small pranks, and now the marshmallow incident, where he finally got caught. John admitted that he himself is the one that Pastor and Aia call Griffin the Gremlin.

Clement listened to John's stories and told him that he doesn't need to be Griffin the Gremlin any longer. If he feels like causing trouble, it is okay because it probably is a normal feeling, but he needs to be careful not to embitter the lives of others. He urged him to come and talk to him instead of acting out, and he'll try to help him work through it. In the meantime they will go together to the church washrooms and flush all the toilets. If the marshmallows will not flush, they will fish them out. Pastor said that together they will make it like the prank never ever happened.

At 9:30 p.m. Ruby and I shared a snack at home. Ruby found a mini-marshmallow today by the door of the ladies washroom and brought it home. We dusted it off really well and pulled it in half. The sweet taste is mediocre, but we mostly enjoyed the distinctive spongy texture we noticed in our taste test.

– F.N.

Tuesday, August 4

EACH AUGUST AN UPDATED PUBLICATION OF THE OSWALD COUNTY CHRISTIAN GUIDE is distributed free of charge to all of the churches in Oswald County. It is a practical and helpful reference directory that lists churches and Christian schools. In addition, Christians pay to advertise their businesses. The new edition arrived today and Ruby and I watched Clement sit in his green recliner while paging through it. He soon called Aia over to read to her the book's contents that were listed under "Funeral Homes and Cremation Centres." Both of the Osterhagens giggled as Clement read out loud to Aia:

Quitz Funeral Home, Trey Quitz, Funeral Director, "Call it Quitz"
　　Holler Funeral Parlour, Mel Holler, Funeral Director, "No Worries, Just Holler"
　　Cease Cremation Centre – The Cream of Cremations, Bern Cease & Ash Cease, Funeral Directors, "A smoke-free facility"
　　Best for the Family Funeral Home, "Best is the Least We Can Do," Adam Best, Funeral Director, "Free coffee, juice, and cookies provided"
　　Grave's Inspirational Funeral Chapel, Donald Grave, Funeral Specialist, "Love and Life Beyond the Grave."

Ruby and I were overloaded with this much information. We needed time to process what we had just heard. We rested on our bed, but unfortunately we fell asleep and slept the day away. At first when I woke up I wondered if Ruby was possibly dead as she was so still. I checked her pulse and found out that blood was thumping. We got out of bed and travelled to the parsonage at 10:45 p.m. Thankfully, we found a snack from something very familiar to the Osterhagens and to us, funeral sandwiches. The Osterhagens eat them frequently because they take very little time to prepare. The open-faced tuna fish sandwiches are generously topped with crushed potato chips. We each got one tiny bite of both a fish and a chip. We decided not to store all of this funeral talk information in our minds. Instead we will focus on the words of wisdom spoken by Mrs. Eleanor Roosevelt which Dr. Simonsen read to us at the last village meeting. She said, "Life was meant to be lived, and curiosity must be kept alive. One must never, for whatever reason, turn his back on life."

    – F.N.

Wednesday, August 5

For Clement and Aia, getting accustomed to having twins has been an overwhelming experience. Aia does very well, but when Clement comes home, she often weakens in her resolve because he is there to catch her and help her up emotionally. Sometimes she has a little breakdown, a moment, in which she usually collapses on the sofa from exhaustion. Fretting about the fact that there is too much work to do every day, she told him that it is impossible to get anything done besides taking care of the twins, even with Gretchen's help. It was 4 o'clock in the afternoon and she was still in her nightgown because she was unable to find a minute to take a shower or to even brush her teeth.

Aia's anxiety is daily, even though Clement and Gretchen are good helpers. Today's plan was for Aia, Gretchen, and the twins to go to the grocery store, return home, and put everything away, but that was not possible. Clement listened to her speak about her feelings of failure. He offered to take on the grocery shopping for now, just for awhile. Also he said he will take care of the children every morning before he goes to his office so that Aia can get showered and dressed. He told her that everything is a bit clumsy now, but together they are finding ways to make everything work.

Before supper tonight Clement headed over to Grocer Dan's and filled up a grocery buggy with essentials like fruit, veggies, dairy products, and meat. Aia warned him before he left that she is trying to watch her waistline, aiming to return to the shape she was in before having babies. He heard what she said, so he knew not to bring home any cookies, desserts, pop, or junk food. Aia chatted with Clement about purchasing dietary shakes, bars, and snacks, but they decided that is not the healthiest way to reduce. Besides, it is expensive. That led to a conversation about joining a gym, but that is costly, too. In reality she is at the point where she can barely find time to get showered, let alone getting dressed in a snappy looking workout outfit.

Aia asked Clement to purchase at least two varieties of gourmet cheese. Yesterday she received a package in the mail that contained a Norwegian cheese slicer that she special ordered over the telephone from Brønla's Blissful Boutique in Washington State. We have heard Aia mention how a cheese slicer will help her dieting efforts, as she will be able to prepare paper-thin slices of cheese instead of chunky slices, thereby consuming fewer calories. Clement's grocery purchases were mostly nutritional, practical food items. Among the items were an institutional-sized can of maple flavoured baked beans and another one of table mustard, along with a very large glass jar of sweet pickle relish. He told Aia that there was a terrific sale on top quality, sturdy, stainless steel, short-blade oyster shuckers. Knowing how much Aia enjoys fresh seafood, he thought that tool might come in handy sometime, so he purchased it.

Ruby and I noticed that Aia was utterly bewildered as to the reason why Clement purchased institutional-sized food items. The containers are so large in size that they wouldn't even be able to store the sweet pickle relish and table mustard in their refrigerator because the space in there is crammed the way it is. They could store them in the refrigerator in the church kitchen, but that would mean running back and forth every time they had hot dogs for lunch.

After telling Clement that she couldn't even imagine purchasing a dozen oysters, Aia mentioned that if they want to eat oysters, it would be better to attend the Oyster Festival held every October in Oyster Bay, New York. If Clement someday were to have a parish on Long Island, then it would be practical for them to own an oyster shucker, but right now it doesn't fit the geographical area in which they live. Right now a kitchen tool that would be extra handy for them would be a plastic hamburger press.

Aia thanked Clement for bringing home the groceries, breaking it to him gently that he should return the oyster shucker, the sweet pickle relish (which she thought would take them approximately five years to consume), the gallon of baked beans, and the mustard and get his money back. Clement agreed with her and said that he plans to return those items tomorrow at Grocer Dan's. He sincerely hopes that Dan doesn't wait on him at the customer service desk, as Dan is a member of St. Pete's and might think badly of him.

At 11:30 p.m. Ruby and I travelled to the parsonage and split what we found on the floor. There were bits of a grilled turkey sandwich with Sussex cheddar cheese imported from the United Kingdom, pressed and toasted to perfection. Ruby and I will never forget tasting the distinctive tang of this superb high-calibre cheese. To us the flavour in the Sussex cheese was monumental, momentous, and most memorable.

– F.N.

Thursday, August 6

SHIRLEY SANDERS AND HER HUSBAND EDDY OWN A GETAWAY LAKEFRONT PROPERTY ON Lake Harvey, which they creatively named "Sanders' Shire." Together they have invested so much time, talent, and treasure in their lakefront place, it is in far better condition and appearance than their home in town. Being only a beautiful fifteen-minute drive away from town, they spend as much time as possible out there in the spring, summer, and autumn months. Weeks ago Shirley invited all of the ladies in the church to the shire for a suppertime summer potluck which started at 5 p.m. today. The mice were aware of this off-campus event because we read about it in a dropped church bulletin found under a pew.

All attendees met at the church parking lot and then carpooled to the shire in several vehicles. Due to Lewis and Clark's ability at being so nimble, dexterous, and quick, they were somehow able to find an ingenious way to sneak into one of the carpool vehicles without being noticed. Their assignment was to discover exactly what happens at the Ladies' Summer Gathering, because our village currently knows nothing about this well-attended event.

All ladies were having a tremendous time sampling everything on the potluck table, mindfully noting which recipes were new and exciting. All chairs were positioned so everyone could enjoy a waterfront view. As they ate, there was a lot of chatting about who made what. As they were halfway through dinner, Ollie Shaw jumped up from her chair and nearly dropped her heavy-duty paper plate. Hardly able to release the frightened words from her mouth, she pointed and announced that there was a monster in the water. Sure enough, there was something that looked just like the Loch Ness Monster. This one had two humps instead of the ancient triple-hump that usually fits Nessie's description. All ladies were dazed and spellbound, especially Shirley, emphasizing that she had never, ever in all these years seen anything like that before, and to think of the danger she and Eddy and their sons Timmy, Tommie, and Tucker have escaped while swimming hundreds of times in Lake Harvey.

After many minutes the monster swam near the shore and walked on land. It happened to be an emu that must have gotten loose from the Hamilton Emu Farm located on the other side of Lake Harvey. No one knew what to do about it, so they called Pastor Osterhagen and told him to call the Emu Farm to come and pick up a loose emu. Aia couldn't believe that they bothered to telephone Clement to get him to deal with the problem. Lewis and Clark thought that one of the ladies should have had the courage to call Hamilton's instead of inconveniencing Pastor with this situation.

The gathering ended shortly after that. Without staying at Sanders' Shire for dessert, the ladies decided to skedaddle out of there after each prepared a take-away dessert on a heavy-duty paper plate. Each lady, with her semi-empty pot-luck dish, dessert take-away, and a large handbag to tote on one shoulder, quickly loaded into the same vehicle that they arrived in. Most ate their dessert en route during the fifteen-minute ride back to St. Peter's.

At 11 p.m. Ruby and I travelled to the parsonage and came upon some tuna macaroni salad that contained teensy-weensy pimentos. Following our snack we were so peppy that we did something very unusual. Together we quietly danced a Cajun Jig until Ruby got dizzy from turning in circles one time too many. After that, we got a move on and returned to our dwelling.

– F.N.

Friday, August 7

THE USUAL SUPPER ON FRIDAYS AT THE OSTERHAGEN HOME IS AIA'S HOMEMADE PIZZA. Tonight was different, though, as Clement took them out to eat at Vandell's Pizzeria. All day long Aia, Gretchen, and Clement looked forward to going out for pizza; Marc and Luc were just along for the ride.

Vandell's is a well known pizzeria in Oswald County, even though the location of it is deep in the woods, really in the middle of nowhere. Even though Vandell's does not advertise, everyone in the county knows just where to find it and how delicious the food is. The establishment is historical as it once served as a dining area for an old lumber camp. It has an immense stone fireplace in the centre of the room. Nowadays it has a dining area as well as a large, well-used dance floor. The ambiance is rich with knotty pine walls, floors, and an attractive beamed ceiling. Amber coloured lights glow from the many old chandeliers that hang from dark wooden beams. Aia told Clement that she is captivated by the building because something about the look and feel of it transports her back to another time in history. She told Clement that she could easily imagine strappingly stout, muscular, burly and brawny woodchoppers eating tall stacks of pancakes at solidly built wooden tables while seated on long wooden benches that are just as sturdy.

Vandell's has a wide range of options on their menu. Because their pizza is so delicious, all of Oswald County ranks it as the best pizza anywhere this side of Italy. A classic pizza at Vandell's is an amazingly delicious twenty-inch crust topped generously with meat, vegetables, and double cheese. After ordering Vandell's supreme twenty-incher, the Osterhagens nibbled on freshly popped popcorn from the help-yourself popcorn machine while waiting for their pizza to bake.

At 8 p.m. on Friday and Saturday evenings the place becomes very loud as it is transformed into a dance hall with a disk jockey. Older clientele and those with young children escape from the place before 8 p.m. to avoid the younger and wilder crowd. The older people also like to escape from the deep woods, returning home to watch the news before bed. One never knows what kind of wildlife will be spotted when they are that deep in the woods: raccoon, deer, fox, coyote, chipmunks, and bats are all possibilities. By the time the Osterhagens left Vandell's on their way home, the nightlife was just coming alive at the old lumber camp. It is a fifteen mile journey on a two-lane highway, at dusk, with solid wooded areas on both sides of the road.

So much transpired on the trip back home from Vandell's that Clement and Aia needed to process their anxiety, talking for several hours after they returned home. Ruby and I clearly heard distress in their voices. Gretchen cried herself to sleep, even though she had a lot of comfort from her folks. She even used an entire box of tissues to dry her tears and blow her nose.

It was dusk when Clement had started to drive his family home. Aia was in the front passenger seat, Gretchen was securely seated in her child seat in the rear of the van, and Marc and Luc were fastened in infant seats directly behind Clement and Aia. Suddenly Clement ran over a big raccoon that had run onto the highway. Only eight miles away from Vandell's Pizzeria, this accident caused such a big thump inside their vehicle that both twins woke up, but went right back to sleep. Gretchen thought it was so much fun that she asked her daddy to do it again. She was completely unaware of what had just happened.

Moving on from the raccoon incident, Clement was safely driving a bit above the speed limit, as he was intent to get everyone back home. After they travelled about halfway, they came upon a steep hill in the next stretch of the road. When they arrived at the top of that hill, Clement and Aia spotted three deer standing in the middle of the road ahead. They were easy to spot because of the headlights shining from the white car in front of them. Seeing two deer bolt off into the words, just in the nick of time, they witnessed the third one freeze and became an actual "deer in the headlights." The white car rammed into the lone deer with the front right side of the car, not killing it, but injuring it severely. That deer could not possibly have made it to safety after it was injured. The eyes of the deer were wide open and looked straight at them as it tried to kick and roll over, but it was unable to stand up. The deer was directly in Clement's path. On both sides of the road were big sturdy trees in a thickly forested area. If Clement swerved at all he would have plowed into the trees.

At that very moment, in the other lane, coming toward them was an eighteen-wheeler. There was no other choice but to proceed forward and run directly over the deer. There was a huge bump inside when the deer went beneath the van. Gretchen, Aia, and Clement were so shook, they were screaming and crying all at the same time. After it happened, Clement pulled over to the side of the road to check the damage to the van. He found a dented front bumper, the front hood of the van bent, and the front licence plate nearly torn off. He told Aia that he was more concerned about the damage that had taken place underneath the hood. Because he wasn't certain that they could drive home in that condition, they patiently waited until another car came along. Aia spent the time trying to calm Gretchen down. Very soon another car came and told the Osterhagens they would go and get help. Soon a highway patrol car showed up, followed by a tow truck and one other vehicle. Immediately the driver of the tow truck recognized Pastor Osterhagen and Pastor recognized the driver, Ernie Schwinn. The Schwinns have attended Historic St. Peter's only twice because he and his wife, Lorena, work most weekends, which makes it impossible to frequently attend the worship services. Before hooking the van up to his tow truck, Ernie mentioned to Pastor that he and his wife would like to join the church, if it is acceptable that they attend just a few times a year. Pastor assured him that they can be members, attend church whenever it works out for them, and that he will be glad to see them each time they attend St. Peter's.

Since the Schwinns live just a mile and a half from the point of the accident, Ernie had asked Lorena to follow him to the scene of the accident. It was a good thing Ernie thought of that, as Lorena was able to give Pastor Osterhagen and his family a ride back to the church. Within a few minutes Lorena and Clement had secured the children's car seats into the Schwinn's van. Lorena told Ernie she would meet him at home after she dropped off the Osterhagens. When the family arrived safely back home, they thanked Lorena as Aia handed their pizza box to her that contained leftover pizza slices. She told Lorena to take it home, warm it up in the oven and enjoy a snack with Ernie when he gets home. Lorena thanked her for the pizza and told Pastor that in two weeks they will see them in church, as they have that weekend free.

This experience was too much for Gretchen to handle as it brought forward so many new emotions she has never felt before. She was sad, surprised, confused, fearful, and fussy. She cried and cried at home and finally cried herself to sleep at 11:30 p.m. Except for the delicious pizza they enjoyed at Vandell's Pizzeria, the Osterhagens did not have a very good time tonight. Clement and Aia held hands in bed and consoled each other by saying that in a small way it was a good day as they survived, they put a deer out of its misery, and now two people want to join the church. They also said that tomorrow would be a better day.

At 11:45 p.m. Ruby and I kept our ears near the crack in the dining room wall as we listened carefully to details about the Osterhagen's terrifying trip. After Clement and Aia went to bed, Buck came over to tell me the details he witnessed on the trip to Vandell's Pizzeria. Earlier in the day, Gretchen was in the breezeway playing with items in her activity bag. When she was not looking, he had been able to hide in her activity bag, knowing that she takes it along with her everywhere she goes. Since so much happened to the Osterhagens tonight, it took a long time for Buck to tell me everything. Ruby grew tired of waiting for me to go out and about to find a snack, so she gave up and went to bed hungry. After Buck left, I, too, went to bed hungry.

    – F.N.

GRETCHEN WOKE UP THIS MORNING WITH PUFFY EYES, THE VERY FIRST TIME THAT Clement and Aia have ever seen her eyes look like that. She told them that they needed to go shopping today to purchase new sheets for Marc and Luc's cribs, because their sheets have lots of daddy, mommy, and baby deer on them with pine trees. She said that she saw their sheets this morning and it reminded her of last night's dead deer, which made her cry again. Gretchen also said that she wanted to get one of those bright yellow warning signs that says "Caution: Deer Crossing" to hang up next to their garage door so that any deer that might come into their driveway will not get run over.

Clement and Aia talked about Gretchen's plans. Concluding that it might be helpful if she talked to someone else about the deer accident, Clement said that Donald Grave, the funeral specialist at Grave's Inspired Funeral Chapel, has recently employed a specialist that counsels young children. Perhaps if she talked to Gretchen, even for just a few minutes, it might help Gretchen to feel shoulders above the way she feels right now.

After lunch Clement telephoned Donald and talked to him about Gretchen and her sadness. Donald told him to bring Gretchen to the funeral home where Misti Stone will help her. Aia stayed home with the twins while Clement and Gretchen went to see Miss Misti. Clement later told Aia that Misti listened to Gretchen and must have said encouraging words. It only took fifteen minutes of time before Gretchen seemed to feel better. After that Gretchen hugged Miss Misti goodbye, but before they parted, Gretchen invited her to attend Historic St. Peter's tomorrow morning. Gretchen added that she will wait for her by the front door and then they can go into the sanctuary to sit together. Since they are new friends, Gretchen also invited her to attend St. Peter's every single Sunday so they can see each other once a week. Since Misti is new to the community, she appreciated Gretchen's invitation, telling her that she would meet her by the front door tomorrow morning.

On the way home from Gretchen's one-to-one, Clement and Gretchen drove directly to the mall to select new crib sheets. They found some that were printed blue, green, and yellow plaid. After that, they drove to the hardware store and purchased a "Caution: Deer Crossing" sign. When they got home, Clement nailed the sign on the wall next to the parsonage garage door. Gretchen was so relieved, because now any deer that might happen to walk down their driveway would not get run over.

Later on Clement also was relieved when he received a telephone call regarding the damage done to their van. He was assured that all of it can be repaired by Wednesday afternoon. Today was a far better day for the Osterhagens than yesterday turned out to be.

At 11 p.m. Ruby and I travelled to the parsonage and split a tiny morsel of a mystery food, something that we have never tasted before. There was a small empty glass jar on the kitchen counter which said, "Capers, Product of Spain," so that must have been the mystery food. We liked the caper but are not certain that capers are meant to be eaten just by themselves. Ruby thought they might be better incorporated into a sauce and drizzled on fish.

Ruby and I conversed about how people at church sing the praises of Vandell's Pizzeria, claiming that Vandell's prepares the best pizza in the region. If we cannot reside at HSP at some point, perhaps the mice village could all move to Vandell's and make that our new home. We're certain that we would be able to find shredded mozzarella cheese morsels at Vandell's anytime, day or night.

   – F.N.

EVERYTHING WAS ALMOST AS SMOOTH AS SILK IN CHURCH TODAY. BEFORE WORSHIP began, Gretchen spotted Miss Misti in the entryway and hurry-scurried over to her, doing her "fast walk" because she knows it is not acceptable to run in church. They hugged each other, after which Gretchen and Miss Misti joined Aia, Marc, and Luc in their usual pew. As the congregation began singing the opening hymn, "As the Deer Pants," one of the mice saw Gretchen's eyes flooding with tears. Misti noticed what was happening and tried to help Gretchen. By whispering a couple of sentences in Gretchen's ear she was able to calm her down, also providing tissues from her purse along with a stick of chewing gum. Whitby, one of our village mice gifted with a phenomenal auditory range, clearly heard Gretchen whisper to Miss Misti that she no longer likes the deer song since last Friday. After church Gretchen told her daddy not to sing the deer song anymore because it reminds her of Vandell, the name she has given to the dead dear. After that, Gretchen gave him a big smile and a hug.

At 11:30 p.m. Ruby and I travelled to the parsonage and snacked on a square of green pepper that fell to the floor from tonight's taco salad. Together we discussed whether or not human beings eat meat from a deer. In our experience, the Osterhagens don't seem to prepare any recipes that call for one pound of ground deer. Since Gretchen named the dead deer Vandell, perhaps news of that will reach Vandell's Pizzeria, prompting them to create a new variety of pizza, a deer meat pizza. Ruby was quick to add that they could name the pizza, "Oh, Deer!" and that the catchy name might tempt customers to be open to experience something new. But, you never know what will go over well with humans. Besides, deer probably tastes just like chicken anyway.

– F.N.

A PHOTOGRAPH WAS TAKEN AFTER THE WORSHIP SERVICE TODAY OF THE CHURCH council standing on the steps in the sanctuary chancel. The council consists of twelve members, thirteen including Pastor Osterhagen. It was a noteworthy day as it was announced that the council was successful in obtaining a $25,000 grant from the synod to apply towards mission work at the nearby Reservation, or "The Rez," as locals refer to it. This photograph is to be submitted to the synod's headquarters to appear in the quarterly magazine along with an article about the purpose of the grant, which is to spread God's Word throughout the Rez.

As the photograph was about to be taken, Aia's hands were occupied with the little ones while she was attempting to pack up the diaper bag. Glancing at the church council for a moment, with Clement positioned centre front, Aia noticed the same old stance she has seen in church photographs numerous times when a group photo is taken. Later on Ruby and I heard her tell Clement that she momentarily thought about interrupting them by saying something in order to vastly improve the photograph, but instead remained tight-lipped. Clement asked her to spill out her thoughts.

She described to Clement that there was a "major fig leaf" issue in the way the council members were standing. Noticing that all twelve members of the church council, men and women alike, were standing with their hands held together in front of their bodies, she mentioned that it just doesn't have a polished, confident look that conveys that they are thankful and excited about this big grant. Reminding Clement that so much information dispatched to the human brain is visual, many people in the synod will not even read the magazine article, but will glance at the photograph and deduce that the people in the photo are just warm bodies, giving their mission work at the reservation a wimpy, feeble, and namby-pamby reception. Aia emphasized that the $25,000 grant from the synod to work amongst the people at the Rez is of paramount noteworthiness, otherwise the synod would not have asked for a photo to be submitted for their quarterly magazine. But, the fig leaf visual does not communicate excitement about the mission work they are privileged to do. The photo communicates twelve people with personal shyness towards their mission work, which is the opposite of the truth. The truth is that the council and parishioners are excited that St. Peter's has been given this opportunity. Aia thanked and hugged Clement for knowing better than to pose in the fig leaf stance, noting that he was the only one who simply let his arms hang down at his side, showing strength and confidence, along with eagerness for the upcoming mission work. He responded to Aia's complement with three words, "You're welcome, Aia."

Later on in the day Clement told Aia that he is going to request that the council retake their photograph next Sunday with all twenty-six arms down at their sides, which will be a far better photo to submit to the synod magazine. Aia thanked him for being so wise and once again hugged Clement, but that is normal behaviour for her, as she wants to hug Clement every time he comes around the corner.

Together the Osterhagens talked about the fig leaf pose and wondered why church people stand that way, as it portrays a look that is sheepish, stiff, and stilted. They stand like that not just during photographs, but ushers all stand that way, too. Small singing groups that use music stands and microphones all stand like that because their arms are free. Clement and Aia understand the reason that greeters stand with their hands in the fig leaf position is because they are protecting their health, especially during cold and flu season. Aia continued her point by emphasizing that simply resting one's arms at the side portrays self-confidence, whereas the fig leaf position looks like an attempt to cover something up. It's not as though they are the naked seventeen-foot marble statue of Michelangelo's *David,* revealing every manly detail. Church people are fully clothed, but when they take on the fig leaf position, they act like ashamed Adam and Eve who haven't had time yet to sew their fig leaves together into a garment.

Aia told Clement that she is thankful for all of the good members on the church council and their steady and thorough work that they do at St. Peter's. But she cannot help herself when it comes to switching the name of the church council to a more applicable name. From now on she will refer to them with the amusing name, the "Fig Leaf Council." She joked with him that she will prepare something containing figs for the members to snack on at the next council meeting. She'll bake a fig spice cake or some type of granny fig bars, or serve chilled blue cheese stuffed figs, or broil some flavourful bacon-wrapped figs. Instead of using any of those ideas, she announced she could make a cold pureed drink fit for a health-nut's palate containing figs, almonds, bananas, and milk which could be served in a Polish crystal goblet, topped with a few caramel coloured banana chips purchased from a specialty grocery. Aia continued on by flippantly mentioning that if she didn't have enough time to prepare anything, she could simply purchase a generic box of fig bars to share at the council meeting. Better yet, she could diligently work weeks and weeks ahead of time to prepare a homemade Christmas figgy pudding for the December meeting. The figgy pudding could be set aflame by soaking sugar cubes in brandy and placing them around the circumference of the figgy pudding. Right before serving it, the lights in the board room could be turned off, which would add ambiance to the upcoming presentation of this specialty Christmas sweet. The figgy pudding could then be ignited by using a long fireplace match. The flames would produce a stunningly sizzling blue glowing flame. After the flame died down, the lights could be turned back on and the pudding could be served with her homemade brandied hard sauce, made with only the best brandy available, imported from France. According to Aia, if the Fig Leaf Council imbibed in a little bit more of Christmas cheer, they might lose the stiffness and be a little bit more flexible, creative, and non-judgemental, which would lead to council meetings being more efficient, faster, and maybe even enjoyable. As a result, they might even drop their arms to their sides and forget altogether assuming the fig leaf position from now on.

I wrote the gist of Aia's and Clement's conversation down because it must be important. After listening to all of it, Ruby and I are absolutely stumped as to what they were talking about. We spoke with Dr. Theodore Simonsen, our village librarian, and asked him if he would be so kind to research this for us. Dr. Simonsen reported back to us this evening that it might have something to do with Genesis 3:7, which he read to us: "Then the eyes of both of them were opened, and they realized they were naked; so they sewed fig leaves together and made coverings for themselves." Ruby and I are beginning to understand the central theme of their conversation, but are still missing the essential point of it all. From now on we'll look to see if we notice the commonly used fig leaf position in action by the members of St. Peter's.

At 11:30 p.m. we travelled to the parsonage and snacked on a couple of crumbs of a fig bar. Aia purchased them at the convenience store this afternoon. Ruby and I finally figured out all of the talk about the fig leaf position while we were snacking. We are certain this must have been "Fig Leaf Sunday" on the church liturgical calendar. That's why the theme of the day at the Osterhagen home was all about the fig leaf.

– F.N.

TWO DAYS AGO AIA PREPARED A LARGE KETTLE OF CABBAGE SOUP TO KICK-START HER weight loss plan. Ruby overheard Aia tell Clement that she has had a successful personal history of losing weight while on this diet. She hopes to shed the weight she gained while pregnant with Marc and Luc so that her clothing will fit better, she will feel better, and most importantly, she will look better. This is another Trinitarian move on Aia's part – fit, feel, and figure. Aia would prefer to purchase dietary shakes to help her lose weight, but they cost a lot more than a head of cabbage and some vegetables. So far she has lost four pounds and is elated that she is making headway. Clement is noticeably hungrier since she began this diet, as he is consuming the same amount of food as Aia, whose portions are much smaller than before. We notice that he also looks a bit thinner and, unfortunately, a bit older from this new eating plan.

This afternoon Clement arrived home displaying a great big smile along with twinkling eyes. His arms held a large box containing fifty single-sized chip bags, a mix of classic potato chips, tortilla chips, and corn chips. After he put the box down on the kitchen counter he went out to the van and brought in two cases of my namesake British beer. He told Aia about his plans regarding the two big purchases. Before bed each night he will enjoy one bag of chips along with one brown ale. He'll continue this ritual until he runs out of supplies, expecting that the last individual bag of chips, according to his calculations, will be eaten on Monday, October 12. He revealed to Aia that this will help him get through her weight loss plan. He will stay on this plan just until she returns to regular cooking. Lately Clement has been emphasizing to Aia that she is the best cook he has ever known and that she makes delicious and satisfying meals. He added that he can hardly wait until she puts an end to the cabbage soup chapter of their lives. Aia told him that, for now, they will continue to watch what they eat and cabbage soup is of primary importance.

At 11:30 p.m. Ruby and I travelled to the parsonage for a snack but came up empty-handed. However, we were not deprived of a nibble tonight because we found a small square of sugar on the church kitchen floor. We are not certain if it is called a sugar cube, a sugar lump, or a cube of sugar. We shared it and remarked at how it ever so nicely dissolved in our mouths. It tasted so wonderful, Ruby and I surmised that each sugar cube, sugar lump, or cube of sugar must be steeply priced at Grocer Dan's.

  – F.N.

INSTEAD OF LOOKING FORWARD TO IT ALL WEEK LONG, AIA HAS DREADED A DINNER invitation from Marty and Lynne Schoenfelder. The Osterhagens are invited to attend five o'clock mass with them at Lynne's Catholic parish so they can hear the musical group that leads the singing there every Saturday. Marty, a lifetime member of St. Pete's, has told Pastor that he much prefers up-beat music to traditional organ music. He has admitted that he is very tired of listening to St. Pete's sleepy sounding organ every single Sunday morning. Attending Lynne's church on Saturdays is entertaining because the music is catchy and appealing, making it far more inclusive and friendly to visitors. Marty is certain that St. Peter's would be better off if some of that style of music were added to liven up each worship service.

Both Clement and Aia have backgrounds of musical training, appreciating excellence in church music. They are attentive to keeping the musical standards high at Historic St. Peter's, but they also seek out new music. After arriving home tonight, Aia commented to Clement that she enjoyed all of the songs at the worship service except for one, which she jokingly said should have been titled "Lovesick for My Lord." Clement agreed with her, adding that the theology on that song was too watered down. Ruby and I picked up that they both enjoyed the new music they heard tonight. We heard Aia singing one of the new songs in the shower, plus Clement was humming the same tune as he got ready for bed.

After mass the two couples met at the Schoenfelder's home for supper. Marty had purchased expensive custom thick rib eye steaks from Jimmy & Son's Butcher Shop. He expertly grilled them, as Marty is a real master of his grill. Lynne had already prepared twice-baked potatoes loaded with cheddar cheese to compliment the rib eyes. She dressed the romaine salad with extra thick blue cheese dressing and sprinkled it with crispy bacon and garlic croutons. She boiled corn on the cob, melted butter in a cake pan, and then rolled the ears of cooked corn in the butter bath and sprinkled them with salt. From the oven she pulled out Italian garlic bread. Later they ate blueberry pie and a scoop of ice cream along with their coffee. Aia told Clement that it was very kind of them to prepare all of the decadent food, emphasizing that they both are great cooks, but said that it took a heavy toll on her diet. She mentioned that the most difficult part of the meal was that Lynne waited on them by dishing up their plates, which made it impossible to control the portion size. Because they were guests at the Schoenfelder's home, Aia said that she felt like she needed to be a part of the "Clean Plate Club" by not leaving even a scrap of food on her dinner plate. Somehow, back in the day, being a member of the Clean Plate Club was crucial to reducing world hunger, especially for the children starving in Africa. Now it has turned into a recipe for obesity, cancer, stroke, and diabetes. Clement listened to her. His only response was that he really enjoyed every bite at tonight's supper and thought the portion sizes could not have been better.

When Lynne placed a full dinner plate in front of Aia tonight, Lynne surprisingly asked Aia if she was a vegetarian. Aia told her that she wasn't, but mentioned to Clement later on that she wondered what Lynne's plan would have been if her answer had been yes. She wondered if Lynne would proceed to take her dinner plate away and quickly put a kettle of water on the stove to prepare macaroni and cheese. If so, Aia thought she would have had fun telling her that she doesn't eat boxed macaroni and cheese because it contains processed cheese and artificial food dye, which is not good for one's health. Aia told Clement that she never would have said that, but she sure was thinking it. After supper Marty got out his guitar and soon had them singing his recently learned praise tunes with catchy refrains.

After Clement and Aia got into bed, Ruby and I heard them discuss the topic of contemporary church music and how to incorporate some of that at St. Peter's. They also talked about how the church could benefit from the cooking skills of Marty and Lynne. Clement's imagination came up with an idea which would use Marty and Lynne's culinary skills to benefit St. Pete's. Clement told Aia that there could be a Steak & Spud Event in Woolcox Hall. Chaired by the Schoenfelders, Marty could be in charge of rounding up grills, selecting the cut of steak, and overseeing the BBQ's. Lynn could be in charge of the potato preparation, as well as the corn on the cob. Many volunteers would help with the work. Musical entertainment could be provided by the praise singing group from Lynne's church, pleasing Marty very much. Both churches would be invited, making it a community get-together, with St. Pete's the event location. If a matching grant is approved, the proceeds would double in size, either for disaster relief or the new clothing bank located in the basement of the Oswald County Library. Aia said that Clement had a fantastic idea but added that she does not want to attend the Steak & Spud Event because of the unfortunate personal consequences it will do to her. It will be another disaster to her weight loss plan, just as she was beginning to make progress.

At 11:15 p.m. Ruby and I travelled to the parsonage, not finding a snack to-night. I must point out that snacking is one of our favourite pastimes, so tonight was disappointing. Together we decided that if snacking was a category in the Olympics like figure skating, cycling, or aquatics, we would certainly win gold or silver.

– F.N.

"MINUTES OF THE ST. PETER'S MOUSE VILLAGE MEETING, AUGUST 23 AT 8 P.M.: Tonight an uncommon request was presented to the villagers by Gustav and Dagmar Christoferson, with Gus doing the bulk of the speaking. While listening to the personal manner of speech that Gus possesses, one can easily detect that the Scandinavian-American expression of *Uffda* is solidly planted within Gustav's speaking repertoire. Gus has a marked pattern to his usage of *Uffda* in which it mostly occurs before sentences begin or it is plunked right into the middle of his libretto as he presents his thoughts. The manner in which Gus uses the word does not project sadness, confusion, surprise, or even a way to express relief, but simply appears to be his day-to-day all-around key expression. *Uffda* is one of those noteworthy words that stands on its own two feet, a complete sentence boiled down and compressed into one all-encompassing word. Just by chance English Toffee, one of our dainty villagers with a disposition as sweet as honeycomb, was at the meeting tonight and kept count of the number of times that Gus used the expression *Uffda* while speaking. She only kept a tab on it as she thought it added such a sugar-sweet feature to his everyday dialogue, suspecting that it may be part of his mother tongue. English Toffee suggested to me that *Uffda* might even have been the very first word that Gus spoke, instead of the word mama. She reported that she heard the word *Uffda* spoken by Gus thirty-one times tonight while he disclosed that he and his family would benefit from the judicious advice from the village, along with a helping hand from their fellow villagers.

"The Christofersons got to the point rather quickly as to the reason why they wanted to address the village assembly. Almost timidly, but resolutely, they asked for assistance from the village to help their family move from Historic St. Peter's to the countryside. Gus explained their reasons as to why they want to move, reinforcing that none of this is being done impulsively or on a whim. Gus pointed out that most of the mice might already be acquainted with the farmstead where they want to reside, as it is not far from Historic St. Peter's. He explained that it is the very first farmstead on the way out of town, going east, which is the site of the Finberg Heritage Farm. Gus remarked that most of the mice might recognize Harald and Vivi Finberg, as they are active and loyal members of St. Peter's. The Finbergs attend church every Sunday by arriving in their charcoal-coloured pickup truck that sports both Swedish and Norwegian flag decals that are adhered to the back bumper. The Christofersons explained that the Finbergs have a Scandinavian heritage like theirs. For example, the Swedish decal was purchased and then stuck on the truck by Vivi because she is proud to be of Swedish descent. After spotting the Swedish flag, Harald telephoned Brønla's Blissful Boutique in Washington State. Harald takes pride in his Norwegian heritage, so it must have been natural to ask Brønla herself to mail him a Norwegian flag decal. According to Vivi they have a mixed marriage, but they overlook the fine points by letting them fall between the cracks.

"With kindness and tenderness in his face, Gus spoke words of thankfulness to everyone in attendance about how much he and Dagmar have enjoyed living at St. Pete's, but divulged that there is something missing and sad at the core of their hearts. Gus went on to explain that they have a pining, an itching, a down-to-earth hunger to return to their roots, their heritage way of life, a life just like their ancestors lived all those years ago in the countryside. Dagmar added that this desire isn't just a revisiting of their past, but a sincere yearning for connectedness with their heritage, a simple going back home. While living at Historic St. Peter's they discovered that they are truly country mice, not church mice.

"Returning to the countryside has been in their thoughts since their girl and boy twins, Dala and Horst, were born. Gus beamed when he spoke of returning to the countryside as he said, "It has so much to offer… *Uffda*… like open spaces, meadows, gnomes, the moon, tranquility… *Uffda*… a simplicity like none other, fresh farm food, wildflowers, exploration, vibrant smells, cool streams, a soothing effect on the heart, mind, body, and soul… *Uffda*… a non-rushed, non-noisy lifestyle… *Uffda*… twigs, berries and blooms, trolls, mushrooms, stars, horses, field corn, a real connectedness to nature. *Uffda*… there is so much more to it than words can express… *Uffda*."

"Gus and Dagmar are aware that the Finberg's Farm is home to two Norwegian fjord horses. Gus took a moment to remind the village mice of one important fact they already know about: mice and horses are able to fully communicate with one another. Because the mouse language is understood by horses, and vice versa, country mice and horses through the centuries have been looking out for one another. An added benefit of this tight relationship is that when danger arises, mice find safety by standing underneath the stocky horses until danger has past. The horses are watchful not to step on the little mice while they are under their protection. Dagmar mentioned that it is only fair to their twins that they have the opportunity to be raised like their grandparents by growing up in the countryside with all of the benefits that way of life provides, including having horses as dear friends. After all, Dagmar enforced her point beautifully by telling everyone that Dala and Horst are named after Swedish Dala Horses, the ever so artfully painted red, orange, or blue wooden ones with colourfully detailed flourishes.

"After hearing the Christoferson's request for help to make their move, a lively discussion ensued and a plan was hatched. By this time most of the mice that listened to the manner in which Gus spoke had taken up the *Uffda* expression themselves and were speaking it frequently. Here is the detailed eighteen-point plan that was contrived, contemplated, and highly analyzed for safety reasons... *Uffda*... and then, finally, passed by the mice. *Uffda*.

1. The move will take place next Sunday morning, August 30. *Uffda*. Shortly before the plan is executed, the entire village will gather in the church basement to say farewell to the Christofersons and to sing "Safety First."

2. A five-foot length of cotton kitchen twine needs to be obtained from the junk drawer in St. Pete's church kitchen under the cover of night. *Uffda*.

3. Two of our strongest male mice will firmly attach the kitchen twine with special knots to one of the tie down anchors located on one side of the Finberg's pickup truck during the worship service... *Uffda*.

4. The Christoferson Family will climb... *Uffda*... one at a time up the kitchen twine to enter the truck bed of the said pickup truck.

5. After Dagmar, Dala, and Horst have arrived in the pickup truck bed... *Uffda*... they will quickly go deep into hiding.

6. Following that, Gus will be the last one to climb up the kitchen twine to enter the pickup truck bed. He will hurry and untie the twine and pull it into the truck bed and hide it so that it is not visible, ensuring that it will not get loose should a big breeze arise. *Uffda*.

7. Gus will join his family in hiding... *Uffda*... in the pickup truck bed.

8. The Christofersons will remain out of sight and noiseless throughout the entire trip. *Uffda*.

9. After arriving at the farmstead, nothing is to happen until Harald and Vivi have gone into the house and are sitting down to their

Sunday dinner which, most likely, will be hotdish, buttered rolls, and pickles. *Uffda.*

10. At this point... *Uffda...* Gus will peek out, checking to see if they are being watched.

11. When the coast is clear, Gus and Dagmar will secure the cotton kitchen twine to one of the truck's tie down anchors. *Uffda.*

12. Dagmar will be the first one to slide down the twine... *Uffda...* and will wait there for Dala and Horst to slide down next. Dagmar will be right there to catch the little ones.

13. Dagmar and the twins will run as fast as possible... *Uffda...* to the area where the horses are kept.

14. Next Gus will slide down... *Uffda...* abandoning the cotton kitchen twine.

15. Gus will skedaddle... *Uffda...* to find his family where the fjord horses are grazing.

16. Introductions will be made between the Christofersons and the horses. *Uffda.*

17. Gus will bravely... *Uffda...* and politely ask the fjord horses if he and his family can live with them until they find a safe dwelling.

18. Lastly the Christofersons will sing "Safety First" and give thanks for their safe arrival to the Finberg Heritage Farm, perhaps one day teaching the safety song to the horses. *Uffda.*"

At 11:15 p.m. Ruby and I travelled to the parsonage and snacked on a couple of spilled morsels of an Amish Haystack Dinner. *Uffda,* that was good! It tasted like potatoes. Ruby mentioned to me that Aia must have made a regular meal for supper tonight in order to get Clement to stop reminiscing about the meal they ate at the Schoenfelder's home last night, and also to get Clement to stop expostulating about eating cabbage soup. We noticed that Aia ate a small portion of her haystack, while Clement ate two big haystacks, and Gretchen ate one-third of a haystack. Clement must have been starved for starch and protein in order to consume two haystacks. He complimented Aia many, many times on the satisfying, mouth-watering supper. Ruby and I wondered if the haystacks that the Osterhagens ate for supper tonight are the exact same recipe that the fjord horses eat in their daily serving of haystacks. *Uffda,* who would know?

– F.N.

THE AUGUST HEAT WAVE IS STIFLING, BUT THE OSTERHAGENS ARE KEEPING COOL IN THE parsonage, thanks to the new air conditioning unit that was installed in June. Two of our mice, newlyweds Colton and Callie Cadwell, have found a cool place to sleep at night during this heat wave. They have made a comfy little bed under the secretary's desk in the air conditioned church office. They were sound asleep tonight, but woke up when the door was unlocked and the lights were turned on. One parishioner with an office key had arrived to use the copy machine. Later on Pastor showed up and found the choir director, Stacey McKinney, making copies. Colton mentioned to me that it seemed to surprise Pastor that she was making copies at such a late hour, which did not qualify as regular office hours.

Pastor told Aia that he observed the second evening in a row the church office lights have been turned on at 10:30 p.m. Instead of wondering what was going on, before he got in bed, he flip-flopped his way down the breezeway in his T-shirt, shorts, and lime green sandals that Gretchen gave him for Father's Day. He was headed towards the church office to find out what was happening there. He found Stacey stationed at the photocopy machine, running off dozens of copies of musical selections. She told Pastor that she recently received a choral sample packet in the mail from "We Sing! Publishing House" located in Oklahoma and was making copies of choral anthems for St. Peter's Choir to sing throughout the fall season. Stacey explained to Pastor that this is top quality music. By selecting this music for the choir to sing, she's keeping the standard of excellence in music high at St. Peter's. If the choir sings this type of music, they feel that it is worth their time to attend the once-a-week choir rehearsals. Plus she is saving the church money, as this music is nearly free of charge. The only cost involved is the wear and tear on the photo copier and the expense of the paper.

Colton and Callie peeked out to see how Pastor was and saw that he was suppressing his displeasure, keeping cool in the air conditioned office. Restraining most of his thoughts, he gulped back and explained to Stacey that if the church gets caught with these illegal photo copies, a huge fine might come their way which might sink the ship, that is, the church. Pointing out the warning section on the bottom of one of the anthems, he proceeded to read the words out loud to Stacey. He read, "REPRODUCTION OF THIS PUBLICATION WITHOUT

PERMISSION OF THE PUBLISHER IS A CRIMINAL OFFENSE SUBJECT TO PERSECUTION." Beneath this wording were the words, "COPYING IS ILLEGAL," which were again written in capitals, in a larger type with bold letters surrounded by a text box. Stacey justified her actions by explaining that the measly amount of money in the church annual budget allotted for choir music expenditures is a pittance, due to the skinflint misers sitting on the church council, who are musical ignoramuses. She went on to say that people are reluctant to recognize that quality church music comes with a price, unless you have a clever choir director. Because of that, she has had to become ingenious in this area. She is able to apply the budgeted money to the end-of-the-year choir party that is held every June. Besides, she has done this every single year and it has worked so far. She explained that she is careful to make the copies under the cover of night so no one will ever see her or catch her, that is, until now.

Colton told me that Stacey set in motion a trick question by asking Pastor if he enjoys the choir anthems that he hears on Sunday mornings. Since he responded positively to that question, she told him that the beautiful music he is hearing, most of the time, is sung from photocopies. She wondered if he was aware of that. He responded that he wasn't. Trying to reassure Pastor that she is not breaking the law by making photocopies, she told him that after a choir anthem is sung, she disposes of the copies. She does this by simply gathering them up and taking them home, burning them in the incinerator located at their farm. She told Pastor that one time she even had an accident by getting too close to the flames which resulted in her eyebrows being singed right off of her face. Stacey said that it was all in her effort to help the church. To reinforce and justify her point, she told him how much time, talent, and treasure she puts into directing St. Peter's Choir.

Stacey revealed that she has often purchased needed supplies for the rehearsals without submitting a request for reimbursement. Reminding Pastor of her faithful dedication to the choir, she said she would do anything for the group, even that of accidently charring her eyebrows off of her face all over again. Clement thanked Stacey for her zeal for good music and thanked her for serving without much pay. But he wondered aloud how long talented musicians could afford to write beautiful music for choirs, if all choirs found no need to purchase music. Stacey listened and wondered back if that is why the cost of music publications keeps rising, and maybe why they are so brash about "copyrights." She said that though she hated to spend the money, on Tuesday she would call and order one or two pieces that she had not yet copied for the sake of the poor musicians who composed them.

Clement simply was exhausted from all of this and was about to drop if he had to hear any more about the copying choral music subject. He returned home and told Aia that he was trying to let it all drop by wishing Stacey good night and going back home.

One of our mice, Celestial, is a night owl, or an evening mouse, spending her evenings posted in the breezeway peering out the windows to observe the night sky. Celestial is an amateur astronomer who watches the sky intently and presents our village with brief reports of her findings at each village meeting. She enjoys the quiet when everyone is asleep and she is able to concentrate. We heard one time that Winston Churchill did the exact same thing, as he also was a night owl and did his best thinking when the United Kingdom was deeply asleep.

Tonight the stillness in the breezeway was drastically interrupted when Clement walked the hallway wearing his flip-flops with the annoying smacking sound which resonated ever so loudly in the empty breezeway. Celestial stopped over to visit me after Clement went to bed, and so did Colton and Callie who reported to us the copy machine exchange between Pastor and Stacey. Celestial was wondering whether people in the Bible wore colourful flip-flops or just wore dusty brown sandals. Ruby was asleep when we had guests, but that is to be expected, as she is an early bird, a morning mouse. She enjoys rising early and often quotes a proverb, "The early bird gets the worm, but the second mouse gets the cheese." We understand the meaning of the first portion of that saying, however we intend to have our head librarian, Dr. Theodore Simonsen, look into the background of the last portion. All of the mice should grasp the concept of that phrase.

Before he fell asleep, we all heard Clement tell Aia that Stacey used reams of copy paper along with hundreds of words to convince him of her good intentions. He seemed to be having difficulty wrapping his thoughts around Stacey assuming her job description included burning photocopied music while risking her eyebrows being scorched. After all, she is just an American woman, not Shadrach, Meshach, or Abednego, who courageously faced the fiery furnace. When he told Aia about all of this, she quickly nicknamed Shirley, "The Triple S," which means "Singed Shirley Shadrach."

At 11:20 p.m. I was so wound up from the late night copy machine ordeal and flip-flop activity that I was only able to unwind by staying up and writing in my journal. I finally joined my main squeeze, Ruby, in bed. I intend to sleep in tomorrow and not be an early bird or a morning mouse.

– F.N.

AT BREAKFAST, LUNCH, AND SUPPER TODAY GRETCHEN DID NOT HAVE AN APPETITE. Aia checked her temperature to see if she had a fever, but she did not, because she was right at 98.6 degrees. Gretchen told her mother that she wasn't hungry, just thirsty, and would feel better if she did not eat anything. When Aia tucked Gretchen into bed tonight, she stepped on an empty potato chip bag that was on the floor that led Aia to discover that there were several other potato chip bags in her bedroom. Gretchen evidently had found Clement's 50-pack individual chip box and helped herself to some. In all, Aia found eleven empty bags of chips in Gretchen's room. Clement and Aia felt sorry for Gretchen, but gently talked to her about the reason for her tummy ache. Up until this point Gretchen did not know that potato chips are to be consumed in small portions. After she was asleep, Clement realized he would have to reconfigure the exact date when his chip supply would run out. Instead of breaking open a bag of chips before going to bed tonight, he just enjoyed the brown ale, because at this point chips have lost some of their appeal.

At 11:20 p.m. Ruby and I travelled to the parsonage kitchen. While there, we looked up and spotted a new clock that was hung on the wall today that gave us the fright of our lives. Added to the kitchen's decor was a shiny red cat clock with a pair of big rolling eyes and a swinging tail that move in sync repetitively. After spotting the cat clock, we were thrown into such a panic that we forgot to find a snack, swiftly returning to the safety of our dwelling.

Noticing the unending tick-tock sound, we wondered whether there was a village of ticks residing in the interior of the clock. We have never seen a tick, but imagine them to be similar to factory workers on a conveyor line keeping the mechanism moving, especially the pendulum tail and the zigzag movements of the cat's eyes. Being uncertain as to the specific type of ticks living inside the clock, Ruby guessed they might be wood ticks. We did not see eye to eye, as I thought they might be deer ticks. After thoroughly discussing the addition of the cat clock in the parsonage kitchen, we are certain that it cannot be of any harm to us as it is not a living and breathing cat, but only a mock-up cat that is formed out of red plastic.

We are confident that on our next outing to the parsonage we will be fearless, choosing to be soothed by the clocks ever present tick-tock sound. Ruby suggested that we name the red plastic cat Paprika, since she is now a permanent resident in the parsonage kitchen, a place where Aia occasionally prepares spicy Hungarian Goulash. This brought back to mind the first time we sampled Aia's Hungarian Goulash. At that moment Ruby and I closed our eyes and pretended that we were shepherds in the beautiful Hungarian countryside. In the future, I think we will close our eyes more often to truly appreciate our food. After accepting that Paprika is here to stay, I recalled Pastor reading First Corinthians 10:31 where it says: "So whether you eat or drink or whatever you do, do it all for the glory of God." Ruby and I have successfully swayed away from our jitters and faintheartedness by seeking to be courageous, calm, and fearless when it comes to Paprika's presence in our lives, just like the first portion of Philippians 4:6, where it reads: "Do not be anxious about anything..."

– F.N.

THE POWER THROUGHOUT OSWALD COUNTY HAS BEEN ON THE FRITZ FOR TWELVE hours. Due to the unrelenting heat wave, the citizens of Oswald County are wilting and practically collapsing. Residents are afraid that the meat in their freezers will spoil. Wafting throughout town is the constantly appetizing aroma of grilled meat: steak, hamburgers, pork chops, ribs, and chicken. Temperaments do not seem very positive either, recently marked by a backyard squabble between Patrick and Maureen Darcy, who are not members of St. Pete's. The particulars were told to me by Pignut, one of our village residents who heard the fiery commotion between them. The gist of the Darcy's argument consisted of whether or not to use direct or indirect heat while grilling their meat. The bad mood all changed when Maureen surprisingly spotted a four-leaf clover while she was attempting to deliver a harsh sentence to Patrick. This good luck find resulted in a whopping attitude change in Maureen, as her words instantly became breezy and even-tempered, instead of snappish and cranky. At this point, the clash between Patrick and Maureen came to an end. Pignut suggested to me that perhaps their demeanour has sunk a bit because their bellies are overburdened from too much protein consumption. Pignut said that as soon as the Darcys awoke this morning, Patrick placed their speckled-enamel coffee pot on their grill, just so they could have their morning cup. Frying bacon, sausages, hash browns, and eggs in order to use up their refrigerated food before it spoils, the morning air that glides over from the Darcy's backyard smells like meals prepared by a cowboy cook who might even have rustled up a skillet of chuck wagon hash.

Aia now washes clothing by hand, only the essentials, just until the power comes back on. Right now the most vital item in her wardrobe seems to be her nursing bras. She told Clement that it is a big heavy duty job to nurse the twins, but she does it because it is so beneficial for their health. To top it off, she mentioned that it saves them a lot of money by not needing to purchase baby formula. Ruby has noticed that nursing seems to make Aia extremely thirsty. She must be tired of filling up one glass of water after the next because she has made a change. After a trip to the Olden T'ings Antique Shop, Aia now drinks her water out of a sixty-ounce plastic pitcher, one that is custom printed with the words, McGuffie's

Bar & Grill. This purchase has cut down on the number of trips Aia makes to the kitchen sink for refills.

Aia seems to have become weary of nursing both Marc and Luc simply because it is a full-time job. She told Clement that her bum is literally glued to the sofa or the recliner. They admit that they made a poor decision when they purchased their bonded leather furniture, commonly referred to in other terms as imitation leather, leather-look leather, or match-bonded leather. Where they have sat and perspired, the leather is coming "un-bonded." Their furniture is shedding worse than an Alaskan Malamute, Belgian Sheepdog, or a Boston Terrier. A major part of doing the household cleaning is picking up, sweeping up, and vacuuming up fake leather pieces that stick to their clothing, their feet, the floor, and especially the steps.

Another problem related to this is that the shower head in their upstairs washroom needs to be repaired or replaced, so they use the basement shower while the upstairs one is out of commission. The basement shower produces such a powerful force that, when the water is running, piercing bullets of water shoot at their bodies while they very quickly try to get themselves clean. After they get out of the shower, their damp feet pick up every little scrap of bonded leather that is on the floors and steps, thanks to their ever-shedding sofa and recliner. Aia told Clement that she wants a new upholstered sofa and recliner for Christmas this year, and although that would be a most generous gift, in the long run it will cut down on her daily housekeeping. She also added that they will save lots of money as well, because after this experience she has no interest in owning another bonded-leather sofa, or, for that matter, ever becoming a dog owner, even if it was a breed that does not shed.

For now, Aia washes her bras in the kitchen sink and hangs them on the clothesline in the backyard. She has two of them in white, plus one in a paisley print. Today the Osterhagens found out that the placement of the clothesline is in a really unfortunate spot. It is located by the back door entrance to St. Pete's. Anyone who enters or exits that door will get a full-blown view of the Osterhagen's backyard life.

One time before the twins were born, Pastor, Aia, and Gretchen were enjoying a picnic supper in the backyard when one parishioner, Erhard Ellison, approached them at their picnic table. Having eyeballed their supper, he told them that he wished that he and his family could afford to eat pork chops, even though he is a farmer who owns and operates a farrow-to-finish hog operation. Today Erhard noticed two of Aia's nursing bras, the white ones, on the clothesline and let his hot-tempered anger get the best of him. Erhard confronted Aia and told her to take her helium balloon-sized brassieres off of the clothesline, adding that it is completely sacrilegious to display them, especially on church property that is in full view for the whole town to see. Aia listened to Erhard but her response was with actions rather than words. She confidently turned away from him, marched over to the clothesline, unfastened the two bras, wildly twirling one in each hand while she trotted to the parsonage back door singing the words of a Stephen Foster song, "I come from Alabama with a banjo on my knee." She walked away from Erhard Ellison and later told Clement that it felt so good to turn a deaf ear to him. Behind Erhard's back she has now bestowed on him the title, "The Bra Monitor."

That night after the little ones fell asleep, Aia suspended a flashlight by a shoestring from the dining room chandelier. She set up the checker board to see if the flashlight provided enough light to play a game. There was plenty, so she asked Clement to teach her the game of checkers. Clement was amazed that Aia had never learned the game, so he started at the beginning and taught her the moves. By the time they were ready to go to bed, Aia was equally skilled or maybe even more competent at the game of checkers than Clement was. Ruby and I peeked through the crack in the dining room wall, noticing that Clement seemed pleased that he had taught Aia how to play checkers. We did wonder, though, if he might feel a bit blue, because up until tonight he had been unbeatable at checkers.

At 11:30 p.m. Ruby and I travelled to the parsonage and snacked on a tiny morsel of a club sandwich that we found under Gretchen's dining room chair. The tastiest part was the droplet of mayonnaise, or perhaps it was hollandaise. Being confused about which "aise" is the right one, we will approach Dr. Theodore Simonsen to seek clarification as to which one is liberally lathered on club sandwiches.

    – F.N.

JUST RECENTLY THERE HAS BEEN AN INCREASE IN PARKING LOT CONVERSATIONS following the Sunday morning worship services. Gathering around Duff McKissick's vehicle, several members of Historic St. Peter's Church Council have been engaged in lengthy and serious-looking conversations. Our mice village has not figured out what is so vitally important, but with help from three outdoor mice who keep their ears to the ground we hope to find out.

This morning's council meeting was scheduled for nine o'clock. Prior to that, Pastor Osterhagen surprised two of our mice, Coffee, and his mate, Cream, by carrying two tables outdoors and setting them up in the church parking lot. After that he rolled out a stack of chairs from Woolcox Hall and placed them around the tables. Ruby overheard Clement explain to Aia the reasoning as to why today's council meeting would be held in the church parking lot. Clement told her that they might as well sit in the exact location where the real-life, bona fide church decisions are made. Aia thought it was a highly insightful move on Clement's part, adding that the fresh air might prove to be conducive to clearing out the cobwebs from some of their heads. She even offered to provide a large pitcher of lemonade and ginger snaps.

Three outdoor mice from the neighbourhood, Paxton, Bronzer, and Trekker, spent the morning hiding behind the largest boulder in the church garden. I asked them to help our community by observing the church council meeting. Even though Paxton, Bronzer, and Trekker are not church mice, they were willing to listen in on the meeting and report the findings to our village. Ruby was concerned about them being placed in this position since they are not church mice, but potential church mice. If one of the council members has something snarky to say at the meeting, the three mice might not want to be involved with the church, stating that hearing any rough talk might burst their bubbles and give them the wrong idea about St. Peter's.

For the last several months, Pastor has been encouraging the members to spread the Word of God by engaging those outside of the church. The church council has been listening to Pastor's sermons and several now feel called to go and make disciples. However, they hope to accomplish this by transferring to the small struggling church located on the other side of town. This news came up at the outdoor council meeting today shared by Todd Klingerman, backed up by Glenda Sinisac. Todd took a deep breath before telling that he and his wife Karla and their three boys will be transferring away from St. Pete's. He said, "I always mean what I say, but I don't always mean to say it out loud." Paxton said that Todd meant that it was easier to tell this information while outdoors than in the board room at St. Pete's. After that, Glenda confessed that she will be leaving St. Pete's also, followed by Tracey Tervis and her family. Just like that Phil Walach said it was a tragic day at St. Peter's as we will be losing fifteen members, six adults and nine children, plus losing the offering that they contribute. Most in attendance looked as though they did not know what to say, so they prayed The Lord's Prayer before adjourning.

Clement arrived home and found Aia, telling her what had just happened. She told him to take a deep breath because he is home. She asked him, "Who needs television when you have church people?" which brought out a big smile on Clement's face. Clement said that he will never have a meeting in the parking lot again as it brought out way to much truthfulness, pointing out that Christians are flawed, but redeemed.

Ruby and I feel sorry for Pastor and Aia when they suffer in times like this. We can see that when members transfer to another church they find it painful to lose them. But, Aia took time to listen to Clement, encouraged him by highlighting that he will continue to preach, lead, pray, teach, and most importantly, love all the members at St. Pete's even though those fifteen members are gone. Aia urged Clement to toughen up his skin, but to keep his heart soft. Clement calmed down and we saw his worry and anger vanish like steam from a tea kettle. After that she gave Clement such a big hug and lengthy kiss that when Ruby and I saw it we were so flustered our cheeks turned red. We turned our eyes away from that scene and let them have complete privacy.

At 10:45 p.m. Ruby and I were beyond delighted to find a cheese croissant crumb on the parsonage kitchen floor. We conversed about spreading the Word of God because it sometimes seems to make people split up instead of stick together. We wondered: if Pastor stopped telling people to spread the Word of God, would they get along better? Dr. Theodore Simonsen, our head librarian, told me once of a strange Bible statement in Matthew 10:34, where Jesus says He did not come to bring peace, but a sword. When I first heard it, I wondered if Dr. Simonsen has simply come unglued, as using a weapon with a sharp blade sounds like violence, instead of putting safety first. But, Ruby and I concluded that neither mice nor men manage to get along with each other without help from above.

– F.N.

THE BIG MOVE AWAY FROM ST. PETE'S WENT WELL TODAY FOR GUSTAV, KLARA, DALA, and Horst Christoferson. We do not know if they arrived at the Finberg Heritage Farm safely, but are looking on the bright side by assuming the best. The last time we saw them they waved goodbye to us from the charcoal-coloured pickup truck as we waved back and blew kisses to them from St. Pete's second floor window ledges.

Stacey McKinney, Historic St. Peter's choir director, recruited amateur musicians within the church to sing or play an instrument during a worship service on a Sunday of their choice this summer. Stacey claimed that it really perks up the worship service if there is some sort of special music, just until the choir starts back up again in September.

There have been a variety of musicians that came forward this summer at Historic St. Peter's to volunteer their talent. One Sunday morning we heard Russell Owens play his harmonica on the Gospel-style song, "Mansion Over the Hilltop." There was a sturdy men's quartet of four bearded men who sang "Heaven came Down, and Glory Filled My Soul." "Be Still, My Soul" was sung by beautiful Anni Kuparinen. After church that Sunday many people told Anni that they want her to sing at their funeral. The Gallagher Family, father Hugh and sons Kane, Davin, and Pearse, played the washboard, fiddle, Irish whistle, and spoons on "Appalachian Hymn." The spiritual, "Swing Low, Sweet Chariot," was sung by Darren Hendrix, who hit unbelievably deep low notes from the basement of his chest. The ukulele was played by Buffy Middlestadt as she sang, *"Ke Akua Mana E"* in Hawaiian, more recognizable as "How Great Thou Art." Tom Lang wanted to play his accordion in church but had much apprehension about it being an appropriate instrument for church, so at first he backed away from sharing his musical talent. Even though Historic St. Peter's is not a Catholic church, Tom felt better and changed his mind when he found out that Pope Pius XII decreed in 1943 that accordions are allowed to be played in all Catholic churches. That news tipped it for Tom and he played his accordion on the song, "O How He Loves You and Me," reassuring himself that he was playing a Christian song, not a dance song like the happy Norwegian on the Lawrence Welk Show. The mice thought Tom played it flawlessly. We liked the optional ending in a rubato style, a slight speeding up of the tempo and then expressively slowing it down. It would have been a shame if Tom had not shared his talent.

Anna Henning, by far the best soprano voice in St. Pete's Choir, provided a rendition of J.S. Bach's famous "Jesu, Joy of Man's Desiring." When it was time for special music, Anna played a lovely orchestral tape accompaniment of the song as she confidently made the haunting, eerie, spooky, and loud hoot sounds of the common loon, scattered here and there throughout the song. Stacey was completely daunted to hear an imitation loon's voice in church, as she fully expected Anna would use her singing voice on the text of this well-known selection, as it is often used at church weddings. Instead, she used her voice to make sounds of the common loon fill St. Peter's sanctuary. The excellent acoustics in St. Pete's sanctuary made everyone feel as though there were actually a couple of common loons right there in the building with them. Stacey did not know whether or not to approve of this, or if she should be embarrassed, so she ignored the loon calls and instead watched to see if the parishioners approved or disapproved of what was happening, a sort of temperature reading on the audience. After taking a weather report of the parishioners, Stacey put a smile on her face because she noticed that the church people seemed to enjoy the special music. All seemed amazed at Anna's unusual, remarkable, and far from common talent. The mice thought that this moment was historical in the life of the church as never before in St. Peter's history has anyone ever made common loon calls to the praise and honour of the Lord and Saviour Jesus Christ.

After Gretchen observed and listened carefully to the various members of St. Pete's who shared their musical gifts these last weeks, she asked her parents if she could sing a song in church like the others had done. Offering that she would like to sing her favourite song, the "Kyrie," the "Lord, have mercy upon us" song, Clement and Aia agreed that she could do that. This morning in church Gretchen left the pew after the confession and absolution and stood next to her daddy, who was in the pulpit. When it was time for the "Kyrie" in the liturgy, Clement lifted Gretchen up in his arms so she was close enough to the pulpit microphone for her voice to be heard. Her sweet, steady, and confident voice sang, "Lord, have mercy upon us. Christ, have mercy upon us. Lord, have mercy upon us." After she sang, Clement put her down and she walked back to her pew as the congregation sang the "Gloria in Excelsis." Gretchen sat next to her mother the remainder of the worship service and helped her with Marc and Luc.

This experience opened the minds of Clement and Aia as it led to the realization that their Gretchen has absolute pitch, as Clement says, or perfect pitch as Aia refers to it. This came about when Aia was playing the piano several days ago and Gretchen sat down on the bench with her. Aia opened Gretchen's songbook and listened as Gretchen began to sing each song a capella without being given a pitch. Each time Aia touched a piano key to check, Gretchen was starting the song on the correct note. Discovering that Gretchen possessed that ability, Aia grew certain that Gretchen has perfect pitch. This happened many times, and then it all was repeated when Clement came home. Clement and Aia concluded that Gretchen can sing a musical note without being given the proper pitch as she somehow finds it on her own. She is very young to have this gift, but Aia told Clement that composer John Philip Sousa also had perfect pitch, which was discovered when he was six-years-old by his violin teacher, so it must be possible.

At 10:45 p.m. Ruby and I travelled to the parsonage and found a pineapple tidbit on the floor that must have fallen when Aia mixed up an ambrosia salad.

– F.N.

EVER SINCE THE POWER OUTAGE, AIA HAS BEEN HESITANT TO KEEP AN ABUNDANCE OF food in their freezer as she fears this might happen again. During that time, some of their food went to waste and that's just not practical, thrifty, or sensible.

Clement has stayed home with her all day today and has been helping her with the children, the laundry, and a general cleanup of the house. His efforts have helped her so much that each time she thanked Clement she planted a big kiss on his lips. Ruby and I notice there was a profusion of kissing between them today.

Since the twins arrived, Clement has developed a new system for being organized by using colourful sticky notes. When he thinks of something he needs to do, look into, find out about, or someone to see, he reaches into his pocket and removes a pen and a pad of sticky notes, quickly jotting down the relevant information. Aia told him that it is a blessing in disguise that he has such poor quality cursive handwriting skills, because no one can decipher what is on them, which makes them private notes. However, Clement's recently developed behaviour is starting to wear on Aia's nerves because she has told him that there are sticky notes in far too many locations: on his dresser, the refrigerator, the washroom mirror, the dashboard of the van, the telephones, his desk, the doors of the parsonage, his office door, and most recently, the breezeway windows. Aia cannot throw any of them away because she doesn't know if they contain important information or not. Clement told Aia that he has never been more organized in his life and she understood his point and agreed with him. She did tell him that if he wants to continue this practice, the cost of sticky notes should come out of the church office supply budget and not out of his own wallet. He agreed with her by assuring her that he would take care of it. Immediately Clement wrote a sticky note and attached it to the dining room chandelier so he wouldn't forget about Aia's thrifty suggestion.

Ruby's nose identified stuffed peppers on the menu for supper tonight at the parsonage. Aia had popped them in the oven shortly before she received a telephone call from Tosca Gardener, an avid fisherwoman, who inquired if she was hungry for fried fish. Aia told her that she is always up for that, especially if they have a bottle of malt vinegar on hand. After that response, Tosca invited her to spontaneously drop everything she was doing and drive out to their place on Lake Harvey and help her clean sunfish. Tosca mentioned to Aia that she could keep as many of the sunfish as she could clean. Having spent most of the day in her fishing boat that she calls "Olde Sweetheart," Tosca admitted to Aia that she pays no attention to observing the silly state fishing limits, adding that she will probably get caught one day, but she will deal with that nonsense when and if it ever happens. Telling Aia that she enjoys sharing her catch, she said that this time she's chosen to share the abundance with them. Aia knows that if Tosca gives the fish away to her, she can go out and catch her limit again that day.

After Aia told Clement about her telephone conversation with Tosca, he agreed to say home and take over for her while she was away. She immediately turned the oven temperature down, permitting the peppers to cook slower. This happens to have been the very first time that Clement has been home alone with Gretchen, Marc, and Luc. We heard Clement assure Aia that he could handle everything and not to worry about anything. Aia made Clement aware that she knows how to clean fish, but isn't very speedy at it, so it might take awhile before she arrives back home. She is certain that Tosca is a whiz at cleaning fish and most likely can clean about four or five fish to Aia's one fish, adding that fisherwoman Tosca probably owns one of those expensive professional Finnish filet knives. Aia said that she hoped to clean quite a few sunfish as they would be a real treat for an old-fashioned, up-at-the-lake fish fry right at St. Peter's parsonage.

After Aia returned home, she told Clement about the lighthearted banter between the two of them while they cleaned fish. Tosca told Aia many things about her life, mentioning that she was especially happy that she had pursued singing and had studied opera. She was thankful for the operatic roles she had been honoured to perform in both Italy and Germany while Sydney was there on business. Tosca went on to say that she does not miss devoting most of her time to learning operatic roles, adding that she especially enjoys that she no longer has to get all gussied up with hugely heavy costumes, thick stage makeup, and wigs for each performance. She and Sydney much prefer getting up every morning, dressing in old comfy clothes, going fishing in "Olde Sweetheart," observing the loons, reading library books, frying fish, working on jigsaw puzzles, listening to music, hiking in the woods, and watching as many movies as they can fit into their busy retiree schedule. One of her favourite pastimes is to take acrylic paints and canvas outdoors. She is in the process of attempting to paint the beauty of Lake Harvey in four separate paintings, one for each season of the year. Tosca also said that she and Sydney are enrolled in a level-one tenderfoot Tai Chi class, noting that it is a gentle way to stretch the body and stay fit. After that class session ends, they intend to progress to the intermediate-level Tai Chi class.

Tosca told Aia that when Sydney retired they were excited to move back to Tosca's home town, desiring to obtain prime lakefront real estate property on Lake Harvey. Finding just what they were looking for, with large windows that look out on the lake, this spot couldn't be more superior of a location.

Tosca gave Aia loads of compliments and praise about St. Peter's and the work that Pastor is doing there. She mentioned that they would not dream of missing church each Sunday. After worship they enjoy going to Lora's Café and ordering Swedish pancakes, which appear only on the Sunday menu. She asked Aia if her family likes Swedish pancakes. After Aia responded positively, she told them that she and Sydney will treat them soon to lunch after church one Sunday.

Tosca relayed that she would enjoy singing solos in church occasionally and Tosca wondered if Aia would accompany her instead of the church organist. Tosca mentioned that she doesn't want the organist at St. Peter's to accompany her because she knows that the music would be far too difficult for her to learn, plus she has noticed that she continually seems to have a cold and covers her mouth with a tissue. Instead of discussing Josie, Aia told Tosca that she would be delighted to accompany her when she sings in church and immediately asked her if she would be able to sing on Thanksgiving Day, which Tosca agreed to do.

Aia told Clement that she placed her cleaned fish in a large food baggie to take home with her. Tosca did the same thing as Aia, but then did something completely unexpected. She handed Aia her large food baggie of sunfish, suggesting to her that she take it home and put it in the freezer so that they could enjoy a fish fry another day. Aia thanked her, gave her a big hug, and headed home to where there were stuffed peppers baking in the oven. Removing the peppers from the oven, she placed them on top of a pair of hot mitts on the kitchen counter to let them cool down. After retrieving her seasoned cast iron frying pan, Aia began the process of gently browning the sunfish, one after the next. She told Clement and Gretchen that she intends to fry the contents of both food baggies because they were going to enjoy an all-you-can-eat sunfish supper instead of the stuffed peppers, which can wait until tomorrow. She explained that she might as well fry up both bags of fish because one never knows when there will be another power outage like there was on August 25. Asking Clement to hurry on down to Grocer Dan's for supplies, it was easy to see that he seemed happy to run this errand. Aia's list included malt vinegar, lemons, cocktail and tartar sauce, plus a bag of frozen French fries, the skinny ones, not the steak fries. We could see that the Osterhagens were excited about their upcoming supper. As she was frying fish, Ruby and I heard Aia's cheerful singing and noticed her managing many tasks at once.

Not only was Aia frying fish, but the clothes washer, dryer, and dishwasher were running simultaneously. Also, she was taking care of Gretchen, Marc, and Luc and their needs. Every free moment she had between flipping fried fish, she spent performing jumping jacks in the centre of the kitchen. Ruby thought that the purpose of the jumping jacks was to burn calories in advance of the all-you-can-eat sunfish event. We know that it is not the same as a pioneer woman weeding a garden while holding a baby, using a walking stick to ward off dangerous snakes, and pocketing buffalo chips for fuel in her burlap apron, but it was pretty close. After Clement returned home from Grocer Dan's and the fish and chips were ready, the Osterhagens sat at the dining room table and dined as though they were at a seafood buffet. Aia couldn't stop talking about her incredibly fun trip out to Tosca's place, mentioning that she hopes they can become really good friends, which they might be already. Aia also said something very sweet during dinner that referred to her dad. She relayed that when she was small her dad would call her his *"fiske jente,"* the Norwegian way to say "fish girl," because her most favourite thing to do at the lake was to go fishing. She said, with delight, that after the adventure today she is now a *"fiske kvinne,"* a real "fish woman," even though the fish were just sunfish.

At 11:30 p.m. Ruby and I travelled to the parsonage and snacked on a morsel of fried sunfish freshly caught today in Lake Harvey along with one-half of a French fry. We thought it was divine but couldn't help but wonder whether walleye, salmon, trout, shrimp, cod, or lutefisk taste the same.

– F.N.

AFTER LUNCH TODAY APPLE BLOSSOM, FLEUR, AND AMARYLLIS, ST. PETER's summertime courtyard mice, watched Pastor briefly stop and stare at the restful beauty of St. Pete's courtyard. From observing his facial expression they could tell that something was troubling him. He looked as though he was in an especially bleak mood, an obvious funk. Before he left the parsonage, Ruby overheard him ask Aia exactly what day it was. She responded by telling him that it was Thursday, September 3. Clement told her that it felt to him more like January 17, Benjamin Franklin Day. He told her the reason was that, after he had placed several unsuccessful telephone calls this morning, it reminded him of a quote he thought Benjamin Franklin said: "He that is good for making excuses is seldom good for anything."

Having spent many hours of the morning at home preparing for the upcoming nominating committee meeting at St. Peter's, he told Aia that it has been a day that should go down in history as "Making Excuses Day." Aia listened to him and heard the struggle he was having finding willing members of St. Pete's to serve three-year positions on the church council. The Recording Secretary, Assistant Treasurer, and Christian Education spots are all vacant and need to be filled by the first of the year. After working on it for hours, he still is without even one name from the congregation to put forth on the ballot.

Since the twins were napping, Aia brewed a pot of coffee and sat down with Clement in order to listen to him vent about how difficult it is to engage volunteers at HSP. Clement told Aia that he has been recording in a spiral notebook a list of excuses he has heard ever since he first entered the parish ministry. Every time Clement hears a new excuse from a parishioner, he records it in his notebook. As of this afternoon, he has recorded two-hundred and seventy-two different excuses of why people cannot do this or that at the church, all written down in this worn out yellow spiral notebook. Aia told Clement that this is news to her and how glad she is that he shared it with her today.

Aia began to understand more and more about the reasons why people hesitate to become a volunteer at church, take on a position, or attend worship, meetings, or gatherings. They often procrastinate making a decision. But if they can come up with an excuse, they know he will have to ask somebody else. Aia then opened Clement's notebook and read one hundred and forty-four excuses out loud. She was exhausted by that time, so she never made it to the other one hundred and twenty-eight excuses.

1.   I have other plans.
2.   I will be at work.
3.   I am too busy that week.
4.   I am too tired to take on anything more right now.
5.   I have a doctor appointment that day.
6.   I can't attend because there is an illness in the family.
7.   I have a chiropractor appointment that day.
8.   I have a dental appointment that morning.
9.   I will be out of town at that time.
10.   I will be out of the state at that time.
11.   I will be out of the country at that time.
12.   I haven't been feeling well.
13.   I can't come to church because there is no bus route near there.
14.   I can't be bothered with that right now.
15.   I have to work at another fundraiser that day.
16.   I have an impending family meal to attend.
17.   I can't do that because it will take up too much of my time.
18.   I need to clean my elderly mother's house that day.
19.   Please excuse me. I always wash my hair on Thursday afternoons.
20.   I have to get my car checked and an oil change at that time.
21.   I don't enjoy baking because I always burn things.
22.   I don't enjoy cooking as I'd rather go out to eat.
23.   I don't enjoy singing in a choir as I'd rather listen to music.
24.   I will try that after I retire, when I have more time.
25.   I need some quiet time, because my life is way too noisy.
26.   I have to take care of my brother's dog that week.
27.   I am power washing my sidewalks that day.
28.   I have to get my car washed and vacuumed that day.
29.   I would love to come – I hope I will be there, if I can.
30.   I am not doing that because it costs too much money.
31.   I have to watch my sister's children that week.
32.   I have someone staying with me at that time.
33.   I have done that before and I didn't enjoy it.

34. I don't like working on a team because I end up doing all the work.
35. I'm too old to do that. You have to involve younger people for that.
36. I'm too young for that much responsibility. You need to find an older person.
37. I have already done that way too many times. Been there, done that.
38. I don't enjoy reading out loud and am tired of being asked to read a lesson.
39. I don't enjoy teaching, it tires me.
40. I don't enjoy following that person. Who would?
41. I am uncomfortable being in that setting.
42. I wouldn't enjoy that now, maybe later.
43. I don't want to help with that project, it is too complicated.
44. I will be there if something doesn't come up at that time.
45. I have an important, hard-to-get appointment at that time.
46. I can't be there as I'm getting together with an old college friend that I haven't seen in years.
47. I am uncomfortable being in that group of people.
48. I will check my calendar, but it's really busy.
49. I won't be there as I've had trouble with swollen ankles and I need to stay home and keep my legs elevated.
50. I will be there if it isn't snowing, sleeting, hailing, or there isn't a blizzard or black ice.
51. I will not attend because you don't charge admission. Nothing free is valuable.
52. I will be there if I get finished with my project.
53. I will be there if the sun isn't out as I need to do the gardening.
54. I will be there if my other commitment/thing gets cancelled.
55. I will be there if you call me to remind me; thanks for calling to remind me, but something just came up.
56. I might have to work, and they need me.
57. I might have to play hockey, go bowling, or another type of sport.
58. I can't be there because that's when I play euchre.
59. I wasn't there on Sunday as I didn't sleep well on Saturday night.
60. I just got married.
61. I just bought a cow.
62. I have fields and commitments that cost a pretty sum.
63. I don't have the skills for that.

64. I can't sit still that long.
65. I have an incontinence problem.
66. I have a tender "bum" and the pews are too hard.
67. I have a tender "bum" and the pews are too soft.
68. I want to, but I can't.
69. I tried that and it doesn't work.
70. I have to get something in or out of the oven at that time.
71. I have a repairman coming at that time.
72. I am expecting a delivery/phone call/visit that day.
73. I don't have the right clothing for an event like that.
74. I don't have proper church clothing.
75. I know that my children/spouse/relatives won't want to come.
76. I can't come to church on the holidays as I host the family dinner.
77. I think it will last too long.
78. I feel it will last too long.
79. I know it will last too long.
80. I am afraid I will be late.
81. I don't want to rock the boat, so don't count on me.
82. I smell fish/skunk/something.
83. I will come next time, if it works out.
84. I have my car in the shop.
85. I didn't know about it far enough ahead of time.
86. I heard about it so long ago that I forgot about it.
87. I just had a baby – it's too soon.
88. I just lost my mother/father – it's too soon.
89. I liked it better the way it used to be, so I won't be there.
90. I notice it is the same every time I go and that is boring.
91. I don't want to make "so and so" uncomfortable by my being there.
92. I had to wait for my pedicure/manicure to dry.
93. I promised an old friend I'd see them at that time.
94. I got divorced.
95. I have a disability.
96. I'm on a new medication.
97. I am off my medication.
98. I didn't know what time it started.
99. I can't make a commitment because my arthritis might flare up.
100. I am allergic to the perfume and cologne at church.

101. I can't come because I have Chronic Fatigue Syndrome.
102. I didn't turn my clock ahead/backward, so I missed it.
103. I didn't come in because there were so few cars in the parking lot.
104. I can't hear well or see well, so I cannot attend.
105. We can't come to church because the brunch buffet at the hotel starts at the exact same time as church, and we like to be the first ones in line to eat at the buffet.
106. I can't stand how loud/soft the organ is.
107. We can't be there because Sunday morning is when we work on home improvement projects.
108. I have to stay home to watch the dog and give him his diabetes shot at that time.
109. Sunday morning is when I talk to my family on the telephone. I can't miss that.
110. My husband doesn't attend church, so I don't either because I do not want to sit all alone.
111. I can't endure listening to the choir or any soloist.
112. I can't bear the sound of handbells.
113. I can't come to church because I have been diagnosed with hyper-hidrosis, a severe perspiration issue with my body and it's a real burden. It is sometimes referred to as a "silent handicap."
114. I can't come because I'm allergic to the food they serve.
115. I can't come because I don't like it when people stare at me, especially when I walk back and forth to Holy Communion.
116. I don't like to come to church because I feel pressure to attend the coffee hour and I don't like the coffee they brew.
117. I couldn't make it to church because I didn't have enough gas in my car.
118. I won't be attending church because our daughters take tap dancing lessons on Sunday mornings until the end of May. After that, we'll be staying at the campground every weekend throughout the summer. We'll try to attend on Christmas Eve.
119. I can't make it on Sundays because I'm too tired from working all week.
120. I can't come because I feel like my thoughts/doubts are not welcome at the church.

121. I don't come to church because someone gives our children a sucker each time we attend. After that, they are given a cupcake at Sunday School along with a sugary beverage. We don't want our children to go through the highs and lows of so much sugar consumption. It's not good for them. It's not just at church. I don't like it at the bank, either, when they give my children candy there, too.

122. I like my church and you Pastor, I just don't like the people.

123. I can't come because I don't feel like my suggestions are appreciated.

124. I can't come to church because of my work, but by reading a Christian devotion early every morning I feel spiritually edified.

125. I can't come to church because the people are too nosey there and are meddlers.

126. I can't come to church because no one talks to me and I feel like a stranger.

127. I can't come to church as Sundays are the only day of the week that I can sit down with a cup of coffee, put my feet up, and read the paper.

128. I can't attend on Sunday mornings because I need to keep my options open.

129. I don't want to go to church because of getting dressed up. I'd rather wear my bummy clothes when I have some time off.

130. I can't serve on the council. After much prayer and soul searching, I feel that it is best for me to serve God in other ways.

131. I can't attend church because someone who is a member there gives me anxiety every time I see them or have to talk to them.

132. I can't attend church on Easter Sunday because I'm helping with the Legion Club's Easter egg hunt for the kiddies.

133. I can't attend church because my face is swollen from having my wisdom teeth removed.

134. I can't attend church because it's too far to walk from the parking lot into the building.

135. I can't go to church because when I arrive there on Sundays all of the handicapped spaces in the parking lot are already taken.

136. I can't attend church from October through May because we'll be in Florida/Arizona/Tennessee/Georgia.

137. I can't read in church because I have floaters in my eyes.

138. I can't attend church or any functions because I'm super busy-busy. It's my fault, not the church's or yours, Pastor.

139. I can't come to church on Sunday mornings. It is the only time of the week available to visit my grandparents at the nursing home.

140. My (fill in the blank) brother/sister/mother/father/child/children/ mother-in-law/father-in-law/grandma/grandpa/cousin/aunt/uncle/next door neighbour/neighbours across the street/ the lady I work with/a man I work with/my best friend/my ex-best friend/ and/or my spouses version of any of those went in the hospital, so I can't come to church.

141. I have a bad bed and I wake up with a backache every morning, so it's too hard for me to attend church.

142. I have a headache most mornings. Can you change church to the afternoon?

143. We live in the country and it's such a long drive to come to church and gas is expensive.

144. I like to watch the Sunday morning services on television. It's so much easier!

Aia paused and asked Clement if these excuses apply mostly to empty-nest employed adults, or to adults that have children in their household. Clement said that it applies to both, but he receives the most excuses from the retirement-aged group. He says that if you ask a retired person, "Hi, how are you?" they respond with an ever-ready pat reply: "Well, I'm retired – I'm busier in retirement than I ever was while I was working!" Clement told Aia that every time he hears that phrase said by a retired person, he almost snaps. It clearly implies that the people who are currently employed are somehow lazy (and aren't even aware of it), whereas the retired people are working harder than ever to keep their heads above water, even though their lives are not dictated by a job schedule. Retired people have the freedom to do just what they please, a lot or a little of it, all done on their own free schedule. This makes them very picky in pursuing all of their pastimes and recreational adventures. They choose activities that are not as draining to them as their employment used to be, finding strength to do them with immense joy, interest, and most importantly, to have fun while doing them. He's seen retired people immerse themselves so deeply in projects, clubs, or groups, that they put way more effort into that than they ever did into their paying jobs. He called it a mismatch between work and passion. He continued on by saying that retirees are not dictated by a job schedule, time clock, or obstacles that are in their way. Freedom is there to do just what they please, which leads to the reason why Clement hears more excuses from retirees as to why they cannot help out than any other age group at the church. They are so busy with the hustle and bustle of their lives, it's probably best to leave all of the work to the younger people.

The kicker yesterday was when Harriet Gilbert, a retired elementary school teacher, dropped by the church to pick up her box of offering envelopes that have been collecting dust in her church pigeonhole for a full eight months, ever since the new year began. Clement told Aia that he asked Harriet if she would consider serving on the Christian Education team, which requires a meeting once every three months. Harriet turned that offer down flat with the excuse that it would be too exhausting and annoying to be on that committee. Clement told Aia that Harriet had a lengthy paragraph for her excuse, all delivered while she was wearing a sweatshirt portraying the hands from Michelangelo's painting, "The Creation of Adam," the one that is painted on the ceiling in the Sistine Chapel. Above the fine art print on her sweatshirt were the words, written in capital letters, CARPE DIEM. Clement continued by telling Aia that carpe diem expresses responsibility, being fearless, having energy, living a life of significance, making positive changes, taking on challenging tasks, expressing oneself, expressing faith in God, living life confidently, and valuing the day, the moment, and life. He didn't witness any of those qualities when he talked to Harriet, and certainly did not see her seizing the day with this offer of a Christian Education opportunity. Aia told Clement that perhaps a more fitting sweatshirt for Harriet to wear would be one that says, "A perfect way to spend your day – WASTE IT!"

Aia suggested to Clement that he is better off without someone that unenthusiastic. Then she recommended to Clement that he discard his yellow book and begin to prepare a "Gratefulness List." When he asked her what that was, she encouraged him to write down everything that fills him with gratefulness, as that is what really matters. Add to that a genuine readiness to show appreciation and kindness to others, all while holding on to an overall spirit of gratefulness. Giving him solid gratefulness examples, Aia included the following:

1. Faith – Jesus loves us. Prayers are listened to. Faith lives and grows.
2. Love – "… my cup overflows…" (Psalm 23)
3. Being alive – the joy of living, the pursuit of a happy life
4. Good health – the capacity of our bodies, the energy to enjoy life, appreciating physical health

5.   Daily bread – being nourished by foods that God created
6.   Our children – they make our heart's burst with love
7.   A roof over our heads – St. Pete's parsonage, a comfy shelter for our family
8.   Time – God never sleeps, but we sleep. He is always there no matter what time it is.
9.   Nature – the unlimited beauty of God's creation
10.   Family – parents and siblings who love, laugh, and encourage us
11.   Support of others – people who help to hold us up in tough times
12.   The opportunity for you, Clement, to serve at Historic St. Peter's in Oswald County...

Aia assured Clement that, with prayer, his gratefulness list will grow. The discouragement of numerous excuses will be cast aside and be replaced by a list full of hopefulness and joy, encouragement and peacefulness. At that point, we saw Clement and Aia clasp hands together as each one prayed a short prayer of gratefulness to God for all of their blessings. Immediately after that, Aia said she needed to make use of excuse #19. Reminding Clement that today is Thursday, she brought their conversation to an end by saying, "Please excuse me. I always wash my hair on Thursday afternoon."

At 11:30 p.m. Ruby and I travelled to the parsonage but before searching for a snack, we talked about how Aia had an absolutely brilliant idea when she suggested that Clement begin a "Gratefulness List." After that, we were grateful that we happened upon a dropped crumb of a fortune cookie. I am thinking about starting a gratefulness list of my own when I am no longer immersed in my recordings. We also noticed that we were grateful when we found the crumpled paper fortune that had fallen underneath the dining room table. Written in both Mandarin and English were these words: "Within the next five months you will find three missing socks." Ruby and I were puzzled and certain that something was definitely lost in translation from Mandarin to English. Besides, doesn't everyone know already that Leprechauns are the ones to blame for missing socks? We went to bed with especially grateful hearts tonight.

– F.N.

THERE WAS NO TIME TODAY FOR ME TO WRITE DOWN DETAILS OF THE MICE VILLAGE celebration of St. Phil's Day in which we honoured the one and only Patron Saint of All Micedom. If I even attempted to explain the pageantry of this relevant event today, it would take an entire notebook to do so. I will note that it was majestically breathtaking to listen to the entire mice village hum "Pomp and Circumstance" by Sir Edward Elgar, which we hummed twice, once when the ceremony opened, secondly when it was finished. Ruby and I returned home spent. No searching for a treat tonight. Enough said.

— F.N.

EVERY SATURDAY MORNING AT 9 A.M. PREPARATIONS ARE MADE BY VOLUNTEERS FOR the serving of Holy Communion for the next day's worship service. The Altar Guild women on duty today, June Phillips and Lizzie Whittaker, visited amongst themselves while they were in the sacristy getting the vessels ready, caring for the linens, and ready to receive the delivery of the chancel flowers. Two mice in our village, Breezy and Clementine, were under the refrigerator listening to their conversation, which they reported to our village today.

Several months ago a professional pictorial church directory company was on site taking photographs of St. Pete's members and families, designed to be a useful resource, plus a keepsake for all of those involved. In the latest issue of St. Peter's Press, the church newsletter, it was mentioned that copies of the new directory will also be given to new members to help them put a name to a face. Three families brought along their family dogs to be included in their photograph, even though Orchid, Saxon, and Rudder-Dudder do not attend the worship services. An exception to that, though, was the time when Orchid was in attendance. Her owner, Nina Hokkanen, tenderly carried her brand new puppy up with her when she went to receive Holy Communion. It must have been difficult for the parishioners to concentrate on their sins being forgiven when a brand new adorable puppy was in attendance.

When entering HSP today, Lizzie walked by the stack of brand new photo directories that were delivered earlier this week. She helped herself to a directory and also picked up one for June. As the ladies were delighting in the fact that they were the first parishioners to get their hands on the new directory, Lizzie declared that she had some "homework" to do this afternoon. Breezy and Clementine listened intently as they heard Lizzie describe what her homework involved. Lizzie relayed that part one was to sit down with her directory and study it carefully. After that she will take a ball point pen and put a big X through the portraits of the people that she is not acquainted with. Part two is to go to the back of the directory and place more X's through the names, addresses, and telephone numbers of those same people.

Clementine whizzed her way to the front of the refrigerator and peeked out to see June's mouth drop as she listened to Lizzie's plan. June took a deep breath and then told Lizzie that crossing out people's faces did not sound like a very kind thing to do. She also said that she might be able to imagine crossing out member's photos if they were obnoxious complainers, gossipers, or dreadfully selfish, but to X-out people who you don't even know is far from praise-worthy behaviour. June reached for Lizzie's hand and together they walked into the sanctuary where two banners are hanging, one to the left of the crucifix, the other on the right. June read the words on the first banner: "Dear friends, let us love one another, for love comes from God." Then she read the other banner: "Everyone who loves has been born of God and knows God. 1 John 4:7." Clementine and Breezy whispered to each other that June must have pinned on her invisible badge of Christian bravery this morning as it took a jumbo amount of courage to admonish Lizzie about her plans in the hope of getting her back on the right track. They also said that both ladies must have realized that the banner's Bible passage was so spot-on and relevant that it might halt Lizzie's afternoon X-ing homework.

On their way back to the sacristy June had one more vital thing to tell Lizzie. She said that if anyone in the church put a big X through Lizzie's photo and also through her name, address, and telephone number, and she found out about it, it would deeply hurt her feelings. June asked Lizzie to rethink her questionable and careless plan and instead do some shoe-shifting, that is, to try wearing someone else's shoes.

Lizzie appeared touched by June's words and assured her that before she does anything, she will take it to God in prayer. For now, she will not be crossing anyone out of the directory. Instead, she will study the directory, find those she is not acquainted with and pray for them, and pray for herself, too, that she will have the courage to introduce herself to them knowing that they are her brothers and sisters in Christ. After hearing Lizzie's words, June said to her, "You go, sister!" Breezy and Clementine told Ruby how confusing June's exclamation was. To their knowledge, June and Lizzie are not kin.

At 8:30 p.m. Rudy and I travelled to the sanctuary and luckily found a wintergreen breath mint. We were quite confused why anyone would choose the flavour wintergreen when it is not the winter season. Today we were tired even though we did not work very hard. Perhaps it is because we have started a diet to reduce the blubber clinging to our tummies. We visited about the subject of dieting, noticing that we already have some issues with fatigue and mood changes. Too, we wonder if this grueling dieting plan we are following might give us gallstones. We will call on Dr. Theodore Simonson, the mouse village librarian, and ask him to research the unhealthy effects of dieting.

– F.N.

SUNDAY SCHOOL RESUMED TODAY AT HISTORIC ST. PETER'S FOLLOWING A THREE-MONTH summer recess. Many children aged three and up gathered together in the sanctuary, each one wearing a name tag with their first and last name written on it. Beneath their names was written the name of their Sunday School teacher. The children sat in age groups, one for each class, and remained with their new teacher and youth helper throughout the opening. Sunday School openings at St. Pete's look a lot like what is described in Luke 13:45, where the children are gathered together, much like a hen gathers her chicks safely under her wing. That is exactly what the teachers and youth helpers were doing this morning. They were being hens that gathered their chicks to safely protect them.

Because this was the first day of Sunday School, there was high attendance. The children were enrolled, similar to Joseph and Mary when they went to be registered for the census taken of the Roman world during the reign of Caesar Augustus. Sunday by Sunday the number of children in attendance dwindles just a bit, until a schedule is printed that announces the dates and times of rehearsals for the children's Christmas pageant. At that point attendance increases as many children hope to be given a costumed part in the program. The parts of Mary and Joseph are desired by most of the children, but, unfortunately only one girl and one boy will be chosen. The number of shepherds and angels fluctuates each year, as the Sunday School Superintendent, Miss Jeanette Grey, aims to make certain every child gets to wear a costume. All mice can see that her heart and mind are well-suited for this position at St. Peter's!

After Pastor Osterhagen led the morning's opening with a prayer, he turned the microphone over to Melody Greene, the Sunday School Music Director, who led the children in singing three songs, with the help of Holly Whitley at the keyboard. "Jesus Loves Me" was an all-time favourite, one was a modern song we mice have never heard before (but enjoyed the catchy rhythm), and the last one was an oldie, "Jacob's Ladder," where the children's arms repetitively moved up-and-down during the ever-so-fun-to-sing "higher, higher" refrain.

Miss Jeanette formally introduced all of the Sunday School staff to the assembly, made announcements, and passed out papers that were to be taken home to their parents. After that, everyone was on their way to their new Sunday School classroom to see what it was like, how it was decorated, and to learn about the Bible lesson for the day. Craft time followed the Bible lesson, in which a craft was made pertaining to the lesson. Near the end of the Sunday School hour there was some time to enjoy a treat.

Virginia Hawkins is the oldest Sunday School teacher at St. Peter's this year. Being newly retired from Cabot's Lumber Yard as the Senior Accounts Receivable Manager, a position that required her to regularly speak sternly with customers who are in arrears of their payments, this will be a brand new challenge for her. Most of the teachers are younger, in their mid-thirties, with their own children registered in St. Pete's Sunday School. Everyone on the Sunday School staff is proud of Virginia for coming forward to teach Sunday School. Being that she is a spinster, she confesses that she honestly doesn't know if she would enjoy being around children because she has had no experience. Earlier this summer Ruby heard Miss Virginia ask Miss Jeanette for a special request, that is, to avoid placing her as a preschool or preteen teacher. Miss Jeanette listened to her wishes, so she assigned her a class consisting of twelve six-year-old children. Our village is pinning our hopes on Miss Virginia noticing how much children welcome the Gospel message that they will hear in their classrooms each week, as the teachers, whether they know it or not, are truly evangelists.

Juniper and Cloudberry, two mice from our village, positioned themselves behind the book rack in Miss Virginia's classroom before today's lesson began. After the class of twelve children were all seated around the large table, she introduced herself as Miss Virginia, saying that this is the first time that she has been a Sunday School teacher. The youth helper, Brooklyn, spoke next and revealed that she has been a helper for three years. Welcoming each student individually by reading their name tags, she asked them to share something about themselves – what they like to do, how many people are in their family, or their pet's names. The children were named Austin, Winona, Dallas, Lincoln, Aspen, Phoenix, Camden, Cody, Jackson, Dacotah, Dakota, and Mary. After meeting each one of the children, Miss Virginia remarked that all of their first names are a match for a certain city or state, except for Mary. She said even she and her youth helper, Brooklyn, have that in common with all of them. Miss Virginia singled Mary out to assure her that she shouldn't feel left out because her name is not a city or state, but emphasized that her name is the only Biblical name in the classroom, noting that she must feel honoured to have been given the same name as the mother of our Lord and Saviour, Jesus Christ. Mary raised her hand after Miss Virginia had finished speaking and told her that she also has a name similar to the others in the class. Revealing that her full name is Mary Fairhope Land, Mary went on to announce that her middle name is a city in Alabama, located on the breathtaking shores of Mobile Bay. It is a place where shrimp, crab, and other fish are sometimes remarkably easy to catch. When this phenomenon happens, the fish and shellfish all come right ashore and it is named a "Jubilee!" She also added that when her first name, Mary, and her last name, Land, are spoken together quickly, it sounds just like the little state of Maryland. Miss Virginia realized that Mary's name surpasses all of the other names in the class, so she pointed out that she is named not just after a city or a state, but after both, and to top it off, she's named after the Virgin Mary. In the wake of that information, Miss Virginia began to teach the day's Bible lesson based on Noah and the ark. From the look on Miss Virginia's face, she must have realized that she had better be well prepared to deliver the Bible lesson each Sunday. She must expect that Mary Land's hand will be raised frequently with various questions.

After today's Bible lesson, the children were each given one half of a white paper plate to colour and embellish. The plates had arches drawn on them by youth helper Miss Brooklyn, one for each of the seven colours of the rainbow. Each child received a red, orange, yellow, green, blue, indigo, and violet crayon to colour today's craft. After finishing the colouring, it was glue time. Miss Brooklyn told Miss Virginia that six-year-olds delight in using glue bottles, something that catapults the craft to a top-notch level. Three cotton balls were glued at the base of each side of the rainbow, and a small piece of paper with the words, "God keeps His promises," was glued in the middle of the rainbow.

Miss Virginia was certainly prepared when snack time rolled around. Armed with twenty-four individually-boxed animal crackers, she made a connection between Noah's ark and the animal crackers, which Juniper and Cloudberry thought was a perfect combination. Announcing that each student could enjoy one box of animal crackers for this morning's treat, she suggested that they take a second box home to enjoy later in the week and remember that God loves us and keeps His promises.

Miss Virginia asked Miss Brooklyn to read the memory verse that she had picked out and stated that they will be tested next Sunday. She read Genesis 9:13: "I have set My rainbow in the clouds, and it will be the sign of the covenant between Me and the earth." Cloudberry could tell that Miss Brooklyn reckoned it was far too lengthy of a memorization assignment for the children, with perhaps the exception of Mary Fairchild Land. Miss Brooklyn's eyelashes gently fluttered as she bravely spoke to Miss Virginia, suggesting that a better memorization verse about Noah would be Genesis 8:1, "But God remembered Noah." Miss Virginia shook her head back and forth, firmly indicating that they would stick to the original plan. We think that Miss Virginia must not know the memorizing limits of her students yet, but that will be revealed to her next Sunday.

Juniper and Cloudberry continued to listen in on the entire Bible lesson this morning while stationed in silence behind the classroom bookshelf. They attended the village meeting tonight to share their knowledge from what they learned in Sunday School this morning. Relaying that Miss Virginia explained Noah's ark by telling that animals boarded the ark two by two, a flurry of conversations started amongst the village. It was clear that two mice were aboard the ark, as well as cheetahs, bees, snakes, lambs, lady bugs, hippopotamuses, hummingbirds, and chipmunks. We now understand that all mice are descendents of Noah's two mice, thus they are our ancestors. Now it all makes sense to us that God created mice, making us special creatures to be saved from destruction in the flood. Everyone cherished the Bible lesson presented to us by Juniper and Cloudberry that was revealed to us today.

At 11:30 p.m. Ruby and I travelled to the fifth grade Sunday School classroom and snacked on a tidbit of a dropped confetti cupcake that was topped with seven-minute frosting. We were perplexed as to why it is called seven-minute frosting, but we figured it out. We kept a keen eye on the wall clock, watching it tick away. It took us precisely seven minutes to eat the cupcake morsels with seven-minute frosting.

— F.N.

EVEN THOUGH IT IS A NATIONAL HOLIDAY, EARLY THIS MORNING PASTOR OSTERHAGEN received a telephone call from Dede Thompkins, mother of eight-year-old Dakota in Miss Virginia's Sunday School classroom. Dede explained to Pastor that Dakota's feelings were hurt yesterday in Sunday School by her teacher. Dakota cried all the way home, nine miles out in the country, until they drove into their driveway, where she calmed down and told her mother what was wrong. She said that she will not go back to Sunday School. At first Pastor thought it might be a discipline problem, but as he listened carefully to Dede explain what had happened, he found out that it all revolves around an unfortunate attempt to distinguish between two children in the classroom named Dacotah and Dakota. It seemed as though Miss Virginia decided it would be easier if one child were to be nicknamed South Dakota and the other to be nicknamed North Dakota. Her precious daughter, Dakota Thompkins, ended up being re-named "South Dakota" by Miss Virginia, even though Dakota explained to Miss Virginia that her name is not South Dakota. Dakota asked Miss Virginia to please not give her that nickname. Dede said Miss Virginia did not listen to her plea and told her goodbye by saying, "See you next Sunday, South Dakota."

Dede told Pastor that this has to stop immediately, mentioning that it can't carry on because things like that can continue on into adulthood, and plenty of adults have scars from nicknames that were plunked on them. Dede mentioned that it is damaging to a person as she personally knows two people who have been saddened much of their adult life because they were nicknamed "Sassy Pants" and "Slacker." It has taken many years for the people within the community to finally call them by their given first names, Glenda and Gary. Dede said that Virginia Hawkins has shown a lack of respect for her Dakota by giving her this nickname. After all, Dakota was not named after the state of South Dakota for any reason, plus they have never been there. She assured Pastor that he will soon be hearing from the other parents, as they are likely unhappy, too, about their Dacotah being nicknamed "North Dacotah." She threatened Pastor by telling him that if this doesn't get straightened out before Sunday, they will have to join another church and start over, for Dakota's sake.

Dede questioned Pastor about Miss Virginia's name, asking him which state she happens to be named after, Virginia or West Virginia. Pastor Osterhagen chuckled and quipped back at Dede by telling her that he would speak to Miss Virginia or Miss West Virginia, whichever name is applicable, about the issue. He further said that Miss Virginia might be a title awarded her in a beauty pageant when Miss Virginia was young, trim, and pretty. He admitted to Dede, though, that he couldn't imagine what her talent portion of the pageant might have been, unless it was getting people to pay their outstanding bills. (Later we heard him tell Aia that remark accidently slipped out of his mouth because he had not yet had his first cup of morning coffee.) That unplanned and sarcastic comment by Clement eased and dissipated Dede's tension, which led both of them to enjoy a huge laugh together. Dede could tell that Pastor cared about Dakota, herself, their family, and also cared about Miss Virginia. Pastor assured Dede that Miss Virginia will be asked not to call Dakota "South Dakota" again. With all the confidence in her Pastor to straighten out this problem, and because of his outstanding listening ability and practical help, Dede thanked Pastor from the bottom of her heart and told him that they will all be in church on Sunday.

After Aia heard Clement talking about the nickname given to Dacotah and Dakota, she felt badly that she has callously given so many church people nicknames behind their backs. Admitting that Historic St. Pete's is full of loving, helpful, and committed Christians, she told Clement that she needs to overcome her bad habit and that she has to come up with a plan to do that. Aia said that if she is able to go twenty-one days in a row without using nicknames, she will have kicked the habit. The same twenty-one day plan applies to most bad habits, like smoking, drinking, and swearing.

At 11:30 p.m. Ruby and I travelled to the parsonage and snacked on crumbs of an indescribably tender buttermilk biscuit.

– F.N.

NOW THAT THE PUBLIC AND PRIVATE SCHOOLS ARE BACK IN SESSION, ALL PROGRAMS AT St. Peter's are back in full swing. Sunday School, Choir, Youth Group, Seniors' Group, Bible Study, the Singles' Group, Confirmation, Handbell Choir, Couples' Club, The Knifty Knitters, Ladies' Sewing and Quilting Group, Overeater's Support Group, Card Club, Ladies' Guild, Book Club, etc. are all on the calendar, but Aia has much more important things to pay attention to at this point in her life than any of the clubs at church. She needs to be very selective about what she will participate in, as she knows that too much will immediately be expected of her, and she really doesn't have any free time. Clement and Aia talked about how they don't seem to have enough time to get their work done. Clement relayed to Aia that he has never been this rushed in his entire life, admitting that he feels like he is in a watertight wooden barrel taking a plunge over Niagara Falls, needing a miracle just to survive it.

Noticing that the little things all seem to add up, he said he is trying to make small changes here and there. Perhaps if he can get more control over those things, he won't be behind so often. For instance, instead of taking a five-minute shower, he now takes a two-minute shower. Substituting his former routine of taking a brisk, refreshing walk to the post office every morning, he now puts on his inline skates and zips to and from the post office. When he runs into parishioners at the P.O., they don't even attempt to chat with him, as they see that he is in a hurry, and this helps to add minutes to his day. We did hear him admit that the only time it feels awkward in his inline skates is when he is wearing his clerical shirt. People look at him during those times with eyes wide open as though they are seeing a version of "The Flying Nun," only he is "The Skating Pastor."

Aia expressed to Clement that she is in need of a break from the children, and added that it is essential that she has an opportunity to go shopping, hoping to find some wardrobe items that actually fit her. Clement promised her that he will take care of the children while she shops at the mall. He told her to enjoy herself and also encouraged her to treat herself to coffee at the food court.

Aia assumed that Clement would stay home with the little ones while she was at the mall, but Clement thought about his time and told her that he could accomplish some church work while she was away. While Clement left the house to fetch Gretchen's little red wagon out of the garage, Ruby and I decided to slip into the twin's diaper bag. We made a snap decision to go along on a mystery trip with Pastor and the little ones. After returning to the parsonage from the garage, Clement got out the cloth baby carrier designed to carry twins. After strapping the carrier on himself, in went Marc and Luc. He asked Gretchen to sit in the little red wagon with her doll and the diaper bag. Off we went, Clement, Gretchen, the babies, and the two of us on a leisurely stroll. Soon we were at Loving Arms Nursing Home, located just six blocks from St. Peter's. Clement told Gretchen that he thought the parishioners in the nursing home would enjoy seeing her and the twins, but his main purpose in being there was to visit three members of St. Peter's and to give them Holy Communion.

After arriving at Loving Arms, the two male parishioners that Pastor went to call on were not in the building. Pastor must have been perplexed as to how they qualified as being "shut-ins" if they were away. Anyway, the receptionist at the front desk explained to him that both of the men frequently escape from the nursing home and travel next door to the gentlemen's club to see in that establishment something other than "loving arms." Ruby and I know that Clement and Aia have talked about this issue frequently and do not understand how city zoning can approve of a nursing home and a gentlemen's club built side-by-side. Clement found out from a nurse's aide that Loving Arms has a friendly arrangement with the Studio Club. When the two show up, a dancer or the bartender quickly phones Loving Arms and immediately one of the nurse's aides hotfoots it over there to escort the two men back to where they belong.

Clement decided to call on the one other member at Loving Arms Nursing Home. He found her resting in her bed. Before visiting with her, he gave Gretchen several quarters, encouraging her to get a treat at the vending machine located in the hallway, right outside the door. He told her to come back right away to the resident's room, which she did. When she came back she held a snack-sized package of hot cheese flavoured sticks, opened them up and immediately told her daddy that her mouth was "big time on fire." Gretchen interrupted Clement during the words of institution by asking him for additional quarters because she needed a drink, and she wanted to get a new snack, as this one must be spoiled. Clement gave her more change from his pocket, at which point she came back soon with a can of cola (too strong of a drink for Gretchen) which made her choke when she tasted it. She also had a teriyaki beef stick, which she announced was spoiled, too. Gretchen interrupted her daddy once again and asked him if they could just go home and have buttered soda crackers and a glass of milk.

Just then the twins woke up and started crying. Clement was in big-time daddy trouble, pointed out by Edwina Gilbert, the head nurse. She walked abruptly into the room and firmly told him that crying babies were not allowed in that particular wing of the nursing centre as noise disturbs the residents. She asked him if he was aware that this particular wing of Loving Arms is designated as a "quiet" wing. Clement told her that he just found out about that.

Clement gave his parishioner the sacrament and a benediction and turned to leave, but at that moment a curious resident walked into the room carrying a baby doll. She discarded her toy baby doll and reached over to Luc and tried to pull him out of the twin baby carrier, claiming that he was her baby. Clement tried to escape from the room, but on his way out he ran into Sharisse Neilson who was walking in the hallway with her mother, Esther Anderson. Sharisse had lost so much weight, maybe one-hundred pounds thanks to bariatric surgery, that Pastor didn't even recognize her. She told him that her mid-life crisis led her to deciding to enter a seminary. She is certain that God wants her to become a pastor, even though it will be a second career and quite a change from being the sales manager at the largest car dealership in Oswald County, MacNeil's Automotive. Clement was so flustered and thrown off-base by both babies crying, along with Gretchen's pleading to go home, plus the tension of Nurse Edwina Gilbert's presence, that he lost control of his words. After eyeing Sharisse's extra-short skirt, her exposed legs with stocking seam tattoos on the back of both legs, he responded by telling her that if she really, really has the desire to become a pastor, the first thing she will need to do is to purchase a longer skirt. After that he pressed on to flee from the nursing home with his three fussy children by speed walking all the way home, pulling Gretchen in the wagon and carrying the hungry twins in the double baby carrier. About one-third of the way home, he noticed, even in the fresh air, that the twins were both in need of a diaper change.

When they arrived home, Clement changed the boys' diapers, while Gretchen fanned the air with a hand-painted silk folding fan that she keeps in the top drawer of the baby changing table for just these special occasions. With the other hand she plugged her nose while saying "PU" at least a dozen times. After that, Clement and Gretchen each held one of the babies and gave them their bottles. When they were asleep, Clement placed them in their cribs. It was finally time to get out the box of soda crackers and start spreading butter. Gretchen and Clement sat at the dining room table with Gretchen enjoying a glass of milk and Clement savouring a big glass of Canadian beer. When Aia arrived home a couple of hours later, he told her everything that had happened while she was away.

Aia was astonished to hear that Sharisse wants to become a pastor. She cannot imagine Sharisse being a pastor simply because she does not seem to have a pastor's heart. He told her about his rough words concerning her short skirt, but Aia told him to overlook it as Sharisse is tough enough to handle any frankness like that. Aia mentioned that Sharisse is far from being a delicate woman who would be mortified by Clement's rude fashion advice. Clement told Aia that he didn't know if he felt better or worse after hearing her words.

Later on he mentioned the unpleasant time he had walking home when Marc and Luc loaded their diapers full at exactly the same time. She commented that they usually do that, and it is not the only thing they do at exactly the same time. They often cry, yawn, and nap at the same time. Aia mentioned that as the twins grow, they will probably crawl, walk, and talk in sync.

Aia said she purchased two new tops, two new pairs of slacks, and a package of six cotton undies at the mall, finishing the outing with a large coffee with double cream. It was an expensive day for the Osterhagens, but Aia so appreciated the break and the improvements to her wardrobe. She told Clement that he is a wonderful husband, the best one in the whole wide world. Clement liked to hear that. They stood in the kitchen and hugged until Marc and Luc started to cry simultaneously.

At 11:15 p.m. Ruby and I travelled to the parsonage and snacked on dropped crumbs of buttered soda crackers and a couple droplets of fine Canadian beer. Yum! We hope to repeat that snack over and over again.

– F.N.

MRS. SORENSGAARD TELEPHONED AIA AT THE CRACK OF DAWN THIS MORNING ASKING her to purchase salmon at Grocer Dan's and then deliver it to her home. It was on a one-day sale, advertised in yesterday's flyer. Since she lives alone and cannot drive a car, she often depends on the Osterhagen's to bring her supplies, especially bananas. Being that she is from Denmark, she has never adjusted to the difference between kilograms and pounds, which makes a very big difference, especially when it comes to purchasing fresh salmon.

Aia left Clement at home with the little ones and hurried to Grocer Dan's to purchase fresh salmon, fearing that if she didn't step on it, the store would run out of the daily special. When Aia looked at the fresh salmon available, she later told Clement that it made her hungry for salmon, too. Aia frugally decided to purchase a can of salmon and make salmon cakes, planning to serve them with white rice and creamed green peas. After leaving the store, Aia delivered the salmon to Mrs. Sorensgaard with the receipt for twenty-three dollars. Mrs. Sorensgaard blew her top, first in Danish, secondly in English, when she found out the steep price, telling Aia that she was only supposed to purchase what was in the advertisement, the salmon special. Aia tried to explain to her that the price was seven dollars and ninety-nine cents per pound, making it almost twenty dollars a kilogram, but Mrs. Sorensgaard was too upset to listen to her and began speaking again in Danish. She grabbed the salmon from Aia and then reached into her handbag pulling out a five-dollar bill from her wallet, saying that was close enough. Then Mrs. Sorensgaard shut the front door on Aia, as Aia stood there completely dumbfounded. Aia was so dismayed in realizing that she did a favour for her and somehow lost eighteen dollars in the process. Aia physically turned around to go back to the car, and mentally did a one-eighty about helping Mrs. Sorensgaard and her requests in the future. Afterwards Ruby and I heard her tell Clement every detail about what had just happened to her. Together they agreed that someone else besides them should help Mrs. Sorensgaard with her grocery needs. The solution would be to advertise for helpers in the church bulletin so that others could physically take her to the grocery store so she can read the prices herself. They agreed that by doing this Mrs. Sorensgaard might learn the vast difference between pounds and kilograms.

At 11:30 p.m. Ruby and I travelled to the parsonage and snacked on nibbles of stale popcorn that we discovered under the sofa, popcorn that has been under there for months, going back to the time when the Osterhagens ate popcorn with their fingers, instead of serving it in a soup bowl and eating with a soup spoon to cut down on spillage. Long ago we tasted popcorn for the very first time. Assuming that it would taste similar to regular cooked corn, we were wrong. We concluded that we prefer popcorn over corn.

    – F.N.

HISTORIC ST. PETER'S BOARD OF ELDERS CONSISTS OF FOUR MEN: DARRYL HOLLEY, Delmar York, Duane Arnett, and Duncan Oaks. For many weeks the "Four D's" have been planning HSP's first annual pork chop dinner, which they have wittily named, "St. Pete's Pork-Out." The elders and their spouses spent several hours yesterday afternoon occupied in Woolcox Hall as well as the church kitchen preparing for this dinner, which was held after the worship service today. By 4 p.m. yesterday Woolcox Hall was entirely set up and all of the food preparations were accomplished, except for the grilling of the pork chops, which was to be done today. Lotus Flower, one of our most attractive, graceful, and delicate mice, overheard the elders and their spouses comment on how they were looking forward to going out for pizza that night at Vandell's Pizzeria. Duane mentioned that it would be his treat at Vandell's, as he wanted everyone to look forward to a reward for all of their hard work, a job well done!

Darryl, and his wife Molly, are friends with Harlan Thornhill, who is a member of the Pork-to-Table Cooperative Society. Darryl, Molly, Harlan, and his wife, Lindsey, often play cards on Friday evenings. Darryl told everyone that during these card parties they have had many conversations about the Society, mentioning that one of the Society's goals is to be of service to communities. The Society brings in professional barbeques to and from various functions to grill pork chops. Their biggest event is the annual State Fair in which they have grilled Windsor chops for forty-three years consecutively. Many weeks ago, Darryl asked Harlan to make arrangements with the Pork-to-Table-Cooperative Society to grill thick-cut pork chops at St. Pete's Pork-Out. Today the representatives from the Society arrived at St. Peter's ready to grill the two-inch thick, centre-cut, smoked pork chops that are their speciality, the famous chops that people can't stop raving about.

Another elder, Delmar, is extremely talented at preparing homemade barbeque sauce. Arriving at church this morning carrying a plastic gallon of his special jazzed-up sauce, he said that it is available for those who want to have their pork chop basted with a kick of heat. Delmar also mentioned that the addition of his BBQ sauce will escalate this church shindig far beyond any old weenie roast, adding that St. Pete's has put on far too many of those routine events.

The four elders sat in church this morning sporting a look on their faces that emitted complete confidence about today's dinner being under control. A few minutes into the worship service Darryl was approached by Harlan Thorn-hill. Harlan quietly whispered words into Darryl's ear that promptly catapulted Darryl from his pew. One of the mice in our village, Tumbleweed, said that he witnessed a troubled and puzzled expression on Darryl's face, and several other details he noticed about the other three elders. After Darryl vaulted from his pew, the three others, Delmar, Duane, and Duncan, wondered if something was terri-bly wrong, so they copied Darryl's actions and dashed out of the sanctuary. The elders gathered together with Harlan in the church kitchen where their conversa-tion quickly revealed that there were no chops at the church. At all. Darryl had as-sumed the Society would arrive not only with their grills and grilling equipment, but also with the pork chops. Harlan had expected that the chops would be there waiting for them in the church refrigerator. At that point, there were five frenzied men in a predicament.

Two of our mice, Fergus and Heather, peeked out from behind the stove to catch a glimpse of the "Four D's" expeditiously working out a solution to their pork chop predicament. They agreed on a brilliant strategy of splitting up and driving in four different directions. This was the master plan: Darryl would inter-rupt Grocer Dan Berry, who was attending today's worship service, and ask him to go to his store to cut pork chops for a quick pickup; Duane would speed south to the only grocery store in Oswald County that is open on Sunday mornings to purchase thick-cut chops; Duncan would telephone his friend, Barry Banfield, the owner of Banfield's Butcher Shop, asking him to prepare chops for immedi-ate pickup; and finally, Delmar would call his brother-in-law, Lennie, the owner of Landon's Fine Meats that is located at the far north edge of Oswald County. Delmar was certain that Lennie would be available to cut and wrap up pork chops since he attends mass on Saturdays at St. Agnes Parish, making him free as a bird on Sunday mornings. Their goal was to return immediately with enough chops to make the First Annual St. Pete's Pork-Out a success. When Fergus revealed to the mice village how speedily the men planned on driving, all had doubts that the elders were putting safety first.

Fergus and Heather reported to us that the "Four D's" strategy successfully acquired the needed pork chops. Trips to all points of the county resulted in all four of them arriving back at St. Pete's minutes before today's worship service was finished. The Pork-to-Table crew had their grills fired up and speedily load-ed the grill racks with pork chops. The thick chops were on their way to grilled perfection by the time the parishioners arrived for Sunday dinner in Woolcox Hall. Fergus and Heather mentioned that many people commented on the wonderful aroma wafting throughout the entire building.

Another aroma that was in the air today was that of gratitude and thankfulness. The four elders responsible for today's dinner spoke to each other about being partners in solving today's debacle. Mentioning how positive it was to work as a team, their conversation revealed how they felt similar to football players who have just won a game. That led to a discussion about how they could apply teamwork to the duties that they perform at church. The thought was expressed that instead of doing so much of their work individually while serving on the Board of Elders, they could apply more teamwork to their elder duties. Heather said that it looked like all four men each had gone through an epiphany of sorts, adding that it was inspiring to observe strong men behave like that. They had put their lives, driving records, and wallets on the line for the cause.

There was only one wrinkle during the round-up of pork. While Duncan was speedily driving back to St. Pete's with his emergency cargo of pork chops, a highway patrol car clocked him and pulled him over for speeding. Before writing him a ticket, Duncan revealed to the trooper that there was a very good reason as to why he was carefully speeding. After listening to Duncan's explanation, the trooper told him that he understood his hastiness. At this point, the trooper introduced himself as Gabriel (Gabe) Horn, the son-in-law of Arthur and Minnie Klingenberg, active members of Historic St. Peter's. Trooper Horn made known that had been invited by his in-laws to attend today's St. Pete's Pork-Out, but unfortunately, he was scheduled to be on duty. However, his wife, Michelle, and their children, Jamie and Jill, were attending worship this morning with the Klingenbergs and were looking forward to enjoying Sunday dinner with them. After Trooper Horn realized that everyone attending St. Peter's today would be highly disappointed if there were no pork chops, he offered a solution. By travelling together at breakneck speed, they will be able to save the dinner. He instructed Duncan to follow him and to stick very close behind him. Trooper Horn got into his police vehicle and blazed his flashers all the way to St. Pete's. Duncan later told the "Four D's" that out of terror he glued his hands to the steering wheel, earnestly watched the road, and took turns grinding and clenching his teeth together. Duncan added that he had a sensation that he was part of the Indianapolis 500 when he followed the patrolman, who happened to be wise enough to recognize that this was truly an emergency.

At 7:30 p.m. Ruby and I travelled to Woolcox Hall in an attempt to locate a scrap of today's delicacy prepared by the Pork-to-Table Cooperative Society. We were out of luck, but we did find a choice morsel of apple crisp that we enjoyed. I mentioned to Ruby that it was unfortunate that we didn't have a little bit of cinnamon ice cream on top of the apple crisp, or better yet, a slice of cheddar cheese. She nodded her head in agreement, but could not speak, as her mouth was overly jam-packed.

    — F.N.

CLEMENT AND AIA HAVE ENTHUSIASTICALLY BEEN PLANNING THEIR VACATION FOR several weeks. Last Thursday Clement called to confirm their rental reservation at Nowlan's Mountain Cottages. After breakfast today Clement packed the van with their suitcases and supplies as well as Aia's Trinitarian boxed lunches that contained sandwiches, pickles, and fruit. Clement also packed up their small cooler with lots of drinks and an ice pack. After that, Clement, Aia, and Gretchen, said goodbye and headed out of town, leaving Marc and Luc at home with Clement's folks, Fred and Nancy Osterhagen. Ruby and I have already noticed that the grandparents are overjoyed to spend time with the twins.

The destination for their vacation is Boone, North Carolina, located in the Blue Ridge Mountains. The rental is located in a wooded area next to a rushing trout stream. The facility has all the conveniences that they desire, especially a hot tub, an indoor swimming pool, and a hiking path. They will be able to prepare meals in a fully equipped kitchenette. So that they can bring home three suitcases of clean clothing, Aia said that they will wash their laundry the final day of their vacation.

Yesterday we overheard Aia mention to Gretchen that her favourite part of their vacation will be spending time in the awe-inspiring mountains, adding that she is really a mountain girl, not a flatlander, even though they live in Oswald County, which is essentially a vast prairie. She repeated what Clement had said, something he thought was said by his favourite wilderness naturalist John Muir: "You are not in the mountains. The mountains are in you." He had told this to Aia because he is of the opinion that it altogether applies to her. Aia continued on by explaining that the first thing she plans to do every morning is to open the drapes so they can look up at the grandeur of the mountains, almost as if they are looking at heaven's gate, where God is almighty, powerful, and in control. Aia mentioned to Gretchen that they will have a peachy-keen time in the mountains. Gretchen giggled at hearing that remark, repeated it several times, and then asked if they could go to Grocer Dan's and purchase three peaches. Aia thought that was a peachy-keen idea, so Clement watched the twins while Aia and Gretchen set off to obtain three fresh and juicy peaches to add to their picnic lunch.

Ruby and I listened to Aia chattering about their vacation plans dozens of times these last weeks. Each day of their vacation Aia intends to pack a wholesome picnic lunch, set off on a little trip, and gather up precious memories for the three of them to take home. She also plans to bring back a large art print of the mountains. Already she has chosen a place for it to hang on a wall in the living room. After their vacation is over, the painting will remind her that everything is peachy-keen and that God is safely holding all of them. Another plan this week is to return daily to the cottage at suppertime to prepare something quick for supper, like fried steaks, tomatoes, and toast. Both Clement and Aia have talked about being on the lookout for a seafood buffet and know that even Gretchen will enjoy it too, as she is already a seafood lover. They are cautious about expenses and plan to eat out only once during their vacation, but they are ready to splurge at a seafood buffet, if they can find one. After they tuck Gretchen in bed each evening, they hope to read their books, perhaps a murder mystery or a self-improvement book (definitely not a church-related book) or they will watch a rented video while enjoying a glass of wine.

For several days Aia has been so excited about their vacation that she hums and sings the words from one of her favourite songs, "In the Pines," that is based on an American folk song that is Southern Appalachian in origin, stemming from around the year 1870. Aia sings, "In the pines, in the pines, where the sun never shines, and you shiver when the cold wind blows." Clement and Aia both are looking forward to being in the "pines," being removed from daily life at St. Peter's, especially to be away from the telephone, the knocks on the door, and the abundant conversations with parishioners about the weather.

At 9 p.m. Ruby and I were able to travel to the parsonage and snack on a dropped morsel of take-away Chinese food. Fred and Nancy were so tuckered out from taking care of the twins today that Nancy had no energy left to prepare a meal. Fred had all he could do to muster up enough strength to drive to the restaurant to pick up their take-away order. We heard them say during dinner that tomorrow is bound to be a little bit easier as they get more accustomed to the twins' schedule. Ruby and I heard them decide that from now on Fred will take care of Marc, and Nancy will take care of Luc. Instead of juggling the boys back and forth, they will each be fully responsible for one. They also comfort each other when they talk about not being as young as they used to be. Clement's folks must have gone to bed around 8:30 p.m. so Ruby and I were able to have our treat earlier tonight. We liked that because we, too, are getting older. We enjoyed the tidbits from Lil's Restaurant, but our favourite was the one crispy chow mein noodle that we shared. We are very familiar with chow mein noodles as Aia makes stir-fry usually once a week.

    – F.N.

Wednesday, September 16

THIS WILL BE A SOMEWHAT LILLIPUTIAN ENTRY INTO MY JOURNAL. FRED AND NANCY Osterhagen have become droopy and completely dog-tired. I decided not to write much in my journal this week about it because I found it exhausting and draining just to watch them. Ruby heard them both agree that the only thing they can do right now is to sit down and hold the babies, lovingly take care of their needs, and that the parsonage dust bunnies and cobwebs will just have to wait until Monday morning.

At 10:15 p.m. Ruby and I travelled to the parsonage and snacked on a couple of crispy taco crumbs that Fred brought home for supper tonight from Eduardo's Taco Take-Out. We gave each other a high five and said *"mucho delicioso"* to each other several times.

– F.N.

CLEMENT, AIA, AND GRETCHEN WILL NOT BE HOME UNTIL TOMORROW. TODAY IS THEIR last day of vacation in Boone, North Carolina. Fred Osterhagen preached at Historic St. Peter's this morning and many parishioners said that they enjoyed his sermon, finding that it was full of words of encouragement. Not so optimistic was Granny Nancy as she tried to hold both Marc and Luc in the confined space of the church pew for one hour. She couldn't wait for the worship service to be over. When Fred spoke the Benediction, "The Lord bless you and keep you..." one of the mice, Whisper, heard Nancy say under her breath as she closed her eyes, "Thank you, God, I made it."

After church the four of them went to Nancy's Lunch Wagon and got settled in a booth with Fred holding Marc and Nancy holding Luc. Nancy has wanted to eat there ever since she saw the adorable sign posted outside of the café, but mostly because she shares the same name of the establishment. Nancy and Fred talked non-stop during lunch. She told Fred that she felt like celebrating and rewarding herself for miraculously being able to hold both twins in her arms and keep them quiet in church for one solid hour.

The fastest mouse in our village, Pinetop Willson, was able to scoot into the twins' diaper bag during worship this morning. Pinetop wasn't spotted by anyone as he is so fast and nimble that he practically flew into the open diaper bag that was positioned on the sanctuary floor. Nancy sat with the babies in the very back pew and the only other person in the pew seemed to be visually impaired, so he couldn't have seen Pinetop careen on by. The gentleman next to her was offered a bulletin, but he didn't take one. He told her that he didn't need a bulletin because he cannot read such small print. He added that he is not missing out on church news because there is never anything in the bulletin. On the plus side, he did mention that he was so happy to be in church.

During the new business portion of our mice village meeting tonight, Pinetop told us information he had heard from listening to Fred and Nancy's conversation at the café. He reported that Nancy said that their week would have been much easier if Gretchen had stayed with them instead of going along on the vacation to North Carolina. After all, Gretchen is almost a mini-mama. As they sat in their booth enjoying California burgers, French fries, and several cups of coffee, Nancy began to relax. She told Fred that they both have gotten the hang of taking care of the twins, just as the week is nearly over. Fred agreed. After lunch they went for a short ride around town before they stopped at Grocer Dan's Market & Deli. Ever since the "St. Pete's Pork-Out" it is open for business on Sundays from 12 to 5 p.m. Fred went into the store by himself and returned to the car with a grocery bag containing a shrimp ring, cocktail sauce, cheese, crackers, green olives, and a box of raspberries. He announced to Nancy that he had supper in the bag. We are aware that Nancy is an outstanding cook in her own home, but while taking care of the twins this week she has been frustrated, even having trouble putting on a hot dog lunch. Fred has even made the coffee every morning. He assured Nancy that he will make supper for a few days when they return home to let her get rested up. He is certain that everything will be back to normal soon, especially their daily exercise routine. He also told her that he misses her delicious cooking, including her gently fried Norwegian medisterkaker patties that she makes using minced pork in combination with special seasonings. Fred said that he cannot decide which is best, the medisterkaker, the sumptuous and extremely smooth gravy, the plainly riced potatoes, or all three of the aforementioned combined. After hearing Fred's kind, uplifting, and encouraging words, Nancy responded to Fred by telling him, "I love you, my Freddy." Fred responded by saying, as he often does, with the words "I love you, too, Nancy pants," just exactly as President Ronald Reagan is remembered saying to his lovely Nancy.

At 10 p.m. we travelled to the parsonage and snacked on a piece of a cracker. Fred and Nancy didn't drip any Chardonnay on the floor, so we missed out on enjoying even a little droplet of a libation today.

– F.N.

AFTER LUNCH TODAY FRED AND NANCY OSTERHAGEN KISSED EVERYONE GOODBYE AND headed home. They intended to travel the eighty-mile trip and arrive home early enough so Fred could catch up on the phone messages, the mail, and the faxes that have been accumulating at his church office while they have been away. Gretchen didn't even cry when they said goodbye because her granny assured her that she will talk to her soon on the telephone. Gretchen ran to get her little notebook and asked Granny Nancy to write down the church telephone number in her book, because she only has their home telephone number. She said that she will call them soon, because she knows how to use the telephone. Three hours later Gretchen called the church to see if they were there yet because she has been learning about seat belts, safety and danger, and how important it is to be careful. She has learned about some of this at school and also from her *Little Red Riding Hood* book that contains the frightful big bad wolf.

Gretchen has become very talkative on the telephone and has dialed up both sets of grandparents several times all by herself. About a month ago, Gretchen talked to her Granny Juliette, and Juliette promised her that she was going to sew something very special for Gretchen and send it to her in the mail. A box arrived today addressed to Miss Gretchen Osterhagen. Right away she knew that it must be from Granny Juliette and she seemed to know exactly what the box contained. She told her parents that Granny Juliette had promised to sew her something special and mail it. It would be exactly like something that is in her favourite book, *Little Red Riding Hood*.

The last time Arni and Juliette were at the Osterhagens, Juliette brought along with her a few of the little books that Aia enjoyed when she was a child. *Little Red Riding Hood* quickly became Gretchen's favourite. Juliette also brought along several *Pepe Le Pew* items, which Gretchen liked, but *Little Red Riding Hood* remains her favourite story. Aia's books are probably antiques by now, but Gretchen likes that they belonged to her mommy when she was a girl. We heard Gretchen say that the books are old and worn out, kind of like her mommy, all because her brothers seem to need her every minute of the day and at night, too. Ruby and I noticed that Aia appeared to be a little hurt by Gretchen's innocent comment, but Aia understood the essence of what she was saying.

Clement and Aia talked about how astonished they were that Gretchen and her Granny Juliette had been able to keep a secret these last weeks, because they had no clue about the arrival of this package. Gretchen told her folks to close their eyes as she wanted to surprise them with what was in the package. The box contained a red velveteen hooded cloak. Gretchen immediately put it on, fastened the hook at the neckline, and then asked her parents to open their eyes. Juliette had indeed sewed something very special for Gretchen. They both told Gretchen how beautiful she looked in the cloak, telling her that the colour red was so becoming on her with her blonde hair. Gretchen told them that she wants to be Red Riding Hood for Halloween and that this will be her costume.

After that, Gretchen dialed up Granny Juliette all by herself and thanked her for the cloak. When they were done visiting, Aia took a turn on the telephone and told her how much she appreciated her sewing Gretchen a gift, adding that Gretchen absolutely loves it. Juliette explained that she found the sewing pattern at a garage sale, purchased red velveteen fabric for the outside of the cloak, and also a warm red fabric that looked almost like satin for the lining. She was able to use the time after work each day to sew, thanks to Arni, as he took over the meals, laundry, and cleaning until she was able to complete the sewing project. Juliette urged Aia to let Gretchen wear it this fall as much as she wants to and to not save it just for Halloween. Aia agreed with her and added that Gretchen will also wear it on Reformation Sunday.

Clement and Aia talked about the issue of safety and how Gretchen is just discovering some of those thoughts because of her fascination with Little Red Riding Hood and the big bad wolf. They chuckled as they talked back and forth about how many phrases refer to safety and danger concerns that people face. Clement began with the phrase, "calculated risks," and Aia came up with, "on the safe side." From then on their conversation continued back and forth including the following: "hang on for dear life," "there's safety in numbers," "throwing caution to the wind," "the coast is clear," "crying wolf," "by a hair's breadth," "playing with fire," "by the skin of one's teeth," "batten down the hatches," "looking clear," "look before leaping," "fraught with danger," "watch your step," and "take cover." As soon as I heard those phrases I got out my notebook and jotted them down so that I wouldn't forget them. Clement mentioned Proverbs 18:10, which he has memorized, where it says, "The name of the LORD is a fortified tower; the righteous run to it and are safe." Aia asked him why he has that particular Bible verse memorized, so he told her that a pastor's life is full of safety issues, and finding refuge in God helps him to do the work he needs to do.

After that they each prayed a short prayer and finished with the Lord's Prayer. At that point, Clement suggested to Aia that they should take cover under the coverlet on their bed, and she agreed and turned off the light.

At 11:30 p.m. Ruby and I travelled to the parsonage and snacked on a morsel of a porcupine meatball. We were amazed at the delicious taste of porcupine, hoping that Aia will purchase more porcupine meat to make meatballs again soon. We talked about safety worries because we heard Clement and Aia discussing it today. Safety is definitely a priority when hiking in a New England or Wisconsin forest and coming in proximity with a porcupine, just as it's a priority to not trip and fall onto a cactus when viewing the desert blooms in Arizona. We think that we are safe at Historic St. Pete's from those two dangers, but anywhere danger is always a possibility. To find some comfort, we went to bed, held paws, and quietly sang our "Safety First" song.

– F.N.

PLEASE NOTE: So, dear reader, you are near and dear to me since you have stuck in there and reached this page in my journal. We are now family! But, for now, I have to conclude *Finley's Tale – Book II: Heaven on Earth*. This part of my journal I have chosen to dedicate to the Osterhagen children: Gretchen, wee Marc, and wee Luc. Not only are they a blessing to Pastor and Aia, but they are a treasure to the parishioners at Historic St. Peter's, including the entire mice community that calls this place home. Our village is watchful of the children as they grow day by day learning new things. We admire how each day is new and fresh in their eyes, showing us that they live life beautifully. It must be because of Matthew 18:3, where it reads, "And He said: 'Truly I tell you, unless you change and become like little children, you will never enter the kingdom of heaven.'"

For many days I have found myself in a stew and have not known what to do. Perhaps it might seem to you to be a simple dilemma, but to me it is a predicament that will require help from the entire mice village in order to be solved. All of the pages in my spiral notebook, the one lacking a cover, are completely full of handwriting. In fact, these words are being written on the margins of the very last page. Until another journal or notebook is found at Historic St. Peter's, I cannot continue to record the goings on. Tomorrow morning I intend to convene a meeting of the village in order to ask for their help in finding more paper. I cannot quit now as so much of the church year is ahead of us and news is in full blossom at St. Pete's, plus there are so many more people and mice that I would like you to become acquainted with. Remember that at Historic St. Peter's there are no strangers. They are just future Christian acquaintances that you simply have not yet met!

Together we will be taking an itty-bitty pause. The final journaling of the church liturgical year at will be recorded in *Finley's Tale – Book III: The Bond of Love*. You have shown love to me by following my tale and I express my thanks to you by saying, *Uqqw weoi* (Mouse), *Mange Tusen Takk* (Norwegian), and *Vielen Dank* (German).

Happy tears are falling from my cheeks as I send you a kiss (X) and a hug (O), and wish all of you Godspeed! I now sign off with hopeful thoughts that one day our paths will cross again. Remember that I have a tale to tell, and you are invited to follow my tale.

Your friend,

Finley Newcastle

(F.N. for short)

Appendix

Characters included in *Finley's Tale – Book II: Heaven on Earth*

Finley Tweed Newcastle, Church Mouse and author of *Finley's Tale – Book I: In the Beginning* and *Finley's Tale – Book II: Heaven on Earth*

Ruby Newcastle, Finley's precious gem of a wife

Pastor Clement Osterhagen, shepherd of Historic St. Peter's, a real keeper

Aia Osterhagen, pregnant and practical pastor's wife, mother of Gretchen, Marc, and Luc, fan of anything Trinitarian

Gretchen Osterhagen, cherished daughter of Pastor Clement & Aia Osterhagen

Ellsworth & Zeb, two mice who located a spiral notebook for *Finley's Tale – Book II: Heaven on Earth*

Lillian Thompson, hurt spinster who did not receive a Mother's Day carnation

Jodie Bernard, asked Pastor for a $20 donation towards her upcoming trip to Niagara Falls, which she instead intends to use to treat her mother to Mother's Day dinner at Sarah's Farmhouse, the newest restaurant in town

Copper, village mouse who overheard the $20 donation scheme

Abbey Whitelaw, church friend of Jodie Bernard who was filled in on her money-making scheme

Cadence Davis, handbell director, victim of Griffin's mischief

Gaynor Babineaux, manure spreader who stinks up the outdoor air on laundry days

Mr. & Mrs. Fletcher, contributors of the parsonage rhubarb bed

Constance Fletcher, the garden thief but gifted baker of anything containing rhubarb

Cécile-Claudette & Hadden, mice volunteers who oversaw the county-wide "Spring Social for Christian Gals"

Dr. Ellen Kam, University professor and humorous speaker

Judith Haugen, President of St. Peter's Ladies' Guild

Claudia Cooke, embarrassed baker of soapy green poke cake

Apple Blossom, Fleur & Amaryllis, three mice that reside in the courtyard during the warmer seasons

Fawne, village mouse with the most beautiful eyes in our entire village

Mrs. Whyte, recipient of Gretchen's hand-picked tulip cups, now known as Auntie Crimson

Chadwick, village mouse that was present when Gretchen was being scolded for picking tulips

Lorinda Hastings, first person that ever scolded Gretchen

Stella Antonelli, hoarder and hymnal thief, among other items

Marcus Antonelli, loving son of Sebastiano & Stella Antonelli

Gail Antonelli, loving and supportive wife of Marcus

Sebastiano Antonelli, Stella's deceased husband and father of Marcus

Presto, expeditious village mouse who overheard all conversations at the Antonelli home

Willow, mouse president of the Garden Girls Club

Cherry Blossom, Linden, Skye, Brooke & Lark, members of the Garden Girls Club

Cedric, bachelor mouse infatuated with bachelorette Lark

Dr. Christoff Kikkunen, assistant mouse librarian of Finnish descent

Christine, Gretchen's babysitter and busy carhop at Diana's Dairy Delight

Aloysius "Tip" Dover, Eileen Dover, Ben Dover, and their dogs, **Roll Dover & Rover Dover,** a family with a red pickup and flowers to plant at the church

Laurel-Leigh & Luna-Leigh, observers of the elderly parishioners at the church picnic

Summer Harris, watering garden girl who could help the church even more by wearing a swimsuit cover-up

Officer King, policeman who followed the Osterhagens to the parsonage to straighten out a switched shoe predicament

Maribel King, Gretchen's friend who has the same running shoes

Trina Steensen, helpful clerk at Steensen's Paint & Wallpaper

Harmony, Spinet, & Celesta, the "Sing it Thrice" mice

Hiram Holmes & Carlton Ferguson, summertime viewers of Summer Harris

Henry Wallace, asked Aia to prepare two hundred servings of homemade potato salad

Grey Neilson, new youth group leader that is not nearly grown up himself

Stacey McKinney, HSP's penny-saver choir director

Sheldon Cunningham, kicked-out choir member

Four mysterious midnight male telephone callers, inquiring of Aia about their "services"

Jayne Brownton, wife of janitor Chuck Brownton, who in her younger days was engaged to Ted Williamson

Chuck Brownton, church janitor who does an excellent job keeping everything clean, and who never uses toothpicks

Winky, attractive male mouse with a rare medical eye condition which causes his right eye to continually wink

Siegfried "Ziggy" Zirkelbach, person who donated the glockenspiel in loving memory of his folks

Hans & Lisbeth Zirkelbach, Ziggy's deceased folks

Ted Williamson, AKA "Toothpick Ted," toothpick addict

Charmaine Reyes, the "Coupon Queen"

Fritz Schmidt, summer flip-flop wearer, but worst of all, flip-flop remover

Mrs. Vargas, frequent washroom user

Caldwell Family, chronically tardy for church

Kennedy & Londyn McCoy, two sisters that often whisper during church

Mrs. McCoy, a fortissimo shusher

Christopher Snyder, wears his baseball cap in church to cover up unwashed hair

Mr. Stephenson, socializes loudly during worship

Church ushers, men who stand in the narthex during worship and visit about sports

Mrs. Jewel & baby Aidan, mother whose son cries continually through the worship service

Angela Fox, teenager who paints her fingernails during worship

Bland "Jett" & Hottie Lablanc, mice couple who disagree about name choices for their female newborn twins

Pandora & Peyton Leblanc, mice twins that nearly got named Blanche and Beige

Adelaide, "Jett" Lablanc's Auntie, who saw a lady hide the book, *Peyton Place*

John Roberts, life insurance agent who claims he has never been served steeped tea in an English bone china cup and saucer by anyone other than Aia

Dr. Joseph L. Melander, delivery room anesthesiologist at Our Lady of Lourdes Hospital, member of Historic St. Peter's

Samantha Hill, delivery room nurse and member of Historic St. Pete's

Elizabeth Carson, also a delivery room nurse and member of HSP

Arni Nygaard, Aia's dad, a university professor

Juliette Nygaard, Aia's mother, a high school French teacher, also an excellent cook

Angelica, towering breezeway statue, given her name by Gretchen

Pistachio & Char, two mice who witnessed the Nygaards claiming the breezeway for their daily morning coffee and afternoon cocktail times

Purity, a female mouse that travelled to the hospital in one of Aia's sneakers and found a way to be completely hidden in the labour/delivery room

Black Walnut, the mouse who rested behind the refrigerator in the sacristy and smelled a full whiff of Josie's breath

Marc Peter Osterhagen & Luc Paul Osterhagen, twin sons of Clement & Aia, Gretchen's brothers

Marc & Luc Barteau, twin older brothers of Juliette Nygaard who reside in Saint-Antoine-de-Tilly, Quebec

Serves You Right Summer Volleyball Club, the "SYRSVC"

Ben Atkinson, leader of the "Serves You Right Summer Volleyball Club"

Catch-a-Wink-Dink, older mouse who sleeps under the church kitchen stove

Viola Worthee, church kitchen patrol snooper who spotted beer cans in the blue recycle bucket

Henry Worthee, deceased husband of Viola, once known as the town drunk

Peter "Rocky" Collinsworth, adult who wants to be baptized and confirmed at St. Peter's

Little Bluegrass, who on his first outing ever, came home with big news about the newest attendee

Bamboo & Belladonna, parents of Little Bluegrass

Matins & Vespers, village mice who attended the Holy Baptism of Peter "Rocky" Collinsworth

Cadwaller's Concrete Contractors, old sidewalk ripper-outers and new sidewalk pourer-inners

Lavender Family, Parsley & Sage, parents of **Rosemary, Thyme, & Little-Herb,** village family in a knot due to Little-Herb playing freely in newly poured cement

Barker, ornery mouse who tried to circulate doubts about Gretchen

Isaac & Hannah Suderman, bewildered guardians of a famous nude painting

Mike & Helen Linden, HSP members and kind neighbours of the Suderman Family

John Becker, person claiming to own the painting he left in the Sudermans' garage

Oswald County Sherriff & two Police Officers, responded to a nude painting emergency at the Suderman Farm

Dr. Cooper, town dentist who has not heard of John Becker

Lance Ramsey, local attorney-at-law who has not met John Becker

Zachary Zimmermann, new pharmacist in town unacquainted with John Becker

Franklin Field, owner of Field's Filler-Upper, who does not know anyone named John Becker

Fred Osterhagen, Clement's Dad who is a pastor

Nancy Osterhagen, pastor's wife and Clement's mother

Carole Browne, human spell checker

Bonehead, a gentle pony that Gretchen got to ride on her birthday that resides at Bracken's Riding Stable

Amanda, lifeguard at the swimming pool and Gretchen's new babysitter

Bettie, Gretchen's birthday gift, a ginger-haired doll with a wheelchair and a rope to tie around her waist so she won't fall out

Canoe & Paddle, two village mice that yearn to travel and hope that someday they can be stowaways on a canoe travelling down the mighty Cedar River, but until then, they travelled to the Swanson Farm with Pastor Osterhagen

Roscoe & Rose Swanson, gave Pastor a trunk load of cucumbers and supplies for canning pickles

Kyle Swanson, helpful grandson who planted and harvested the cucumbers at the family farm

Aggie Cox, AKA Aunt Bee, emergency pickle canning helper

Beacon, one of the brightest mice in the village who witnessed the whoopee cushion prank

Will Anderly, Board of Property Chairperson

Ellie Crowley, sign-up sheet lady attempting to provide a perfectly productive and well-planned potluck, wearer of numerous fashion *faux pas,* AKA "Potluck Patrol Ellie"

The Tomato Lady, hangs out in the parking lot at the Salvation Army Thrift Store, generously giving away her abundant supply of homegrown tomatoes

Oaken, brawny mouse who keeps Ellie Crowley under surveillance as she walks to pew number eight

Speckle, village mouse that prefers to hang out in the ladies washroom behind the wastebasket

John Overby, Church Gremlin named John, after his father, who plays pranks, often stealing something but later returning the items

John Overby & Marit Ellingson-Overby, parents of John, "Griffin the Gremlin"

Agnar, Vor, & Sindri, three Norwegian forest cats that belonged to the Ellingson Family

Trey Quitz, Funeral Director, Quitz Funeral Home, "Call it Quitz"

Mel Holler, Funeral Director, Holler Funeral Parlour, "No Worries, Just Holler"

Bern Cease & Ash Cease, Funeral Directors, Cease Cremation Centre, "The Cream of Cremations" (a smoke-free facility)

Adam Best, Funeral Director, Best for the Family Funeral Home, "Best is the Least We Can Do" (Free coffee, juice, and cookies provided)

Donald Grave, Funeral Specialist, Grave's Inspired Funeral Chapel, "Love and Life Beyond the Grave"

Grocer Dan Berry, member of St. Pete's and owner of Grocer's Dan's Market & Deli

Eddy & Shirley Sanders, sons **Timmy, Tommy, & Tucker**, owners of Sanders' Shire

Ollie Shaw, Loch Ness Monster spotter

Ernie & Lorena Schwinn, tow truck owners and operators

Buck, village mouse that travelled along to Vandell's Pizzeria, who dreams of living in a forest

Misti Stone, funeral home employee who specializes in children's grief

Whitby, village mouse with a phenomenal auditory range

Vandell, deer that was accidently run over, so-named posthumously by Gretchen

Colton & Callie Cadwell, mouse observers of illegal photocopying of choral music

Celestial, amateur mouse astronomer

Historic St. Peter's Church Council, renamed the "Fig Leaf Council" by Aia

Marty & Lynne Schoenfeld, very skilled but heavily calorie-laden cooks

Erhard Ellison, "The Bra Monitor," nicknamed by Aia after he criticized her for pinning nursing bras on the backyard clothesline

Duff McKissick, owner of a vehicle that the council members gather around when holding a parking lot meeting

Coffee & Cream, two mice who noticed Pastor carrying tables and chairs to the parking lot for a *real* council meeting

Paxton, Bronzer, & Trekker, three mice who overheard the parking lot council meeting as they hid behind a giant boulder in HSP's garden

Todd & Karla Klingerman and their three boys, transferring away from HSP

Glenda Sinisac, along with her husband and two girls, transferring away from St. Pete's

Tracey Tervis, along with her husband and four girls, transferring away from St. Peter's

Phil Walach, Council member who declared October 29 a tragic day at St. Peter's because of the loss of fifteen parishioners and especially their offering

Gustav & Dagmar Christoferson, truly country mice, not church mice

English Toffee, a mouse with a honeycomb sweet temperament who thinks the word *Uffda* is unlike any other word

Harald & Vivi Finberg, owners of both a heritage farm and a charcoal-coloured pickup truck

Pignut, one of the mice that has a preference for living outdoors during the summertime

Dala & Horst Christoferson, girl and boy twin mice named after Swedish Dala Horses

Paprika, a red coloured tick-tock cat clock that recently has been hung in the parsonage kitchen

Patrick & Maureen Darcy, short-tempered neighbours that live next door to St. Peter's

Russell Owens; Anni Kuparinen; Gallagher Family consisting of Hugh, Davin, and Pearse; Darren Hendrix; Buffy Middlestadt; Tom Lang; Anna Henning; and Gretchen Osterhagen, summertime musicians at Historic St. Peter's

Sydney & Tosca Gardner, retired couple who enjoy the outdoors life on Lake Harvey far more than living in Europe and the world of opera

Harriet Gilbert, retired teacher who is completely uninterested in becoming a volunteer at HSP

June Phillips, Altar Guild Lady that discourages "X-ing" member's photographs

Lizzie Whittaker, came close to doing her "X-ing" homework, but instead is praying about it

Breezy & Clementine, two sacristy mice that overheard June and Lizzie's "X-ing" discussion

Orchid, Saxon, & Rudder-Dudder, three dogs photographed with their families for the church pictorial directory

Nina Hokkanen, loving owner of Orchid, her newborn dog that she loving carried in her arms with her to Holy Communion

Melody Greene, Sunday School music director

Holly Whitley, Sunday School pianist

Virginia Hawkins, oldest (and newest) Sunday School teacher

Austin, Winona, Dallas, Lincoln, Aspen, Phoenix, Camden, Cody, Jackson, Dacotah, Dakota, & Mary, Miss Virginia's Sunday School class, all named after cities or states

Miss Brooklyn, helper of the first grade Sunday School class, also named after a city

Juniper & Cloudberry, two mice who listened to Miss Virginia's excellent Sunday School lesson based on Noah's ark

Dede Thompkins, upset mother of Dakota

Glenda, nicknamed "Sassy Pants" and still having emotional troubles from it

Gary, nicknamed "Slacker" and still suffering anxiety from it

Edwina Gilbert, head nurse at Loving Arms Nursing Home

Sharisse Neilson, tattooed potential pastor with far too short of a skirt

Esther Anderson, mother of Sharisse

Mrs. Sorensgaard, shut-in salmon lover who shortchanged Aia eighteen dollars

Darryl Holley, Delmar York, Duane Arnett, and Duncan Oaks (known as the "Four D's"), members of the Board of Elders, hosts of the "First Annual St. Pete's Pork-Out"

Lotus Flower, the most attractive, graceful and delicate mouse in the village

Molly, Elder Darryl's wife, card player

Harlan Thornhill, member of the Pork-to-Table Cooperative Society, card-playing friends of the Holleys

Lindsey Thornhill, wife of Harlan, card-playing friend of the Holleys

Tumbleweed, sanctuary mouse who witnessed the four elders flee from the worship service

Fergus & Heather, two kitchen mice who heard firsthand the elders' plan to gather up pork chops

Barry Banfield, owner/butcher of Banfield's Butcher Shop, ready to cut chops for an emergency pork chop run

Lennie Landon, owner/butcher of Landon's Fine Meats, brother-in-law of Delmar York, also available to cut chops for "St. Pete's Pork-Out"

State Trooper Gabriel (Gabe) Horn, led the way to St. Peter's, speeding with his flashers on

Arthur & Minnie Klingenberg, state trooper's in-laws, active members of St. Peter's

Michelle, Jamie, & Jill Horn, Trooper Horn's wife and children

John Muir, American wilderness naturalist who loved the mountains and wanted them protected for future generations

Whisper, a church mouse that watched Granny Osterhagen miraculously cradle both twins in her arms during an entire worship service

Pinetop Willson, the fastest mouse in our village

About the Author

Greetings! My name is Sandra Voelker. Originally I hail from the United States having grown up in Austin, Minnesota, a mid-sized city that is known worldwide as "SPAM Town, U.S.A." Taking up residency more than twenty years ago in Canada came about when my husband, a Lutheran pastor, accepted a call to a parish in Windsor, Ontario. In 2004 we took the oath of Canadian Citizenship. For the last thirty-three years I have held church organist positions in three different locations, Michigan, Minnesota, and Ontario. A published composer of hymn tunes and settings, I have also worked in church offices, banks, an art gallery, and Hormel's corporate office.

We have four daughters, and God has also blessed us with two granddaughters and two grandsons. Topping my daily delights of favourite things includes breathing God's fresh air, selective types of music, spending evenings at home, my Northern attempts at Southern and international cooking, reading, popcorn and movie nights watching British murder mysteries, word search, daily tea or coffee at four p.m., being a friend, home wine-making, growing flowers and herbs, thrift store shopping, writing and painting.

My daily prayers are thankful to God for the many people I love, but included also are those who are far from loveable. I know that one day Christ our Saviour will take me home to heaven, but I hope that He procrastinates that for a while yet.

The side-splitting groundwork of the *Finley's Tale* series springs from actual "church" experiences during my lifetime. Being a P.K. (pastor's kid) and a P.W. (pastor's wife) are blessings that have provided me with a fragrant potpourri of priceless encounters and experiences, a panorama of parish life that only those on the "inside" witness. *Finley's Tale* Books I, II, and III exists because I was in seventh heaven writing about that which I know best of all, "church musings."

Soli Deo Gloria

Follow Finley's Tale online at

finleystale.com

where you can find:

• discussion questions for a book group or Bible study

• periodic blog articles about Historic St. Peter's

• recording of "Safety First," the mouse anthem and more!

978-1-4866-1531-5

In the Beginning, the first book in the *Finley's Tale* series sets in motion the journal of Finley Newcastle, a literate church mouse who writes his observations of the people (and mice) who populate a small-town church. Keen to monitor, study, and write about the parishioners and his fellow mice, including what others might think of them, Finley is unaware that his account may prove comical to human readers.

His favourite humans are Pastor Clement Osterhagen, his wife Aia, and their daughter Gretchen who reside in the parsonage. They are merciful, quiet, quick to forgive, prone to worry, adventuresome, big-hearted, and extra good-looking. Finley's observations lead him to conclude that they possess a strong faith in Jesus Christ.

978-1-4866-1668-8

The Bond of Love, the third book in the *Finley's Tale* series, completes Finley Newcastle's journal of experiences involving church people and church mice. Highlighted are the state-sponsored Underground Railroad tours, the eye-opening discovery by the mice that Historic St. Peter's is a "Lutheran" church, a sheep-stealing debacle, and umpteen other developments. At last, Finley says farewell to his journaling days, turning his attention to another goal on his bucket list.

Years later, his journal is rediscovered by a new generation of church mice who are riveted to learn of St. Pete's past. Finley Newcastle becomes a hero in the mouse world, the only mouse who has picked up a pen and written a journal about the most important place on earth: Historic St. Peter's Lutheran Church in Oswald County.